Bound together by their oaths and by friendship...

Brave and talented Knights Leopold, Hugh and Tristan are determined to serve their King and country. Destined to be the greatest warriors in all the lands, their reputations are risked by a jealous enemy.

Now, they must each complete a task lest they lose their Knighthoods. But as each Knight sets off on their individual mission, they find themselves embarking on the greatest of quests...love.

Follow these valiant warriors and the women who have captured their hearts!

Read Leopold and Arianwen's story in
The Knight's Rebellious Maiden

Hugh and Bronwen's story in
The Knight's Bride Prize

And Tristan and Catrin's story in
The Disgraced Knight's Redemption

All available now!

Author Note

This is the final book in my Knights' Missions trilogy. I always love stepping into a world of chivalrous knights and feisty heroines, and these three books have been such fun to write.

This is Tristan's story, and ever since I wrote the first book, I have had a soft spot for this character. Writing his story didn't disappoint; he's been a joy to get to know and I will miss spending time with him. I adore his physical confidence and his inner vulnerability as well as his fierceness in battle. He does not let anyone harm the people he cares for!

When I started The Knights' Missions series, I knew Tristan and his heroine were going to experience conflict over a patch of land, but I knew nothing else about Catrin. It wasn't until I met her on the first pages of this novel that I realized how much of a strong personality she would need to hold her head high in a world dominated by men. She came at me with passion and fire, in much the same way she does Tristan in the opening scene, and I have loved her ever since.

I hope you enjoy getting to see these two fall in love, as much as I did.

If you liked The Knights' Missions series, then please check out The King's Knights, which is set in the same world. You can also visit my website to find out about all my books: www.ella-matthews.com.

THE DISGRACED KNIGHT'S REDEMPTION

ELLA MATTHEWS

Harlequin

HISTORICAL

If you purchased this book without a cover you should be aware that this book is stolen property. It was reported as "unsold and destroyed" to the publisher, and neither the author nor the publisher has received any payment for this "stripped book."

Harlequin®
HISTORICAL

ISBN-13: 978-1-335-83157-6

The Disgraced Knight's Redemption

Copyright © 2025 by Ella Matthews

Recycling programs for this product may not exist in your area

All rights reserved. No part of this book may be used or reproduced in any manner whatsoever without written permission.

Without limiting the exclusive rights of any author, contributor or the publisher of this publication, any unauthorized use of this publication to train generative artificial intelligence (AI) technologies is expressly prohibited. Harlequin also exercises their rights under Article 4(3) of the Digital Single Market Directive 2019/790 and expressly reserves this publication from the text and data mining exception.

This is a work of fiction. Names, characters, places and incidents are either the product of the author's imagination or are used fictitiously. Any resemblance to actual persons, living or dead, businesses, companies, events or locales is entirely coincidental.

For questions and comments about the quality of this book, please contact us at CustomerService@Harlequin.com.

TM and ® are trademarks of Harlequin Enterprises ULC.

Harlequin Enterprises ULC
22 Adelaide St. West, 41st Floor
Toronto, Ontario M5H 4E3, Canada
www.Harlequin.com

HarperCollins Publishers
Macken House, 39/40 Mayor Street Upp(
Dublin 1, D01 C9W8, Ireland
www.HarperCollins.com

Printed in U.S.A.

Ella Matthews lives and works in beautiful South Wales. When not thinking about handsome heroes, she can be found walking along the coast with her husband and their two children (probably still thinking about heroes, but at least pretending to be interested in everyone else).

Books by Ella Matthews

Harlequin Historical

A Season to Wed

Their Second Chance Season

The Knights' Missions

The Knight's Rebellious Maiden
The Knight's Bride Prize

Brother and Rivals

Her Warrior's Surprise Return

The King's Knights

The Knight's Maiden in Disguise
The Knight's Tempting Ally
Secrets of Her Forbidden Knight

The House of Leofric

The Warrior Knight and the Widow
Under the Warrior's Protection
The Warrior's Innocent Captive

Visit the Author Profile page at Harlequin.com.

To the Swansea Girls: Gemma, Emma, Helen B., Charlotte, Haf, Sian B., Sian T., Helen W. and Donna

Chapter One

Wales 1337

The blade at Tristan's throat didn't waver, the metal glinting in the summer sun temporarily blinding him. For a moment the world stilled, the breeze ceased and the birds fell silent, even the bees stopped working. All that existed was the hard blue stare of his assailant, the one that seemed to see through to his very soul and recognise his unworthiness beneath his warrior facade, and the cool, sharp steel against his skin.

Darrow, only five paces away, whinnied, breaking the quiet, his hoof pawing the ground as if impatiently reminding Tristan of all that he was. Years of training, instructions burned into him, thousands of sword fights played out with men twice the size of his current opponent had him assessing the situation with a calm reserve. The sword wielder, face covered aside from the eyes, was slight, physically no match for him if one discounted the blade, but he couldn't ignore the deadly edge pressing against him, no matter the size of his adversary. To forget he was at a disadvantage could cost him his life. His knees weakened, the idea that he might not finish his mission, might not redeem himself suddenly a real possibility.

If he died, he wouldn't be around to witness how his failure impacted the men he considered his brothers, but that was scant consolation. Letting them down would dishonour his memory and their years together. Besides, he was a trained warrior, one of the best England had produced in years. This was not the end because he would not allow it to be.

His sword was strapped to Darrow. His fingers moved, involuntarily reaching for it. His hand found only air, the blade too far away to reach. He bit back a curse at his own foolishness. He'd not have made such an error if he hadn't been so wrapped up in his dark thoughts repeating the same ground in his mind as he had for months—a pointless endeavour. Even though this mission should have been an easy one, it was still vitally important and he should have been focused on every step of it.

The strap of his dagger was wrapped around his thigh; he could reach it easily so long as his movement did not nudge the sword against his neck. His fingers twitched…

'Stop.' The blade pressed deeper into his skin, still not cutting him but more uncomfortable now, reinforcing his challenger's message. The steely gaze had not left his face and yet his enemy had somehow seen the slight flicker of his hand. He pressed his lips together, repressing his jolt of shock. He had not expected a worthy opponent so far away from the country's centre of power, an arrogance that had led to his current disadvantage.

And then, finally a break. Blue eyes flicked to his neck and then back to his face—a hesitation, something he could use. His charm, after all, was legendary.

'You do not want to kill me.' He was friendly, almost jovial and not a threat, not yet anyway.

'That doesn't mean that I won't.'

The voice was high, not yet broken. Tristan's eyebrow twitched; it would be humiliating to die at the hands of a child, especially on a mission that was supposed to be not only his redemption but also proof to himself that he was worthy to be a great knight. He would have to find another way to win, because his life would not end today.

Darrow whinnied again, perhaps in protest at his master's treatment or maybe in annoyance at the host of sparrows flitting around the pommel, using it as a place to rest and view the drama. In his peripheral vision, Tristan could see the birds fluttering and dancing, revelling in their freedom.

Slowly, Tristan raised his hands. He could fight and win. He knew how to twist away from the blade, where he would put his hands to snatch the sword away, how he could end the life of his opponent. But...he might not escape completely unscathed; a small graze could fester and kill him as easily as a slit to the throat. He needed to be physically fit to complete his mission, surrendering, or at least appearing to, was his best option in this moment. 'I mean no harm. There's no need to kill me.'

'So you've already said.' The blade still did not drop but Tristan knew from experience that it was harder to kill a man whom you'd engaged in conversation.

'You don't need to hurt me either.' He smiled. He'd been told many times that his smile was beautiful. His two friends were by turns amused and annoyed that he often got what he wanted just from using it. They would not blame him for it now as it was the only weapon at his disposal. Even though it was like wading through something sticky, something it would take an age to wash off, he made his best move. Glancing down at the ground as if bashful, submissive, he paused for a beat and then peered up at his assailant through his lashes. 'I'm no threat,' he said softly.

If his friends could see him now, their mockery would be merciless, given that he often pontificated on how he would rather use his fighting skills than his looks in order to win at anything.

The eyes watching him grew colder. 'Has that foolish expression worked for you in the past? Surely no fool has ever been taken in by such a pathetic display.'

Heat rushed across his skin, scalding his face. No one, man nor woman, had ever failed to respond to him when he used his charm on them; some only had to look at his face to be persuaded by what he said. Not even those closest to him were immune to it all the time, and they knew he sometimes wielded it like a weapon. It had been both a blessing and, more recently, a curse, but it had *never* failed. 'I...'

The figure opposite him sighed, a slight relaxation in their stance. 'You're right. I'm not going to kill you, at least not right at this moment, provided you do not prove problematic. In which case, I will end your life without remorse.' Although the tone was almost conversational, Tristan didn't doubt that this was true; warrior called to warrior in this instance. 'For the time being, I need you alive to find out what your master's plans are. Does he think that by sending you here I am not going to put up a fight?' Tristan had no idea what his opponent was talking about. 'When I am sure of your answers, I'm going to return you with a message of my own.'

Tristan could have responded, could have reached for his dagger and fought for his freedom, but shock rendered him paralysed. He wasn't sure how he had not noticed before—perhaps the sword at his throat had dulled his wits or maybe his mind had been trying to calculate his escape route—but now he realised that the voice threatening him was not that of a young man but of a woman. A woman had held him at knifepoint and had failed to respond to his charm. *That* had never happened before.

Too late, he realised that his assailant was not alone. Meaty hands grabbed the arms he was still holding above his head and roughly held them behind his back. His muscles protested at being turned at such an unnatural angle but he kept his mouth tightly closed. He needed a moment to reassess, to plan his next move.

'Get the dagger on his thigh,' the woman told her companion.

The rough hands began to feel amongst his clothes; thick fingers brushed against the top of his thigh. Rage, hot and molten, flooded through Tristan's veins, burning his skin and bringing life to his muscles. He spun, wrenching away from the man who held him and reached for his dagger. The handle was smooth, worn away from being held a thousand times, handled so much as if it was an extension of him. He brandished it at the giant who had tried to hold onto him before spinning and locking eyes with the woman.

If she was frightened by him there was no sign of it in her cool eyes or the steadiness of the hand that held her sword aloft.

Behind him, he heard the sound of more people emerging from the woodland around him, the snaps of undergrowth so plentiful that he wondered how the hell he had missed so many of them moving through the forest until they'd made themselves known to him. He'd been trudging along, paying no heed to the path he was following, wallowing in his misery and confident there was no one else around in this wild and desolate corner of Wales. For that he deserved to be run through with the woman's sword.

She still had it pointed at him, although now it was levelled at his chest rather than his neck, just as deadly but not as close. The lines of her body were smooth, her outstretched hand balanced by the way her legs were parted. She only needed to step forward several paces and she could run him through with her blade, not that she would get that close. She might have the sword and he only a dagger, she might have the stance of the warrior, but he already knew what he would do to block her thrusts if she went left and how to bring her to her knees if she went the other way. She might be good, but he was better.

He risked a glance away from her, to see how numerous the newcomers were. He swallowed as he caught sight of men and women, all clasping some sort of weapon, albeit some old and rusty, and all with their focus locked on him.

'No one needs to get hurt,' he said. His gaze darted from the woman to the giant and the people with them, before turning to concentrate on their leader. Her eyes gave no hint as to her intentions, whether she was about to attack or command her people to do so. Normally adept at reading people, their almost lack of response was causing his jaw to clench so tightly it hurt.

'*You* don't need to get hurt,' she countered. 'You could surrender your weapon and come with us.'

'Why would I do that?'

There was no fear in her eyes, no sense that she was concerned that he was waving a dagger around, that she was the closest to its sharp edges, that he could act like a cornered animal and lash out at her.

'Your master has sent you here for a reason,' she replied calmly. 'You won't be able to complete it if you are gravely wounded or dead.'

There was no way that this strange woman knew the details of his mission. A mission given to him in England, many miles away from here. He could not believe she had ever heard of his liege, Lord Ormand, let alone know what had been said between the two of them many weeks ago.

It could only mean that she was involved in some other conflict that he'd had the misfortune of wading into.

'I am not the person you think I am,' he said, his feet still hip-width apart, his dagger clutched in his right hand, mirroring her stance. He would not relax until she did. 'I'm on a very specific mission to meet with Lady Catrin and…'

The blue eyes narrowed, a flash of something in their icy depths. 'Then you are in luck because you have found her.'

Tristan's heart thudded once, painfully. That could not be right; this coolly composed person could not be Lady Catrin because if she was, then his carefully crafted plans of the last few months were well and truly ruined. He'd been told that Lady Catrin was a young innocent woman who was stubbornly refusing to leave her family's castle after the death of her male relatives. She was gently bred, the daughter of a lord, she'd lived a pampered life and, it was said, did not seem to understand that she could not stay where she had always lived.

King Edward would not allow such a thing; he could not afford to. A woman could not raise young knights who would swear loyalty to the King. A Welsh woman born and bred would be no ally for the man who wanted total English dominance in his lands. King Edward wanted to gift the castle and the surrounding land to a man he knew to be loyal to him.

It wasn't that the King wanted harm to come to the lady—it was not her fault her father and brother had died—but he also did not overly care what became of her. Tristan's liege, ever a sycophant to King Edward, had promised he had a knight who could achieve the King's aims with no bloodshed. He had just the man to complete the task, even if the man, Tristan, wanted nothing to do with it.

Tristan and his charm had been dispatched to do the deed. Complete the mission and he would be rewarded; fail and he would spend his life in obscurity. Maybe if Tristan had only had to consider himself, he could have refused. His two friends, Leo and Hugh, were on equally obscure missions and, although they would never blame him, Tristan knew it was his fault. If it hadn't been for him the other two would not have been framed for a crime they hadn't committed. It was Tristan's face that had caused a young woman to believe she was in love with him. The consequences should not have been devastating, she wasn't the first person who professed to love him without knowing him, but he was usually able to let them down kindly. This time, a jealous Sir Robert, a fellow knight, had hated him because of it and had made his life hell. Again, it need not have led to disaster if the knight had not been petty and small-minded, but he had targeted Tristan and his friends in his pointless revenge. Revenge that meant they'd all been sent on missions beneath their abilities.

This mission was to be his redemption, to repay his friends who had stood by him even when their plans had turned to dust. They had not blamed Tristan for Robert's spite, but the fault lay with Tristan nonetheless. Charming a young woman into doing his bidding should have been easy; he'd thought redemption nearly in his grasp, until now. Nowhere in this plan did anyone mention that Lady Catrin was a sword-wielding warrior with nerves of steel and a look so clear and pure it seemed as if it could slice a man in half.

'As you are looking for me,' Lady Catrin continued, 'and as we are already in discussion, you should hand your dagger to me and come with us peacefully.'

That idea had some merit, although giving up his dagger was not an option. 'As your prisoner?'

A flash of amusement flickered in her eyes. 'I'm sure Lord Ogmore wants you returned in one piece. If you comply with my wishes, you need not worry about your reception at my castle.'

His suspicion was confirmed. Lady Catrin was embroiled in some conflict that had nothing to do with his mission. He loosened his stance slightly. His mission might even help her. A strong man in charge of Pwll Du Castle would solve any physical battle.

'My liege is not Lord Ogmore. I have never heard of the man. I am here from Lord Ormand. He...'

She rolled her eyes. 'You do not even have the ability to come up with a different-sounding name for your made-up liege. You could have chosen anything, Rhys or Owain, but no, you went for Ormand. Are your opponents normally so lulled into a false sense of security by your looks that they lose their wits?'

She had noticed the way he looked then, although from her words he didn't think his face was going to do him any favours. On this vitally important mission he had finally met someone immune to his supposed attractiveness. He'd have laughed if the situation hadn't been so dire.

'I have not made Ormand up. He is a large landowner in England. I...'

'Listen.' All amusement left her eyes as they flashed with anger. 'I do not tolerate liars, so don't repeat this nonsense. Ogmore wants his hands on my land and he is not going to get it, no matter how many raids he sends or how many men he tries to sneak past my borders. You have a choice. You can hand me your dagger and walk on your own legs to our castle as someone almost resembling a guest, or have the weapon taken from you by force and get dragged by Dafydd.' She nodded to the man who had tried to take his dagger before. The man's arms were like tree trunks, his chest like a barrel of ale. Dafydd would not move quickly in a fight but a punch from him would hurt.

In the end, the choice was easy to make. Lady Catrin

was the woman he wanted to talk to; there was no need to make an enemy of her. Walking would allow him to hold his head up high and was less likely to end with him covered in bruises. Tristan wanted to reach over and pull the covering from Lady Catrin's face; he wanted to read her expression, to see if there was a softening in her lips when she looked at him, or a telltale flush high in her cheekbones that showed she was not totally immune to him.

'You can't win this,' she told him as he deliberated, nodding towards the rest of her people. 'Give up the dagger and come with us peacefully.'

He half-turned. Either there were more emerging from the woods with every moment that passed or he had missed some before. His hand was slick on the handle of his dagger and sweat was forming on his forehead. He resisted the urge to wipe it away. 'Do I have your word that you will return it when I leave?'

There was a long pause while she regarded him steadily. He held himself still, forcing his hand to remain steady.

Eventually she nodded. 'I swear to you that I shall return the dagger to you when you leave my castle.'

He would have to be happy with that. He straightened, throwing the dagger casually so that it landed directly in front of her feet. She didn't flinch as the blade entered the ground, even when her people gasped. A better knight would have handed it to her with respect for her womanly status but he had no such compunction. She was not acting like a lady, so he would not treat her as such. A tiny act of rebellion, but an important one.

Slowly, almost casually, she leaned down and plucked

it from the soil. His shoulders tightened as she inspected the handle. She would not be able to read the words inscribed in the wood. They had faded and worn away over years of handling, but they were important to him; the blade was not just a weapon. *'Simul vigemus'*—*Together we thrive*—a gift from Leo not long after they'd formed their band of brotherhood with their third friend, Hugh. The phrase was there, always reminding him that if the world turned against him, those two men would stand beside him, as he would them, reminding him that he could not fail this mission because to do so would ruin them, the only people who had never let him down.

She tucked the dagger into her belt and gestured for him to walk in front of her. His legs almost refused the command and he had to remind himself that he wanted her on his side. If he had to play the subservient prisoner, he would do it for now.

'Darrow.' He half-turned towards the stallion. Tristan was not leaving without the horse; he was more family to him than his own.

'He is a magnificent beast. He will receive the best care my people and I can provide.' Her voice was warmer when she spoke about Darrow than at any point during their interaction. He believed her when she said she would look after him, but he didn't think he was about to receive the same care. It was no matter. He'd lost this initial skirmish but he would not lose the war.

Chapter Two

He was an arrogant devil, the latest man sent by Lord Ogmore to try and get past her defences. Perhaps if she hadn't already been fooled and betrayed by a pretty man whose lies had cost her dearly, this attempt would have had some success. There was no denying his face was pleasing on the eye. Those eyelashes…so decadently long and thick they were almost hypnotic. When he'd peered at her through them with his dark eyes her heart had fluttered like a bird in a cage. She'd experienced that foolish reaction once before, years ago when she'd been young and naïve and had believed in love.

She'd learned the hard way that a beautiful face did not mean there was a beautiful soul inside. A handsome man could lie as easily as any other. It didn't matter how full this stranger's lips were or how square his jaw, she would not spin dreams in her mind about how things could be between them. That was a girl's folly and she had not been one of those in a long time. Ioan's betrayal had seen to that.

This latest attempt by Lord Ogmore to manipulate her would fail as surely as all the others. Although, given the timing and the rumours they had heard, his arrival did not bode well.

Ffion, her right-hand woman, moved up to walk beside her. 'Do you think he is telling the truth?' she murmured in Welsh, nodding towards their captive. 'About his liege, I mean.'

The two women watched the man as he strode along at the front of the column. Despite his distinct disadvantage, he held his head high, striding forward, his long legs eating up the distance with a confidence the situation did not warrant.

'No, of course he is lying. If Ogmore is truly planning a siege, he will want to know our weaknesses. What better way than to send in a handsome spy?'

Ffion nodded slowly. 'I agree. The two names were too similar, as if he made it up in the moment. Perhaps the Englishman thinks us as simpleminded as Ogmore.'

'Perhaps.' Although she didn't think so. His gaze had cut into her as if he could see right into her soul—a fanciful idea, the type she had stopped having as life had taken a harder turn than she'd been expecting, but one that she could not shake.

'Do you think Ogmore really believes we will fall for this one's lies?' continued Ffion.

'Maybe he believes us womenfolk will be so overcome by the sight of those shoulders we will give him what he wants.' Years ago, when she had been young and gullible, it might have worked but not now.

Ffion grinned, her gaze flicking to the knight. 'Surely Ogmore has to know that we are not so easily swayed.'

'The stranger's magnificent horse has more brains in his left hoof than Ogmore,' Catrin reminded her friend.

'Remember when he tried to take our castle with an army of ten men.'

The two women laughed grimly. Ogmore had not been expecting a castle led by a woman to have any defences in place. On that very first attack, his soldiers had arrived expecting to walk into the courtyard and announce that they now ruled, some of them too drunk to stay upright on their horses. The shock of Catrin's people's retaliation had soon sobered them up and they had abandoned their first attack within half a day. Catrin might not have been trained in warfare but the drunken men had been no match for her fury.

Ogmore had tried again with more men, but he had still underestimated her people's will to stay where they were with Catrin as their leader. He was persistent though. Persistent and continually annoying. Just as this latest attempt showed. He believed, as the nearest male in this corner of Wales, that her castle should belong to him, despite owning a sizeable stronghold of his own. As he had known her awful father, he thought she should hand it over to him without a qualm. He didn't seem to understand her consistent message, that she was not giving up her home for him or for anyone. Once she had thought to flee her father but, now that he was gone, she valued the steady routine the castle gave her. It gave her peace.

She continued to watch her captive. He was studying the land around him, his head turning slowly, taking in every detail, glancing every now and then at the horse he'd called Darrow. He seemed concerned about the animal's wellbeing and, if he hadn't been sent to try and take her castle from her, this might warm her to him. He moved with an easy grace, despite his size. He had the body of a warrior and the stance of a man who knew how to hold and use a blade. Catrin had no doubt he would have won any skirmish between them had she not been able to take him by surprise.

When she could, she sent scouts out, checking the boundaries of her land, making sure that they had plenty of warning of whatever Ogmore was up to. The rumour of an impending siege was the first serious threat in a while. When they'd reported a lone man, clearly a warrior, following the River Ewenny, she'd guessed this was Ogmore's next step.

With many of her people, she'd set out to investigate. They'd kept to the densely packed forest, barely making a sound as they'd followed routes they knew better than anyone, watching and observing his movements. He had walked alongside his magnificent stallion, seeming in no hurry to reach his destination. The weapons strapped to his horse had marked him out as a warrior but his head had been bowed as if he were carrying a weight of which only he was aware. His size had marked him out as a formidable opponent, the weapons strapped to his horse superior to any she had seen before. So they had waited, not wanting to give away their advantage to a man who could easily harm them.

Their opportunity had come when he had left his horse to fill a water bag at the river's edge. Catrin would never ask her people to put themselves in danger and so it was she who strode towards him and held a sword to his throat. She did not revel in bloodshed but if he had tried to use that dagger then she would not have hesitated in ending his life. The safety and welfare of her people took precedence over everything else.

She palmed the man's knife, the one he had insolently thrown at her feet. Her father would have killed a man for showing such disrespect but Catrin had understood the man's action. He'd known he'd lost and he was trying to make parting with this piece of him easier. She studied it from every angle. This was a blade he'd carried around with him for a long time; the worn handle was smooth from being held. It had some sort of hold on him. His reluctance to hand it over was not, she thought, because he minded being weaponless. She'd seen the way he had moved away from Dafydd. Dafydd wasn't fast but he had an unmatched brute strength, or at least not matched until now. Her captive had pulled himself away with a power she had not seen before. So no, the man was not worried about that; he would be able to do much damage without a dagger. She turned the handle towards the sun; words had been etched into the wood but she could not make them out. Perhaps it held the key to the man, perhaps it was merely decoration. She intended to find out. It was best to know everything about your enemy, after all.

'What is your plan?' Ffion asked as Catrin tucked the dagger back into her belt.

'Interrogate him. We need to know whether this siege is a rumour or reality.' Catrin hated uncertainty. What you didn't know had the potential to hurt you far more than if you were prepared.

'We could always keep the man hostage,' Ffion suggested.

'Do you think Ogmore will care about his fate?' Catrin was sceptical that Ogmore cared for anyone other than himself. He certainly showed no sign of caring for his wife and their children, or those he had with his many mistresses.

'I doubt he would rouse himself to be bothered by a hostage but if he is planning a siege then a warrior such as that one would be a benefit to him.' The two women gazed at the large man striding through the countryside; physically, he was a cut above Ogmore's other warriors.

'I cannot understand how someone like that has come to Ogmore's castle.' That was a puzzle she could not resolve in her own mind. He had protested that he did not know who Ogmore was, but surely that was a blatant lie to try to appease her. There could be no other reason for a knight to want to speak with her. She tugged at the veil hiding her face; the heat of the day was rising and beads of sweat were forming underneath the material. She pushed aside the niggle of doubt in her stomach; if her sources were correct, a new attack from Ogmore was imminent and she could not afford to get distracted by a side issue that probably did not exist anyway.

'Perhaps he is a mercenary. He is young, not much older than you. If...'

'I am not young,' Catrin interrupted her friend. Some days Catrin felt a lot older than her twenty-one summers suggested she should.

'At a guess,' said Ffion, ignoring her interruption, 'I would say he has not long qualified as a knight. He looks as if he has skills but that lovely face of his had no battle scars. Maybe he fell out with his liege and is roaming the country looking for mercenary work instead.'

'Rather than speculate, I will see what he has to say for himself.'

Catrin moved forward through her people, nodding

and muttering words of encouragement. They had done well today—there would be feasting later, perhaps a contest of some sort—but for now she wanted everyone alert. Until he was locked up, the man was still a threat.

She came to walk beside him. She was tall but her head only reached his shoulder. His hands, which hung loosely at his sides, were wide with a smattering of dark hair across the backs.

'What is your name?' she asked. She could not continue to think of him only as 'the man'.

'Sir Tristan de Boutellier.'

She smiled at his emphasis on the 'Sir', confirming that he'd had a knight's training. She doubted it was with Ogmore—his looks were striking enough that she would recognise him or word would have travelled the short distance between Ogmore's stronghold and her own.

'And where is the de Boutellier family from?'

She caught him glancing at his dagger tucked into her waistband but he did not reach for it. His restraint was remarkable for a man who had clearly been raised to assume the world was his for the taking.

'Deep in the middle of England,' was his low-rumbled response. He did have a strong English accent, with no hint of a Welsh lilt.

'How do you find yourself in Wales?'

'I am on a mission for my liege, as I have already told you.'

'Ah, yes, it concerns me, does it not?'

She studied him while she waited for his response. There was no denying he was a handsome man. His skin had almost a golden hue, his cheekbones were high, his jawline was sharp and his dark eyes were framed with those lashes she'd found so enticing. But that wasn't all that made him so compelling to look at. There was something about the way his full mouth moved almost imperceptibly as he thought that made her want to reach across and touch it lightly with her fingertips.

'It occurs to me,' he said after they had walked several paces in silence, 'that I only have your word that you are Lady Catrin.'

She was glad she was wearing a veil for it hid the parting of her lips. 'Why would I lie about that?'

He shrugged and she cursed herself for following the line of his wide shoulders. 'To get me to surrender my weapons, at a guess.'

'I am telling you the truth.'

He shrugged again.

She turned away from him, releasing her curled fingers. He was deliberately trying to get a reaction from her, first with his contemptuous throwing of the dagger and now this nonchalant response to her questions, and she was dangerously close. She couldn't really explain why. She had trained herself to be calm, no matter what she faced. It was odd that this man was getting to her with two lifts of his shoulders. Maybe it wasn't only that. Perhaps it was the way he'd tried to manipulate her with his soft smile, or perhaps he was inherently irritating. It had to be the last one because otherwise it reflected more on her and her lack of control than on him.

She waited until she found that inner calm she had taught herself to summon—she visualised it as a soft, meandering stream, cool on a summer's day. Over the years, reaching for it had become instinctive and she would find it now in this moment.

'Perhaps a few days of our hospitality will convince you,' she responded blandly when she was sure she had her temper under control.

His lips quirked and her heart did that odd flutter again. 'By that am I to assume I shall be thrown into some dark dungeon and forgotten about until I am willing to concede that you are, in fact, Lady Catrin?'

'Pwll Du Castle does not have a dungeon, but we do have a chamber for you to call your own for the duration of your stay.'

He nodded slowly, understanding the implied threat. 'I have never been a prisoner before. It will be an interesting experience.'

He did not seem despondent at the idea. If anything, the weight he'd appeared to carry as he'd wound his way through the countryside was lifting. There was something sharper, more defined about him. There was almost a swagger to his stride now—where before it seemed as if he had been trudging through the countryside, he now seemed to be quickening his pace, as if eager to reach her castle.

Next to them, the wide, shallow river tumbled over its pebbly bed. Catrin fought the childish urge to push him into the water. She wanted to see this calm man ruffled, or afraid or something. Ever since she'd had him at knifepoint he had done nothing but confound and confuse her. He was not acting how he should, cowed and essentially beaten. His bearing was more that of a man returning successfully from war. A dip in the water would serve him right but to follow through on such an action would be to show just how irritating she was finding his serene countenance. She couldn't allow him to know that he was getting the upper hand. Already, so early in their acquaintance, she knew it would be like that with him.

They rounded a bend in the stream and Pwll Du Castle, her home, came into view.

'Picturesque,' murmured Tristan as he paused slightly and took in the small stronghold.

Resting on top of a steep man-made mound, Catrin's home was not a grand one. The moat was drained from the river and ran deeper around the castle than it did naturally, its dark water giving the castle its name of Black Pool. The wide, flat valley floor that surrounded the area was fertile and, yes, pretty to look at, if she could find the time to do so between her duties and protecting it. While it wasn't the grandest or most strategic castle in the area, it belonged to her and to those who lived within its walls and she would be damned if anyone took it from them. Certainly not the insolent lord who lived nearby and who had been plaguing her with increasingly determined attempts to take it from her.

'Indeed,' she agreed with Tristan, nudging him slightly to get him moving again. Her elbow met a solid wall of muscle that she would not be able to move by herself. Fortunately, he obliged her by starting to walk again. 'But, as you can also see, it is not a castle that needs to be fought over. It is not imposing enough to house an army, nor in a vital position for the country's defence. You can tell that to Ogmore.'

'As I don't know who this Ogmore is, that will be difficult.' They began the well-trodden path towards the castle gate, the worn stones crunching beneath her boots. 'Why does he covet it, if this place is nothing special?' he asked.

'Because he is a mangy, flea-ridden dog who thinks that because of what swings between his legs he has a God-given right to take what he wants without consideration to others.'

Tristan grinned, although she had not intended to be funny. She ignored the way his smile was like the sun coming out on a winter's day. She would not allow any positive feelings for this man; he had been sent to manipulate her and softening towards him would mean her downfall.

'You can tell him exactly what I said when you return to him.' Reminding them both that Tristan was her enemy and lying to her.

'If I ever meet him, I will,' was the infuriating reply.

'Why not admit that you are his man?'

His dark gaze slanted down at her. 'Why do you find it so hard to accept that I am not?'

'Because it is wildly improbable that I hear rumours of another attack from Lord Ogmore days before a man appears claiming to have word from a Lord Ormand, of whom I have never heard.'

'What would I stand to gain by lying to you?'

'My trust.'

He was not to know that her trust was almost impossible to gain.

'And when I had that?' He turned towards her as they stepped through the castle gateway, the shadow of the arch a welcome relief from the strength of the sun.

'You never will.'

'But if I did?'

'You would manipulate me into giving up my castle to Lord Ogmore.'

Something flickered across his face, gone before she could tell what it meant.

'I wouldn't want you to give anything to this man because I don't know him.'

She sighed. 'Has anyone ever told you that you are extraordinarily irritating?'

He paused. 'No.'

'Well, you are.'

He laughed, the sound rumbling in his chest, and she was once again glad of the veil, this time because it hid her answering smile.

Tristan shouldn't be enjoying himself. He was separated from his friends, on a mission that appeared to be more complicated than he'd expected and humiliatingly captured by a ragtag group of people from whom he should have been able to escape easily. And yet…and yet he was in a far better mood than he'd been in for weeks, months even. He'd been living under the weight of a dark shadow, a gloom that had not been of his making and yet was somehow still his fault. Working towards his redemption while fearing it would be impossible to achieve.

Worryingly, the improvement in his mood seemed to be down to the person walking next to him, his enemy, who was trying to hide how much he was getting to her. Despite the fact that he had only seen her eyes, she was becoming surprisingly easier to read as their interaction had continued. Every time he said something that irritated her, her shoulders tightened; every time she decided to shrug off his comment, they would loosen. His life had been like wallowing in horse manure for so long that the simple pleasure of interacting with someone who was annoyed with him for something he *had* done was making him happy.

Even the thought of being thrown into a locked room didn't daunt him. He'd been trained in how to escape and now he'd be able to put it into practice. Fine, so this mission wasn't going entirely to plan. He hadn't expected to become a prisoner of the woman he was trying to charm into doing what he wanted. Nor had he expected her not to be. But, for the first time he could remember, he was being presented with a challenge, something to pit himself against, to use the skills for which he'd trained.

Being captured had initially tied his mind in knots. He'd imagined the look of disappointment on Hugh's face and the devastation on Leo's when they realised that he had failed to make things right. They were his friends so they would forgive him, but in a way that would be worse. He didn't want forgiveness, he wanted redemption.

As they'd strode along the banks of the Ewenny, his blackness had lifted. He was exactly where he wanted to be, he was heading into the stronghold he had been hoping to gain access to and he was in conversation with Lady Catrin. With all the setbacks of the last year or two, even the smallest victory was pleasing. And it wasn't just that. Perhaps it was the way the sun sent sparkles of light across the burbling river or the low call of cattle on the wide valley plains, but there was something about the land that reminded him that life didn't have to be shades of grey.

Inside the castle walls, a fire roared in the far corner of the courtyard. A blacksmith poked at it, sending sparks into the sky. A group of young children peered out from behind an open door, their round faces alight with curiosity. They squealed with delight or fear when they caught his gaze, disappearing, apart from one braver, dark pair of eyes. Tristan winked and was rewarded with a giggle.

Lady Catrin said something in Welsh and the laughter faded instantly before the gaze disappeared. 'You're to have nothing to do with the children,' she told him, indicating that he should head towards the right-hand side of the courtyard.

'I'm not here to harm anyone,' he said. His heart ached at the thought that anyone might think him capable of such a thing; he was not a monster and he would rather fail a thousand missions than lay a hand on a child or destroy their happiness with cruel words. He knew all too well what sort of misery that could cause.

They approached a wide doorway and the group paused before entering the inner recesses of the castle. A rapid exchange in Welsh followed. Tristan tried to follow it; he'd been taught the language a few years ago, but had not paid enough attention, never expecting to need it. He'd never practised and the long, complicated words had slipped from his mind as quickly as glasses of rich red wine were consumed on feast days. Instead, he gazed about him. The sun spilled over the ramparts, the walls shielding any cooling breeze, and the temperature rose. Sweat began to pool at the base of his spine and he wondered if prisoners were ever allowed to swim in the cool-looking waters of the river. He very much doubted it, but it did not spoil his fantasy.

Darrow clattered into the courtyard, his dark coat gleaming. Tristan watched him being led towards a small stable building near the blacksmith's. A young boy rushed out to greet them, the smile on his face widening as he took in Darrow's magnificence. The horse began to nuzzle the boy as he whispered in his ear. Tristan's only ally had already moved on.

Sweat beaded across his forehead and he wiped it off with the back of his hand. He'd been accused of being arrogant, one of the reasons he was being punished with this mission in the depths of Wales, so far away from Windsor it might as well have been France. He'd never truly believed the accusation. He'd had the confidence knocked out of him as a child and any poise he showed as an adult was an act.

But perhaps it wasn't the fake bravado people were referring to when they'd accused him of this trait. He hadn't seen any use in learning Welsh and so he'd put it to the back of his mind, casually dismissing an entire country because the idea of going there was not part of the future that he and his friends had planned for themselves.

The three of them had known they were the best squires to be trained at one of the best strongholds in England. That wasn't vanity, it was fact. Everyone who had seen them fight and train over the years had said so, even those who did not like them. Their plan had been to gain their knighthoods and present themselves to the King's most trusted man and leader of an elite band of knights, Sir Benedictus. In their naivety they had never doubted that Sir Benedictus would realise their potential. That they would not even meet this famed knight had not once occurred to them in all the years of planning. It should have done. The three of them should have plotted like their enemies had done. If they'd had a second or even a third plan, they would not be in this mess. He should have learned from this lesson, should have prepared for his mission by learning to speak Welsh or finding out more about Lady Catrin, but once again he had rushed forward, safe in the knowledge that he was a *great* knight. This hubris had punched him in the face and brought him to his knees.

He was here, in Wales, on a mission that was punishment for a crime he had not committed, having never learned to understand the language that was now being used to discuss his fate. Or not. He had no way of knowing. He shook his head; he was a fool and deserved everything fate threw at him. He had failed to plan for the worst twice in his life, but there would not be a third time.

The long, lyrical debate finally came to an end. Most of the people who'd emerged from the forest trudged off to a long building that took up most of the west wall and which must be their Great Hall. Lady Catrin remained, along with the giant Dafydd and a lean older man who glowered at Tristan as if he were the devil.

Tristan held his palms up. 'I'm not a threat.'

The older man snorted.

Lady Catrin rolled her eyes. 'I agree with Wynne. You're about as trustworthy as a drunkard at a game of dice.'

He pressed a hand to his heart. 'I'm wounded.'

She stared at him for a long moment, no sign that she appreciated his attempt at humour in those cool blue eyes. 'Let's go.'

She turned and made her way through a narrow doorway. Inside the stone walls it was mercifully cooler and his sweat began to dry against his cool skin. Lady Catrin moved at a brisk pace, leading the way; the two men stalked close behind him. For all their lack of trust in him, they did not bind his hands or cover his eyes. As she took him through various tunnels, Tristan memorized the route, glad he had paid attention to *that* part of his training.

'This is where you will be staying during your short visit.' Lady Catrin came to an abrupt stop and indicated a plain wooden door, before stepping past it and gesturing for him to open it. He reached out and touched the door handle. The handle was smooth and cool beneath his skin.

'Is there a problem?' demanded Lady Catrin.

He glanced to his right. In the dim light of the corridor, he could not clearly make out her eyes, her arms hung loosely by her sides.

'Well?' she demanded, impatience lacing her words.

'There's no problem at all.' He grinned at her, even when his fingers didn't relax their hold.

He pushed open the door and light from the corridor spilled into the chamber in front of him. He could make out fresh rushes on the floor and a blanket folded in the corner.

'Were you expecting me?' he asked.

'We keep this for any visitors.' She gestured for him to step inside. 'As much as you are enjoying the sound of your own voice, I need to get on with my day. Please make yourself comfortable.'

He whistled. 'That was harsh.' He glanced at the chamber again. 'Although I'm looking forward to a good, long rest, I'm slightly concerned that I won't be able to see anything.' There was no window; once the door was shut and locked, he would be in complete darkness. He wasn't afraid of the dark, he was a grown man and any such childish nonsense was long conquered. But darkness would make it harder to get out of the chamber, not impossible but not as easy.

'Wynne will bring you a candle.' Wynne looked about as pleased with this task as being asked to clean out the latrines. Never had a man hated him on sight as much as this one. With his face, Tristan had plenty of male enemies who viewed him as a threat. Not that Tristan had ever *tried* to take a married woman; it was not his fault that bored wives wanted to use him for entertainment. Tristan would not cuckold a man; he knew from his mother's experience how much pain and suffering a cheating spouse could cause, but that didn't stop some of the men from hating him anyway. Never as much as Wynne though.

'Excellent,' said Tristan, beaming at Wynne. His overconfident attitude might be inappropriate but he would be damned if he'd show any sign of fear to any of them.

Wynne snarled and stalked back down the way they had come.

'He'll be back shortly,' said Lady Catrin, beginning to close the door.

Tristan stuck his foot out to stop her closing it all the way, not ready to lose the light. 'How quick is shortly, incidentally?'

'Very soon.' She yanked on the door, banging it against his foot, but he held firm.

'That's not very precise.'

Her eyes narrowed. 'You do realise that you are a prisoner, yes?'

'Yes, I do understand. Only I thought you and I were becoming friends.' He winked at her, already anticipating the tightening of her shoulders that told him he was getting to her and knowing that was perhaps not the best road to travel but doing it anyway because it kept her talking to him.

The blue eyes narrowed and something in his chest moved, a sensation, near his heart, close to pain. 'Don't act the fool. It demeans you.'

Maybe, but the longer the door was open, the less time that he would be plunged into darkness. He'd dance for her if that was what he had to do to keep her there.

'Look, Sir Tristan...' she said softly, leaning against the doorframe closest to him. In the close confines he could smell the soft hint of rosewater she'd used to wash. Instinctively, he leaned closer. Too late, he realised his mistake. She took advantage of his momentary inattention and slammed the door shut. He heard the lock turning in the door as darkness enveloped him.

He stood staring at the place where he knew the door to be until his eyes adjusted and he could make out dim light around the edges. Sweat gathered around his hairline, his palms damp. Forcing his breathing to remain slow and steady, he took stock of the situation. He knew nothing about Lady Catrin, but he did not think she would leave him here for days; she appeared to be efficient. Besides, he could get out of here. All he needed was a moment... He was fine.

This was not like when he was a child; he now had the means at his disposal to get out of the chamber. He did not have to reside in the dark, listening to the rats scurrying about the floor, they would not run across his bare feet when he least expected it. He was wearing good, solid boots and, from his quick glance around the chamber before the door closed, it had looked clean and well-maintained; perhaps there would be no rats at all. There was no need for his stomach to writhe and his thoughts to swirl around his head like angry hornets in a disturbed nest.

Heavy footsteps sounded outside, Wynne returning. He held his breath as they slowed, coming to a stop by the doorway. He stepped backwards from the door, two paces, then another one. The lock turned and Wynne's scowling face appeared. Tristan could have kissed him. He thrust a tallow candle in Tristan's direction. Tristan stepped forward to take it from him. '*Diolch*,' he managed, the word of thanks the only Welsh one he could remember.

Wynne's steely gaze faltered, obviously hearing Tristan's true gratitude at being given a light, at not being forgotten even though he was a potential threat to the people of this castle. He grunted before slamming the door closed and locking it once more.

Tristan's heart rate slowly returned to normal. The candle threw shadows across the floor as he made his way to a sconce on the far wall. He placed the candle in its position. He was where he wanted to be, he had the means and the training to escape and, although she might deny it, he had a rapport with Lady Catrin. In all, not a bad morning's work.

Chapter Three

Catrin rubbed the corners of her eyes with her thumbs. When she'd taken over as leader of Pwll Du Castle she'd vowed to make sure that all her people could contribute to the way things were run. She wanted something different from her father's iron but capricious rule, something that allowed everyone to feel safe but free. She wanted to create a legacy that people admired, one that had nothing to do with the way she looked and everything to do with her actions. It was these principles she intended to stick to, but now tiredness dragged on her shoulders after this afternoon's lengthy debate in the Great Hall as they'd discussed what to do with their prisoner.

If she'd thought about it beforehand, she could have predicted Eluned would suggest they keep Sir Tristan and make him work for them for as long as possible. It had obviously not escaped the young woman's notice that the man currently locked in one of their chambers was very easy on the eyes. Lloyd had suggested Sir Tristan be hanged in order to show Ogmore they were not to be messed with, but as the young, passionate lad was madly in love with Eluned that comment, born of jealousy, had been ignored by almost everyone.

In the end, they had agreed with Catrin's original plan, which was to question Sir Tristan for any insights into Lord Ogmore's plans. They needed to know if the rumours of a siege were true. They had been amassing food supplies to weather a siege, had talked endlessly through imagined scenarios, but it would help to know for sure. This was where their lack of experience showed. The castle contained no trained knights and her father had never imagined he would die of the ague without a male heir. As a daughter and not a son, he had not trained Catrin in warfare and sometimes she felt as if she was fumbling in the dark, trying to find her way. She knew they needed more weapons but finding the ore to mine for iron was proving difficult and there was no one whom she could ask for help. The uncertainty was getting harder to endure; it followed her around, reminding her that things could change in an instant if she was not careful.

Catrin let herself into the private corridor that ran from the Great Hall to her antechamber. The air was still and quiet, cool here despite the heat of the day, the thick stone walls of the building protecting her from more than invading lords. She walked softly, a habit born of the days when her father was still alive and she'd done everything she could to avoid him. Today it helped her burgeoning headache to move silently over the rushes that lay on the floor.

There were two entrances to her antechamber, this one she used to enter without being seen by the rest of the inhabitants, allowing herself a few precious hours alone. The entrance was hidden inside the antechamber by a large tapestry that hung across the length of one wall. The main entrance that members of the stronghold could enter, should they need to talk to her, was just like any other door in the castle. She was the only one who came this route and only those closest to her knew of its existence.

Before pushing through the thick fabric she paused, her fingers grazing the rough interlocking wool. From this angle the tapestry was a swirl of colours. She preferred it this way to the other side, the ordered bucolic scene on display in her antechamber was not as interesting or as pretty and sometimes she would pause out here to take in the disordered beauty, the crisscrossing pattern revealing the hard work of the women who had made the piece of art.

Today her stop was not about appreciating its charm. Today her pause was caused by the breathing she could hear on the other side of the fabric. No one should be in her antechamber. Her people were accounted for and none of them would invade her personal space without express permission; she had earned their respect through sheer will and hard work.

That left only one potential trespasser.

Surely it was not possible for Sir Tristan to have escaped the locked chamber. Wynne had hated the man on sight and he was the most efficient man in the stronghold; she knew he would not have forgotten to lock their prisoner in after he had delivered the candle. His brisk nod to her when he had arrived at the Great Hall had confirmed he had carried out his duties.

A thrill of fear ran down the length of her spine, her fingers tingling as she slipped her dagger from its sheath. She'd been virtually silent on her way here; he would not be aware of what the tapestry hid. With trembling fingers she lightly lifted the edge of the fabric, clamping her lips together to stop herself from gasping out loud at what she saw.

Not only was Sir Tristan in her antechamber, he was sitting in her chair, hands resting behind his head, his feet up on her table.

She let the tapestry fall softly back into place, her fingers tightening around the handle of her weapon, hard resolve flooding through her, tightening her muscles. How dare he treat her belongings with such casual ease? He was making a mockery of her and her people, acting as if it was fine to stroll into her private space and treat it as if it was his own.

She took a long, silent, calming breath. She could not allow her emotions to cloud her thoughts. She needed her inner calm to plan her next move or else she could find herself dead or, worse, captured by the enemy.

Sir Tristan was a big man with muscles as thick as the branches of the old oak tree just beyond the castle walls. He'd pulled away from Dafydd's arms without even pausing for breath and Dafydd was the biggest, strongest man Catrin had ever encountered before today. To fight Sir Tristan would find her at his mercy; they were so far away from her people that he could do with her what he wanted. She could retreat, but after a lifetime of giving in she found it difficult to do that, now that she finally had a backbone.

As she stood there contemplating her options, she heard the scrape of her chair on the tiled floor. She held herself still, not even daring to breathe as she heard footsteps slowly coming her way. The sharp sound of his boots, precise and direct. He could not possibly know that she was here and yet...the noise stopped directly opposite her.

'Are you going to enter?' His rich voice was laced with laughter and liquid rage surged, hot and fiery, through her veins. She resisted the urge to run the knife through the tapestry and straight into his stomach, reminding herself that she liked this wall-hanging; it would be expensive and time-consuming to get a replacement and, for the time being, she needed him alive. 'Or are you going to stay there?' he finished.

Hell, he was a smug bastard. It would serve him right if she did ruin her tapestry with a well-aimed thrust.

'How did you get out of your chamber?' she asked, deliberately avoiding answering his question.

'I picked the lock.'

She pressed her lips together; she would not give him the satisfaction of asking how he had done so.

'Why?' she asked instead. It was a valid question, although he was hardly likely to tell her the truth if he intended to either kill or abduct her.

'Because I wanted to see if I could.' She blinked. That had not been the answer she had been expecting. 'And then I wanted to find your antechamber so that we could talk.'

'I have nothing to say to you.'

'Now, that is not true, is it?'

He was right, it wasn't. She had a lot to say to him, only she wanted to do it on her terms, not his. 'Has anyone ever told you how exceedingly irritating you are?'

'Only you, although I am sure many people would agree with you.'

'Could you try to be less so?' She had never had a

prisoner before, but she was certain this was not how an interrogation was supposed to go. He was meant to be at least a little concerned about his life and welfare.

'Hmm... I don't think I can. My personality is fixed at this point. However, if you wish to say nothing to me, then I can do the talking. I know you want to know why I am here. I can tell you all about it and thereby spare myself the torture young Lloyd was so keen to mete out.'

She muttered a curse word under her breath. She should have kept that meeting in the Great Hall purely in Welsh, but she'd had no idea Sir Tristan would be listening. Lloyd had been quite graphic in his description of what they could do with Tristan. The conversation, like most that took place around the castle, had meandered from Welsh into English and back again.

No, better yet, she should have kept someone guarding the chamber so Tristan could not have escaped in the first place and listened in on their plans. From now on, she would do just that. She pushed down the small voice that reminded her that she might not be able to get him back into his chamber. She had overcome worse difficulties; she would overcome this.

'We don't have a rack,' she informed him. When her father had died, she'd had it ceremoniously burned. It didn't matter what someone had done, they did not deserve to be slowly pulled apart.

'That is reassuring.'

'But I suspect Lloyd is out building one right now.' He wasn't. Catrin had set him the task of sorting through the wool pelts. It wasn't something that needed doing but it would allow the headstrong lad the time to cool off.

'I see.'

He didn't ask why Lloyd was so against him. With features like Tristan's, jealous men were probably something he had to deal with frequently. She wondered briefly whether he'd had many lovers, before deciding that it didn't matter.

'If you found your way from the chamber, perhaps you would like to take yourself back there.'

She heard his soft laugh.

'After you've spoken to me, I will return. I'll even be kind to the guard you will no doubt post outside and stay there until you next have need of me. Before I do so, I would be grateful if we could speak face to face. Although I am enjoying staring at this scene of…is that meant to be a sheep or a dragon?' She was glad of the tapestry because he could not see her smile; she hated that she was responding to his light-hearted charm. 'I think it's a sheep.' His voice was louder now, he had obviously leaned closer to get a better look. 'But that is a very long tail, with a suspiciously pointy end. Unless, is that how a ram looks? Huh, how is it that I don't know that?'

'I know what you're doing.'

'Looking at your interesting tapestry?'

'Trying to make me like you.'

There was a quiet beat. 'Is it working?'

Surprisingly, yes.

'Not at all. I am in awe of your lack of intelligence. I cannot believe a man of your age does not know what ram genitalia look like.'

'What can I say? I have never thought to look until confronted with this…intriguing scene, but now I shall make it the first thing I do when released from your captivity.'

She pressed a hand over her mouth; she did not want him to hear the laugh that was trying to escape.

'I will join you in *my* antechamber,' she began when she was sure she had erased all trace of her amusement from her voice, 'but I want to hear you move away from the tapestry.'

There was little she could do if he attacked her but he'd had the opportunity to do so for the whole time they had stood talking. He could have killed her ten times over and he hadn't. She was going to have to trust that he would continue to respect her person. Unease writhed in her stomach; she did not count on people acting honourably easily.

'Of course,' he said immediately. 'I would never hurt you, Lady Catrin.' The teasing note had gone from his voice too.

Despite his words, and the sincerity she could hear in them, she waited until she heard his footsteps move away from the other side of the tapestry.

'I'm on the other side of the room,' he called out.

She lifted the edge of the tapestry, her dagger still clutched in one hand. Sure enough, Tristan was leaning with his back against the far wall, his legs crossed at his ankles, his arms folded. She slipped around the tapestry and stepped into the room.

She knew the moment Tristan caught sight of her face. His cocky grin faded as the skin of his neck turned red, the colour spreading up before washing over his cheeks. His lips parted and his hands fell to his sides. She bit her lip, once more stopping a smile.

He must have wondered why she hadn't fallen prey to his charm earlier and now he knew. She was just like him—people had been falling for the way she looked since she'd been a young girl. It was both a blessing and a curse. She knew every trick he did, had undoubtedly deployed them herself at some point in her life and had once revelled in the adoration she could elicit just from the way her features were aligned. She'd learned the hard way that that type of veneration could cause problems, vicious, harmful problems that could destroy lives. She'd lost friends through jealousy, unwittingly made enemies through envy of her looks and been betrayed and heartbroken because she had believed someone loved her, because how could they not when she looked like this? She made it a point to never try and win someone over by employing her wiles. She was firm and she was fair and she worked hard to earn her people's respect that way. She would never use her beauty to manipulate.

She had not met anyone new for a while and it was fascinating to watch Sir Tristan compose himself, closing his mouth and recrossing his arms. It was hard to keep herself still, to not allow her head to tilt or to show a smirk at his reaction.

'I can see why you would want to keep that face covered, your ears are uneven,' he said eventually.

She laughed, unable to stop the sharp burst of amusement. She watched him swallow as his gaze never left her face. His reaction made her feel better about admiring his shoulders on their walk to the castle earlier. 'Better my uneven ears than those eyebrows.' She nodded to his forehead, where two perfectly symmetrical eyebrows rested above deliciously dark eyes. He reached up and smoothed them; she gazed down at her dagger to hide her growing smile. A point to her in this skirmish of words.

'Do take a seat.' She gestured to the chair opposite her own on the other side of her desk. It was smaller than her own, one of the few of her father's tactics that she'd kept. She wanted the person sitting opposite her to remember that she was in charge here. Her people were seemingly loyal but she was still a woman in a role that was traditionally a man's. It didn't hurt to subtly remind people of her place as their leader.

They both lowered themselves to sitting slowly, as if moving too fast would give the other person the upper hand.

He glanced at her face before focusing on straightening out his clothes. 'You're remarkably beautiful,' he said after a while.

'I know.'

Laughter huffed out of him like a punch of air. 'Of course you do.'

'Just like you are particularly handsome.'

His grin was infectious. 'You think so?'

'Despite the abomination of those eyebrows, you are pleasing to the eye, yes. But handsome is not the same as attractive.'

'Ouch,' he said. 'You are one of the most brutal women I have ever met.'

Good. She wanted to be different, for him to realise that just because his mouth looked as if it was made for kissing she was not going to fawn over him. If her own experience was anything to go by, she expected that women had fallen over themselves to please him before now.

'You may have well-proportioned features but it does not mean you can charm me into doing what you want.

Even if I found you attractive, the future of my castle is of paramount importance to me.'

'I understand.' He nodded slowly. 'And if I could get past the hideousness of those ears, your beauty would not stop me from trying to complete my mission—nothing will.'

'Then we understand each other.'

'We do.'

They gazed at each other for longer than was strictly necessary. The air between them seemed to warm as something indefinable flickered around her heart, something she was going to ignore. Not only was this man her enemy, he was also over-confident. Two very unattractive qualities.

'You were going to tell me why you are here,' she said when the weight of silence began to press down on her. 'Or do I need to encourage Lloyd to hurry up with building that rack?'

He shuddered dramatically, breaking their locked gaze. 'There is no need for any sort of torture. I was willing to tell you the reason for my visit from the moment we met. I am here on the behalf of His Majesty the King of England, Edward. He requests that you...' Tristan shifted in his chair. 'He requests...' He cleared his throat. 'That is to say, he asks that you leave Pwll Du Castle so that he can install one of his loyal followers as liege. He understands that this has been your home since birth and he is willing to compensate you accordingly.' Tristan rubbed his hands along his thighs, pressing on his knees as if to stop them from moving.

Catrin's heart thundered in her ears. This could not be true. Lord Ogmore and his increasingly absurd plots must be behind this. Her bothersome nemesis had to be the source of this ludicrous story because to think otherwise was a nightmare Catrin had never considered. One could ignore a bumbling fool but to refuse an order from the King was treasonous. Sir Tristan must be lying because the truth would upend her world.

'Do you really expect me to believe that King Edward knows about this tiny castle in the depths of Wales with hardly any occupants?'

'King Edward is aware of many things,' said Sir Tristan loftily.

Catrin scoffed.

Sir Tristan leaned forward, resting his forearms on his legs. 'Look, I don't know how King Edward knows, in truth. It is not as if he and I have sat down for a conversation about this. I am merely a knight sent to do the bidding of the great man. In my belongings I have a seal from the King's household to verify who I am. If you return them to me, I will be able to show you.'

Catrin's stomach tightened. It could not be true. A seal could be stolen or copied. It might not mean anything. Sir Tristan must be a wonderful liar because she could see no falsehood in his expression.

'And what, pray tell, is the way I will be compensated accordingly?'

'You will receive a sum of money.'

'Money,' she repeated. 'What use have I of that? Where am I to go?'

'A nunnery. No, I can see by the way your eyebrows are nearly tunnelling into your skull that suggestion is not a good one.' He glanced away from her, scratching his neck. 'Marriage?'

'To whom?' she demanded. Leaning back in her chair, she continued to frown at him, trying to set him alight with her gaze. Then a horrific thought occurred to her. 'Hell, not to you.'

He flinched and she ducked her head to hide a triumphant sneer, pleased to have landed a blow to the arrogant knight's pride.

'I don't know to whom,' he said frostily. It was the first time his charade of the pleasant, affable knight had broken down. She was pleased to have found a chink in his armour. It was one she would use again if she had to. 'All I know is that I was to take you to Windsor, so that appropriate arrangements could be made for your welfare.'

No. This was an utter outrage. As if she would travel anywhere with this man. She would not even be the one to escort him back to his chamber, that was how little time she wanted to spend with the fabler.

'As you can see, my welfare is fine here. If you are telling the truth, you can return to Windsor right now without me and inform the King that while I am grateful for his offer, it is unnecessary. I can swear an oath of allegiance to him, my people will be loyal to him and his heirs. Alternatively, you can return to Lord Ogmore and tell him he needs to come up with some better story if he really wants me to leave my home unguarded.'

The knot of anger in her stomach was growing, becoming harder and hotter with every breath. She'd been enjoying their repartee through the tapestry, her headache had gone as he'd made her laugh about those awful sheep and she'd started to like him. That was exactly what he had wanted, and she had fallen for it. She was a ninny-hammered half-wit who almost deserved to have her home taken from her.

'Is that all of your message?'

He nodded, his jaw tight.

'In that case, I shall return you to your chamber.' She had no idea how she was going to do that if he did not want to comply but a show of confidence had worked well for her in the past.

He regarded her for a long moment. He must be thinking along the same lines, must know that she was no match for him physically. She forced herself to hold his gaze. This would not be the first time she had faced a tough opponent and it would not be the last.

'Very well,' he said finally. 'I will leave you to think about what I have said.'

'There is nothing to think about. You already have my answer. But I will give you some time to rest in your chamber before sending you on your way with a message for Ogmore.'

He shook his head. 'I swear to you that I am telling you the truth. I have never heard of this Lord Ogmore of whom you speak. You need to think about King Edward's demands because if you disobey him, I am the least of your worries.' He made to stand but paused, his hands on the arms of the chair. 'He'll send an army, in case that wasn't clear. Are you prepared to risk the welfare of your people over your own desires?'

'It is not *my* desires that keep me here.' How dare he suggest such a thing? 'It is the welfare of those who live here that concern me.' The inhabitants of Pwll Du Castle had suffered under her father's rule and she had only been able to watch, helpless. She would not put her people through anything like that again, not if she could help it. She had brought order and steadiness to their lives and her own and she did not want to let that go for anything. Even if Sir Tristan was telling the truth, surely her castle was not worth the time and effort, not if the rumours were true and King Edward was about to go to war with France. 'And I hardly think King Edward will bother himself to send an army.'

'Then you are more naïve than you look. King Edward, and his father before him, have campaigned hard to make Wales a part of their Kingdom and he will not give up control easily.' Sir Tristan's expression was grim, no trace of the laughter she'd encountered when she had first stepped into the antechamber. He stood, his height and breadth seeming to take up a large part of the room. 'I can see myself back.'

She laughed incredulously. 'I don't think so. In fact, wait here.' Amazingly, he stayed exactly where he was. 'You must have some sort of tool on you in order to get out of the chamber. I want you to give it to me.'

He spread his arms wide; his palms were callused, his fingers were long and thick. 'I have nothing on me.'

'That cannot be true.'

'You are welcome to search me.' Amusement danced in his eyes once more. Perhaps he thought she would not accept the challenge.

'And you'll just stand there and let me do so?'

He shrugged. 'Consider this my show of good faith. I swear to you I am not lying about the message and I swear to you I am not lying about having nothing on me either.'

She came closer. He did not move. She was not afraid

of him, he'd had plenty of time to hurt her since she'd entered the antechamber, and yet, as she stepped up close in front of him, her heart hammered in her chest. This near, she could smell the leather of his tunic and the faint salty tang of his skin. She cleared her throat. 'Spread out your arms further.'

He lifted them so his palms were shoulder height, the same level as her eyes. The soft material of his shirt clung to the curves of his muscles. With a briskness she didn't feel, she ran her hands down his left arm, the heat of him burning her palms through the softness of his clothes. She grasped his wrist, turning his hand both ways. A thick scar ran across the palm and she traced it with her fingertip. He inhaled sharply but when she turned to look at him, his gaze was fixed on a point in front of him. She moved to the other side and repeated her search, a strange sensation swirling in the pit of her stomach.

She stepped behind him and ran her hands down his back, his muscles twitching as she moved over every inch of him. His hair curled at the nape of his neck and she swept it to one side in one swift movement. His breath hitched again and the small hairs at the back of his neck stood to attention.

She moved round to his front, sliding her hands over his broad chest and down the sides to his waist. There was no sign of any weapon, only the solidity of his strong body.

'Keep your arms up,' she demanded when he started to lower them. To her surprise, he returned them to their original position. 'Move your legs apart.'

She heard his deep inhale and long, slow exhale as he complied with her demands.

Her hands trembled, a strange headiness flooding through her as this big man obeyed her commands. She flexed her fingers before resuming her search. She travelled down one leg, her hands systematically moving from front to back over his thick thigh and strong calf, her fingers dipping into the edges of his boots, searching for hidden knives or lockpicks, but there was nothing to find. She moved to his other leg, biting her bottom lip. She reversed her search, over his knee, the inside of his leg, the curve of his hip. By the time she stood up, his chest rose and fell quickly.

She had been the leader of Pwll Du Castle for nearly two years but she had never experienced the potent power that was racing through her veins in this moment. This man could snap her like a twig if he chose to do so, and yet it was as if he was completely at her mercy. It was probably some trick, some way of making her think she was in control before seizing it for himself. Even knowing this, it didn't stop the pull towards him she was experiencing in this moment. This close, she could see the crease of a dimple in his left cheek and the dip in the middle of his top lip and she wanted to stay like this, to study his features, to find his imperfections, to map them and to know him.

She moved her hands to the front of his chest and swept them out to the edges of his body. His eyes fluttered closed as his heart pounded beneath her hand. She continued her search, slowly now that it was nearly over, checking each rib, each taut muscle of his stomach. She was almost done when she encountered a hard length. He grunted, colour staining his high cheekbones. He did not pull away and for a beat she stayed where she was, the urge to stroke, to see this man come completely undone was so strong that her knees weakened.

She dropped her hands to her sides. His eyes remained closed, his arms still raised. When she was sure her voice would not betray her trembling hands, she said, 'You may return to your chamber.'

He lowered his arms. Opening his eyes, his gaze slanted to her. She tilted her chin and his lips twitched.

'As you wish,' he murmured and a fine tremor ran through her.

'Wynne will bring you something to eat later.' She didn't know why she was telling him this, only that she was deliberately prolonging their interaction.

He nodded, still gazing at her through hooded eyes.

She walked around him. Opening her antechamber door, she spotted a couple of her men walking in the direction of the courtyard and she called out to them in Welsh, asking them to escort Tristan to his chamber and instructing one of them to remain outside until a rota could be established. Both men seemed pleased to have been given such an important task and made a big show of coming to march off with Sir Tristan.

Tristan was easily the size of both of them put together and from the way he winked at her as he passed, he knew it. She knew his compliance was an act, that he was behaving obediently in order to get on her good side, so that she would fall for the act and do as he asked. She was aware of it but a small part of her was still responding to it and especially to the hard length of him—that part of him had shown he had enjoyed her hands on him as much as she had.

She closed the door quickly before she could do something dim-witted, like run after him and ask him to help her with the strange ache that had built up inside her as she'd touched him.

She sank down into the chair Tristan had recently occupied. There was no way it could still be warm from his body and yet she fancied she could still feel the residual heat of him. Her fingers ran over the wooden armrests, gathering herself.

It was a shame that Sir Tristan was her enemy, whether he was working for Lord Ogmore or the King. When they were talking she could forget that unpleasant fact and when she was running her hands over his magnificent body that knowledge went completely out of her mind.

That she liked the way he spoke to her, that his body was divine, that running her hands over him had nearly brought her to her knees changed nothing. Or rather it reaffirmed that she must stick with her plan. If she developed a softness for him, he could easily claim victory over her. If she let him, she knew that he could persuade her to leave her castle and walk away with him and that would not do. She had allowed herself weakness over a man before and the consequences of that had nearly destroyed her. She'd built herself up and become the woman she was today: a leader.

Their time together in her antechamber had shown her that he was not going to be honest about his involvement with Lord Ogmore. That meant it was time to move onto the next part of her plan involving Tristan. When it was over, he would not stand obediently in front of her. In fact, she would probably never lay eyes on him again, which was for the best. He was a distraction she did not need.

Chapter Four

Tristan waited until he heard the door to the chamber locking before he checked under his blankets. His lockpicks were where he'd left them. He slid them back into their hiding places in his boots and then settled his back against the wall.

That had been...there weren't really words for what he'd just experienced. He'd been touched by a woman before and it had been fine, much like sitting on these rushes staring at the flickering candle was fine. But that...that moment in Lady Catrin's antechamber when she had run her hands over him had been something else entirely.

As she'd approached him, he'd known that he could have easily overpowered her. She was no match for him physically—she was muscled, yes, bigger than most women he knew, but she was small in comparison to him, half his width, if that. It would have been the work of moments to gain the upper hand. If she had managed to fight back, she might not have even been able to inflict a bruise. But the moment she had commanded him to stretch out his arms so that she could inspect his body for hidden weapons, something hot and liquid had raced through him. Before she'd laid a hand on his arm, he was the hardest he'd ever been. He had submitted to her search entirely and that had been...intoxicating. Better than any red wine he had ever consumed, better than any rich meal. And when she had touched him, hell, he'd forgotten his own name, would have given anything, absolutely anything for her in that moment. Everything had centred on that one press of her fingers. He'd had to fight with everything that he had not to make any sound. Just thinking about it now, locked in this dark chamber, had him standing painfully to attention. Nothing he'd ever experienced had been like those long, exhilarating moments in Lady Catrin's antechamber and he'd been entirely clothed.

Maybe it was because she didn't fawn over him. For as long as he could remember, women had vied for his attention. But not this woman. She treated him with hostile disdain at worst and polite indifference at best. She hadn't been repelled by his interest in her but she hadn't seemed...triumphant, or pleased.

It was all irrelevant anyway. He wasn't here to bed the lady of the castle. He did not use his looks to seduce women into providing him with something he wanted. He would not sully his body to achieve his aims, despite what his liege and others thought. He had never done anything like that and never would.

The candle made strange shadows flicker over the white-washed walls. Tristan watched them dance as he tried to sort through his plan of attack. Lady Catrin didn't fully believe him, didn't trust him, hated anything to do with his charm and wanted him gone. She seemed practical and resolute, a woman who liked order. It was a difficult starting place but he was in the castle, he had his lockpicks and she was talking to him, so it could have been worse.

Whoever this Lord Ogmore was, he was hindering the communication between himself and Lady Catrin. Tristan was going to have to find a way to deal with the situation because the lord was obviously causing big problems for her, dominating her thoughts and not allowing her to see that his own message was the truth. He wasn't sure yet how he would do such a thing, but it was essential that it was done and done soon.

He had no idea how long he stared at the wall, but at some point food and drink were delivered by a scowling Wynne. Wynne barked a few incomprehensible words of Welsh at him before slamming the door shut. Tristan held his breath as the air from the moving door caused the flame to burn low for a moment, but relaxed as it roared back. He was a grown man and a respected knight…he was not afraid of the dark. It would be easier to…think if he was not plunged into darkness.

He caught a waft of the richly cooked meat coming from the trencher and moved over to it. He picked up a cut and held it towards the light to work out what it was. A leg of poultry of some sort. He put it to his lips, it had been cooked in something sweet and sticky, normally his favourite, but he could not bring himself to wolf it down.

This whole experience of being locked up was a world away from how he'd been treated as a child. His mother, an angry woman, had adored her husband but loathed his many affairs. Tristan, his father's image in looks, had borne the brunt of her fury when she could not punish her large, powerful husband. A locked chamber with no light was a staple of his early years. He'd long since conquered his fear of the dark—grown men did not curl into a ball and cry, not like a little boy who had only a vague understanding of what he had done to deserve such a punishment.

The echo of his memories dampened his normally voracious appetite. He forced himself to take a bite; he had no idea when he would next eat and he needed to keep his strength up if he was going to escape from the chamber again. Especially if he was going to engage in another battle of wits with Lady Catrin. The food was good, no scraps for the prisoners of Pwll Du Castle. Even so, the meat stuck in his throat as the walls seemed to close around him.

At some point he must have slept; dreams of reaching for something just outside his grasp haunted him. He woke to the sound of feet pounding past the locked door, more than one person; by the heavy thud of their boots, he guessed at men. He sprang straight to standing, rubbing his eyes, brushing away the vague nightmares that clung to him. Another hurried set of footsteps passed by and another. He strode the few steps to his prison door. He didn't need to press his ear to the wood to hear shouting coming from deeper into the castle; it was sharp and fast.

He knew those sounds, even though he could not make out any individual words. They were cries made by men in battle. Without pausing to think of what might become of him, Tristan pulled out his lockpicks once more and put them to use. When the heavy door swung open, the noises became louder, more insistent. He raced towards them, not knowing what he would find, his years of training making it impossible for him to do anything other than throw himself into the path of danger.

Outside, dawn was breaking, the low sun throwing long shadows over the crowded courtyard. Men were running towards the battlements, women and children bundling stocks of food and fuel and hurriedly carrying them inside the thick castle walls. From the clamour, it was clear now that the castle was under attack. One woman glanced at him but it was obvious she didn't see him, not when her gaze was full of panic.

Men were hastily pulling on armour as they ran towards the ramparts, calling and shouting to one another in a mix of English and Welsh. No one paid him any attention as he rushed through them, scanning the crowd, searching for Lady Catrin. He could not imagine what the fiery leader of the castle would do, had no idea why it was important to him that no harm befell her. By the time he made it to the other side of the courtyard he had not set eyes on her. He stopped running, his pulse hammering in his throat, his gaze searching the battlements.

He spied her and his breath caught in his throat. She was striding along the walls amongst the men defending the castle. Over her chest, she had pulled on a breastplate but, despite her height, it swamped her frame, surely becoming more of a hindrance than a help.

He swore, climbing the steps two at a time in his haste to join her.

Before he could reach her side, a young man yelped and fell backwards against the opposite wall, a bow and arrow clutched in one hand.

'Lloyd!' cried Lady Catrin, running towards her fallen

soldier, but Tristan reached him first. He dropped to his knees, assessing the damage.

'It's all right,' he told the man, whose skin had lost all colour. 'It is only a scratch.' An arrow had grazed the lad's shoulder but the cut was not deep. He would live but it was clear from his pallor and his wide eyes that he was in shock. 'Here, put your hand on it like this.' He pressed Lloyd's hand to the wound. 'Tighter. That's it.'

'They shot at me,' he said.

Tristan's heart clenched at the naivety in the young man's statement. 'The bastards,' he agreed.

'What happened?' asked Lady Catrin, dropping to her haunches beside them.

'He's been clipped by an arrow, but the wound is not deep,' Tristan told her. 'He's going to make a complete recovery.' He did not mention infection, the lad was already terrified and they would both know the horrors of a cut turning septic. 'Do you have someone attending the wounded?' he asked instead.

Lady Catrin licked her lips, her gaze darting between him and the blood slowly seeping from between Lloyd's fingers. 'Ffion is in the Great Hall; she is setting up somewhere for the injured to go but...' She rubbed her fingers over her forehead. 'We have barely even started. I don't...'

Lady Catrin had been calm and collected when she had accosted Tristan yesterday and she had kept her composure during the interrogation in her antechamber but Tristan could see her unravelling.

'Excellent, Ffion is doing the right thing. Take Lloyd there and explain what has happened.' The further Lady

Catrin was away from the action the better, especially in her ill-fitting armour.

It seemed she did not agree. 'I cannot leave the battlements.'

'What are you hoping to achieve?' he growled. 'You have no weapon and your armour isn't fit for a donkey.'

She straightened, worry leaving her gaze, replaced by anger. 'Who are you to tell me what to do?'

'*That* should be obvious. I'm the man who is going to get you out of this situation.' An arrow flew over the battlements, dangerously close to them. Lloyd moaned, leaning away from it. 'I need your bow and arrows.' Tristan held out his hand to Lloyd but the young man glanced at his mistress.

There was no time to be impressed by the loyalty Lady Catrin had instilled in her people or to argue with either of them. Tristan snatched the weapon from Lloyd, pivoted on his heel and stood in one fluid motion. Spying an enemy archer, he wasted no time in loosing several arrows in that direction. He had a moment to see that his hit had been successful before dropping back down. Further down the wall, some of Lady Catrin's men cheered in acknowledgement of the successful shot but he paid them no attention.

'Who are they and what do they want?' he demanded.

Lady Catrin bit her lip, her gaze darting down to the courtyard below, where her people were still scurrying about, some still storing goods, others building piles of weapons.

'I was telling you the truth yesterday,' he reassured her. 'I am a messenger. I am not here to make war with you. I have no stake in what is happening with the people outside these walls. I *am* a trained warrior. I can help you if you let me, but if you lock me in that room again and I die in there, I am going to be furious with you.'

She half-smiled at that and he was struck once again by just how lovely she was to look at. He knew that if someone was pleasing to the eye it meant nothing. It did not mean she had a good nature or was a strong leader, but it was somehow hard to stay irritated with her as her blue gaze followed her people's activities in the courtyard below. Next to them, Lloyd continued to clutch at his arm but his colour was returning, the shock receding.

'We heard rumours that Ogmore was planning a siege, but this…' She shook her head. 'This is different from anything he has ever done before.' She turned and faced him, the brilliance of her blue eyes hitting him. 'It is like he has learned how to organise himself and his men.'

Tristan raised his hands, the wood of Lloyd's bow brushing against his forehead. 'I know nothing of this, I swear to you on the life of my stallion, Darrow.'

She gazed at him assessingly. A shout from further down the ramparts broke her concentration. More arrows passed overhead, none of them having the force or accuracy to do any damage. Tristan swore. Standing, he saw that the original archer was down, probably never to rise again, but two more now stood in his place. He swore again and the next few moments became the feel of the shaft between his fingers, the pull of the string and the soft thwack of the arrow as it released.

'More,' he demanded when the quiver was empty, forgetting that he was not with his knightly companions. But he needn't have worried; the arrows were replenished and he carried on his one-man attack.

It was working, the opposing army was retreating, falling back so that they were no longer in his firing range. A thrill raced through him as the last of the stragglers moved behind an invisible line where his arrows would not reach. He set the base of the bow on the floor beside him, his eyes still on the retreating men. He had held them off for now but they would be able to regroup and plan a different line of attack. What he needed was to...

'Sir Tristan.' He turned, blinking at the woman beside him. In the flurry of battle he had forgotten his surroundings, his mission and all that rested on its successful completion. All he had thought about was beating the enemy, bending them to his will. This was what he lived for, what he was good at and the reason he had trained his whole life.

'Sir Tristan,' repeated Lady Catrin, who was crouched low by his side, Lloyd no longer anywhere to be seen. 'Is it safe to stand?'

'It is.' He reached down a hand to help her straighten.

She gazed at it as if it was a strange sight and he thought that she might not take it, that perhaps the death and destruction she had witnessed made his touch disgusting to her. Slowly, as if she could not quite believe herself, her palm slid against his, her skin warm and soft. The clamour of activity beneath them fell away, the sound of men calling to each other faded. The world stilled and slowed, time changing its meaning as the moment spooled into eternity. There was only her touch and the tranquil blueness of her eyes.

Then she was standing, pulling her hand from his and adjusting her terrible breastplate. She turned from him, peering over the battlements at the scene outside her castle walls. He could not tell from the still way she held herself how she was feeling. She could be triumphant that her enemies were retreating or she could be horrified by the bloodshed. Beyond her, further down the battlements, the faces of the men of the castle were easier to read, a plain mixture of shock and awe. Next to him, their lady remained silent.

He cleared his throat. They would need to plan for the next stage, to regroup faster than their opponents, but before he could say all that, she was turning back to him.

'I believe you now,' was all she said.

Chapter Five

Sir Tristan had been a god full of vengeance and fire as he faced Lord Ogmore's assault. Catrin had called to her people so that he had a constant supply of arrows delivered to him. She could see from the way his gaze had locked on his targets that he had been unaware of everything around him, that she and her castle had ceased to exist. All that had mattered to him was success. He had single-handedly driven Ogmore's army into retreat. Without him, they would already be losing, unprepared for this new, more deadly version of their opponent.

'I believe you now,' she said to him again and he responded with a curt nod.

'Good.'

'That solves none of our problems, however.'

His mouth hitched at one corner, the ghost of a smile flickering in his dark eyes. 'I agree. It is not ideal for anyone, not least for that miserable cur.' He nodded in the direction of the attacking army. They were organising themselves away from Tristan's range, heated discussions appearing to take place between the men, one of whom was definitely Ogmore. She could tell by the way the morning sun shone off the top of his smooth head.

'I currently feel he has the advantage,' she admitted.

Tristan shrugged. 'For now, perhaps. But I am sure that we will prevail.'

'We will, will *we*?'

His smile was broader this time. 'Whether you like it or not, Lady Catrin, you need me and my training.'

She folded her arms across her chest. 'Be that as it may...'

'Be that as it is,' he corrected. His eyes were dancing now, humour sparking in their depths. She had the strangest conflicting urges to either throw him over the side of the ramparts or pull him closer and press her mouth to his.

She did neither. She was a calm leader, someone who did not give in to passion but who followed logic. In her youth, she had been ruled by her feelings but not now. She was not going to panic. She would plan every possible response to this turn of events.

'This is my castle and I will not have you striding in and taking over.'

His humour fled. 'I would not do such a thing.'

'Hmm.' Lady Catrin had never met a man of Sir Tristan's stature that hadn't tried to stamp their authority over everyone around them.

He straightened his shoulders. 'I have never sought to be the leader of a grand castle. I have only ever wanted to become a great knight. All I have ever wanted is to be good enough to join the King's Knights.'

She whistled. 'You have a high opinion of yourself.'

He raised an eyebrow. 'I suppose you think I am going to tell you it is warranted after your display.'

He grinned, flashing his teeth. 'Do I think you are

going to say it? No, I do not. In our short acquaintance, I have discovered that you are the most stubborn woman ever to have existed. It will require a much wider display of my abilities before I get anything approaching praise from you. However, your eyes are expressive and I can tell that you are greatly impressed by my daring prowess.'

He was right, she was. She had never seen anything like the skill or the power that Sir Tristan had displayed. She had never met a member of the King's Knights but, from the stories she had heard, she knew them to be a formidable band of warrior knights and, from what she could see, Tristan was the same. But he was also right in that she would be damned if she told him. He was arrogant enough as it was without her compliments adding to his confidence.

'Whatever you think you are reading in my gaze is most likely down to the morning breeze stinging my eyes.' She blinked rapidly as if there were strong gusts up on this high wall when, in reality, it was a perfect summer's morning with no wind stirring.

He grinned again and she turned away from him, disliking the way her heart kicked at the sight of his smile.

'I know I have already sworn to you on Darrow's life—and you do not know how important that beast is to me—but I will swear to you on his life again, for what it is worth, that I do not seek to take over as Lord of your castle, or indeed any castle. I have told you why I am here and you have said that you believe me.'

'I do.' That Sir Tristan was an emissary from King Edward was something she would have to face but it was a problem for another day. She could not give the message the breadth and space it needed for her to consider what it would mean for her ordered life and for her people. Not when she had an army at the gates.

'I cannot complete my mission with this lord of yours preventing us from leaving the castle,' Tristan said. 'Like it or not, we have a common enemy.'

Even though she was not looking at the knight, it was as if she was aware of the space he took up, his warmth somehow radiating out to her.

'We do.'

She bit the inside of her cheek. She hated to do this. Hated that she and her people had been blindsided by the strength of Ogmore's attack, that she'd thought them ready, only to be horribly wrong. She had spent the years since her father's death building a community, a place where everyone could feel safe and happy and as if they were all responsible for each other. It was the exact opposite of her father's way of ruling, which had been all about himself, rules being bent to suit him. Now she would have to ask for help from a stranger, a man who was also hellbent on destroying her life but in a different way from Ogmore. At least if Tristan had his way it was only her who would suffer and not her people. If Ogmore managed to seize control of Pwll Du Castle then they were all doomed. That made the choice easier. In fact, it wasn't a choice at all; her people's safety always came first.

She turned to him, losing herself in the warmth of his dark gaze. 'What should we do now?'

She had expected him to gloat a little at her question but she was proved wrong yet again.

'Have your men stand guard. Make sure they are seen to be moving; we want Ogmore to think we are stockpiling weapons up here. Light some fires, get some water boiling. Do you have tar?' She nodded. 'Good, get that heated up too. I do not think they will be coming close any time soon, but we need to be prepared if they do. Your men can alert us if Ogmore begins to move again.'

'And us?'

'I would like you to give me a tour of your weapons and supplies. I need to know what is at our disposal and what we need.' He paused, his gaze flicking over her body. 'We also need to find you some better armour. That is no good.'

She glanced down at herself. 'It was my father's.'

He reached out and ran a finger around the top, lightly brushing the skin of her neck as he did so. His breathing didn't alter, there was no sign that his pulse beat any faster at the accidental touch but her whole body sprang to attention, as if every nerve-ending was alight. It had been so long since a man had made her body sing and, for a brief flash, she wanted to lean into it, to forget everything and let herself feel. The desire was over as quickly as it had come; if she had a need then she would have to find someone else to satisfy it. Not this man—anyone but this man.

'It is a good quality piece of armour,' he said, dropping his hand as if nothing had happened, which, for him, it clearly hadn't. 'I am not doubting that. But it does not fit you and therefore it is as good as useless.'

'I don't think...'

He gently tugged on the edge of it. There was very little force involved but she still stumbled to the right slightly. His other hand caught her before she fell, his fingers curling over her forearm. 'Do you see what I mean?'

told him. 'It needs to be made to fit Lady Catrin as a matter of urgency.'

Catrin scowled at him; that distinctly sounded as if he *was* taking over after all.

He caught her look. 'I am not going to apologise for being concerned about your safety. The health of the leader takes priority in any battle.'

'It won't be enough,' interjected the blacksmith before an argument could begin. 'Not at the rate he's going.'

Catrin nodded. 'We shall add the acquirement of iron ore to our goals,' she told him, although how she was going to do that without leaving the castle, she had no idea. They had no supply. 'In the meantime, do you think you would be able to alter my armour? Sir Tristan is right, it is currently far too big for me.'

'Aye,' said the older man. 'Take it off and I'll see to it straight away.'

The metal armour weighed down her shoulders, the extra layer adding to the heat of the day. She pulled it off, shuffling away from Tristan when he made to help her. If it had been another man she would have accepted, but it was better if he didn't touch her.

Leaving the armour with the blacksmith, they made their way to the Pwll Du Castle stores. The door was already flung open, a pile of bows tipped over, like drunks at a celebration. Swords were stored in a far corner, the stock depleted as men had come and taken them earlier, the rush of action clear in the disordered mess left behind. Other than that, they had a few long lances left over from when her father had enjoyed jousting with his cronies and a slowly rotting axe.

Heat crept up her neck as Tristan ran his gaze over

His touch was scrambling her thoughts; she
away from him. 'I understand,' she agreed quickl
perate for him to stop touching her so she could
her wits. 'I shall look for something more suitabl

'Or have your blacksmith change this one. It
not be too hard. This bit could be removed.' He r
out as if he was going to feel the edges of her a
once more but she stepped backwards. She nee
think and his proximity was not making it easy.

He dropped his hand, a small frown creasing h

'That is a good idea,' she told him before he
her to explain her behaviour. 'I shall get him to
to it right away.'

She strode away from him, towards the other
the battlements, so there could be no more touch
cidental or otherwise. He followed her, waiting p
while she gave the orders, yet another point in hi
that he did not go around barking out commands.
questioned Sir Tristan's involvement in their c
even though he had been their prisoner only ye
No one who had seen him fight could doubt tha
currently their biggest asset and from the punish
had meted out to Ogmore's men, it was clear he
on their enemy's side.

Back in the courtyard, she headed straigh
blacksmith's forge, Sir Tristan's stride matchi
The man's face was dark with soot as he hamm
arrow heads. 'We'll need more iron,' he said b
a greeting. 'The knight is using it up fast.' He
in Tristan's direction; already news of his pro
spread.

'You can take some from this breastplate,' S

their pitiful stockpile. In his previous attacks, Ogmore had thought he could take their castle easily; it had been effortless to rebuff him with very little, far less than they had now. She and her people had been in the process of creating more but Catrin had prioritised food over weapons, believing that Ogmore and his men would be as ill-prepared for a fight as they had been in the past. Something had changed, somehow Ogmore's tactics had become better and under the stern warrior's assessment she felt woefully naïve.

'We have barrels for heating water and tar,' she told him. He already knew this but it seemed important to emphasise that their defence was not all that was in front of them.

He nodded slowly and her toes curled in her boots, shame cutting her deeply. She would prefer him to be arrogant and rude; this gentle acceptance of their inadequate weaponry was somehow worse than any of his teasing taunts.

'The gates and stonework of the walls look in good condition,' Tristan said, further compounding her misery with his faint praise.

'You can say it,' she said, not able to take another moment of him being polite.

'Say what?'

'That we are unprepared.'

He rubbed his forefinger along the length of his jaw. 'I am not going to criticise you, not when you are finally treating me as an ally and not your worst enemy. Besides, I have seen worse.'

'Have you?'

He paused. 'No.'

Unexpected laughter burst out of her, his answering grin dulling the edges of her embarrassment.

'I was trained by Lord Ormand,' he told her. 'You may not have heard of him, but his stronghold is one of the most impressive in the country, if not Europe.' She rolled her eyes. 'I am not telling you this as a boast, you insufferable woman. I am merely pointing out that if this was his weapon store, we all would have died quickly.'

'Oh.' Her amusement fled as quickly as it had arrived.

'Again, I am not saying that to scare you, so there is no need to look as if I have just kicked several babies. I am telling you that he was more likely to be under attack from greater forces than your Lord Ogmore. He also liked to train knights; it added to his sense of self-importance to have one of the largest, most successful training castles in the country. His stockpile of weapons could probably rival Windsor. My parents' stronghold was not as impressive but it was a larger one than this and so they had to have more weapons. I have not lived anywhere else so I cannot comment on whether this is normal or not.'

'I am not sure whether you are making me feel better or worse.'

He gazed down at the weapons. 'We can work with this. Your blacksmith looks competent and your people are efficient. Do not feel worse.' Somehow, this man she barely knew was soothing her worries. She'd been alone for such a long time, was still alone really, but Sir Tristan was sharing some of the burden, which she hadn't even realised was resting so heavily on her shoulders. 'What are your food supplies like?' he asked.

'Better than this,' she told him, pleased to have some

good news. 'We have been gathering food supplies and I believe we can last at least a month on what we have without having to leave the castle. Perhaps longer, if we are careful.' It would be difficult to be stuck within the walls, not to be able to leave and bathe in the river in this intense heat, but they could do it.

'And water?'

'There is a well.' She pointed towards it. 'The source of it is a secret, known only to me and one other. It is not from the river that runs directly outside and will not be easy for Ogmore to poison.'

'This is all good. We can always make weapons—' he gestured to the store at their feet '—but we cannot conjure food and water out of thin air. It is better this way around than having no food.'

Her heart lightening, they stepped back into the courtyard. The sun had risen and was now streaming over the ramparts, lighting up every corner of the wide expanse.

'Do you have a chain of command already set up?' he asked.

Her optimism faded as quickly as it had risen. She did not. She hadn't needed one in previous bouts with Ogmore. There had been her and Ffion leading, and Dafydd intimidating their enemy with his size. Their opponents had expected an easy victory and had been shocked by women willing to fight for their home. They'd been backed up by the men of the castle who at the time had been willing but young. The simple strategy had worked and they had not needed to plan anything complicated. In the intervening time, all of them had trained. They did not have a master-of-arms or anyone with experience but they had weapons and they had made targets and her people were better equipped than they had been in previous attacks. Ogmore had been better equipped than his two previous attacks, not to mention better organised, but his men had still been beaten back by one knight. If Tristan hadn't been here... Her knees gave way, unable to support her as the horror of everything settled on her shoulders.

Strong arms came around her, holding her up, guiding her away from the storeroom entrance, back to the courtyard and to a barrel lying sideways a few steps away. 'Take a seat,' said Tristan, his voice gruff with kindness.

She lowered herself down. There was something wrong with her chest. It was tight and she couldn't get enough air into her lungs. She inhaled rapidly but it made no difference.

She was vaguely aware of Tristan sitting next to her, the wood creaking under his weight. A hand settled on her back, the soothing stroke of it anchoring her to the world. By her feet, the gravel was bone-dry; a quick scuff of her feet had a small plume of dust rising into the air.

'You must think I am pathetic,' she said when her breath had settled back to something approaching normality.

'Not at all.' She half-twisted to look at him and his hand dropped. She missed the comfort but there was no way to ask him to continue; it would be too strange, too personal. 'You are doing remarkably well for a person whose home is under attack,' he said.

She barked out a laugh. 'It is only morning and already I have lost the ability to both breathe and stand.'

'You are breathing perfectly normally and it is usual to want to sit and contemplate what's happening. For now, there is nowhere you need to be. Everything is under control. We will take this time to calm down and assess.'

'You do not seem as if you need to relax.'

His large back was slightly curled, his arms resting on his knees. His chest was rising and falling steadily. There was no sign of the despondent man she had seen trudging through the Welsh countryside yesterday, or the arrogant knight who had tried to charm her in her antechamber. If she had not seen him before this moment, she would not have thought those other versions of him could possibly exist. This was a man carved from the earth, solid, dependable, possibly their way out of this crisis. But also, possibly, the bringer of her own personal nightmare. She couldn't think about his message from King Edward now, not when her breathing was finally back under control.

'I am calm,' he agreed, reminding her of what they were talking about. 'But that is because situations like this are what I have trained for my whole life.'

'That and you do not know or love anyone in this castle.'

He straightened. 'Is there someone *you* love here?'

'Everyone,' she replied simply.

'Of course.' He settled back down.

'What did you think I meant?' she asked, knowing full well that he thought she had been talking about a man.

His eyes narrowed. 'I thought perhaps there was someone you were pining over.'

She laughed. 'I am too old for that, too jaded also.'

'Ah, I sense a story there.'

There was and there was nothing happy about it.

'One you will never hear. I noticed,' she carried on

before he could protest, 'that you did not comment on my age.'

'Oh, well, I can see you that you are ancient by the deep lines carved into the skin around your eyes and the grey hairs in your braid.'

She laughed again, amazed that she could do so after the morning she had experienced. 'I care about everyone here. We are family. If they hurt, I hurt.' She recalled Lloyd's pale face as he'd gripped his arm. 'Do you really think Lloyd will be fine? I did not see the wound, only the blood seeping over his fingers.' She knew the image would haunt her dreams. Lloyd was always eager to prove himself but he was young, far younger than her, maybe not in years but in experience.

'I do. He was more shocked that someone had the audacity to shoot an arrow at him than anything else. I do not blame him; there is something quite unbelievable about it the first time you are hit. It was his first taste of warfare but I fear it will not be his last.'

She pressed her hands together. She wanted to ask him what he had experienced before he'd appeared in their lives but she sensed the story was long and they did not have the time.

'We need to make a chain of command then.'

'We do.'

For a while they discussed a simple strategy, deciding on who would report to whom. He did not try to take over; occasionally he would make suggestions but never in an overbearing manner and always in a way that meant she had less work. She still did not fully trust him but it helped to have someone like him with whom to share thoughts.

'But I am doing very little,' she said when they had finished.

'On the contrary, you are doing most of the work.'

'A lot of it seems to be listening to what people are saying rather than doing anything,' she said in protest. She had always been at the centre of any fighting, although admittedly that had been nothing like this. Still, she did not want to be seen as a coward. If anyone was leading anyone into battle, it should be her.

'Until that breastplate is fixed, it is better for you to stay off the battlements. But it is more than that. There has to be someone coordinating everything. Without that, there will be chaos.'

She studied his expression, trying to find the trace of a lie. He stared back steadily, holding her gaze.

'I am not spinning you a child's tale,' he said after a while. 'As the leader, you need to be seen to lead, to have all the answers at your fingertips. If you are running around trying to involve yourself in every situation, you will lose track of the scope of the attack.' He held up a hand. 'Before you argue, I mean "you" in the general sense. I would advise any leader, male or female, to act in this way. It is also about perception.'

She leaned forward, adjusting the strap of her boot, which had become loose; the leather was old and worn, the material soft under her fingers. 'What do you mean?'

There was a slight hitch of his wide shoulders. She shouldn't be studying them, was trying not to, but it had been a long time since she had touched a man and she was only human. She hoped he hadn't noticed her attention, although she doubted it. She had noticed the slight catch of his breath every time he looked directly into her eyes, after all. Neither of them was as oblivious to the other as they were pretending.

'It is obvious to me that you are valued by your people,' he said eventually.

'This is true.'

He grinned. 'And you're modest, everyone likes that.'

'You may sound sarcastic, but I have worked hard to be well respected for my leadership and not for...' She gestured to her face and his smile faded as he looked at her.

'I see what you mean. When there is time, you must tell me how to achieve that. I feel I have only been successful twice in my life in getting people to like me despite the way I look.'

She wanted to ask him more but he was right; this was not the time or the place and really, his past and his future should not matter to her.

'You were saying...'

'Ah, yes. Your people respect you and are remarkably willing to follow your orders...'

She stood abruptly, any serenity or goodwill towards him vanishing instantly. 'What do you mean by *that*?' He pushed himself upright, towering over her, but it didn't matter; with anger surging through her she was sure she could win any confrontation. 'There is no need to answer. You meant that people follow me despite the hideous disadvantage I have of being born a woman.'

His eyes flashed. 'It is not an insult and I have not treated you any differently to how I would a man, so there is no need to act like an angry hedgehog.'

'Deny that it is what you meant then.'

She waited. The calls from the courtyard had died

down, all she could hear was the sound of heavy footfalls on the battlements above and the repetitive clanging of the blacksmith as he worked. After an age, he glanced at the floor. Triumph shot through her, quickly followed by a bone-aching disappointment. She had not wanted to be right.

'It is remarkable and, yes, I mean that because you are a woman,' he said slowly. 'But I do not understand why you think that is an insult. You have achieved something I have never heard of before. I am not suggesting it is a bad thing. Trust me, I have lived under an egotistical leader and a careless one, and what you appear to have here is something far better than I have ever seen, but that does make it unusual. The point I was trying to make, although badly it seems, is that as the person in control you need to be seen to be so by being at the centre of everything that happens here. We've established a chain of command, now you need to implement it and then you need to run it as tightly as you can. Standing here, under the clear blue sky, the enemy taking their time to regroup and this task seems easy. But if this siege goes on for weeks, then you will soon realise how hard you are going to have to work, how many difficult decisions will fall at your feet. As I've said, I have never sought to be leader of anything. I am a knight and a damned good one, but the role we have outlined for you is much harder than anything I have experienced or ever hope to.'

It was her turn to drop her gaze. Phrased in that way, her response to him seemed excessive. She was used to derisive comments from men. Her father had not thought any of her suggestions worthy of acknowledgement; his less pleasant guests had taken one look at her face and thought that all she deserved was pretty comments at best and wandering hands at worst. The one man she had thought she'd loved had tricked her, making her believe in a bright future, taking what he wanted from her and leaving her when it was obvious that everything he had ever told her was a lie. So, yes, she always did presume the worst, but it shouldn't follow that the man standing in front of her, offering her help when she needed it the most, was deceitful. She wasn't used to trusting those who had not proven themselves worthy, but it seemed she was going to have to take a leap of faith with Sir Tristan.

When she said nothing to his short speech, he continued, 'Where shall I send everyone for you to run through your plan—the Great Hall?'

She nodded.

'I will take over the watch on the ramparts while you do that.'

She nodded again. He paused as if waiting for more, but when she remained quiet he strode off, his long legs carrying him quickly out of sight.

Chapter Six

Tristan rested against the high stone wall, hidden from view. From this angle he could see the sweep of the defensive walls disappearing into the dark waters of the moat and Ogmore's men, their armour glinting in the sun.

After this morning's surprise attack had ended with a volley of his arrows, the enemy had made no further movement to come closer to Pwll Du Castle, but now tents were being erected further back from their frontline, an ominous sign that this was far from over.

Tristan ducked and moved to the next high section of wall. It did not really matter if he was seen by the enemy; they would no doubt recognise him from his earlier attack. He would prefer it if they did not know he was watching them; he wanted to lull them into a false sense of security, hoping that they would make a rash move if they thought they were unobserved.

Behind him, all was quiet within the castle walls. Lady Catrin had taken his advice and everyone, aside from him, was inside listening to her plan of attack. *Their* plan of attack really, but he was happy to take no credit for it. The quicker this whole thing was over, the faster he could get on with his true mission.

With Ogmore blocking Tristan's way, he could not get Lady Catrin out of the castle. For now, he and the lady had a common enemy. By the time this was over, he hoped she would trust him enough to come with him willingly, leaving Pwll Du Castle and its inhabitants for whoever King Edward saw fit to rule this small slice of Wales. If she did not, he would have to throw her over his shoulder and carry her out. He would have no time for charm after he'd dealt with this unexpected attack. He smiled ruefully. His charm hadn't worked anyway. The first time he had ever truly had to use it and it had failed him.

The way Lady Catrin had leapt straight to anger when she'd thought he had insulted her abilities suggested that, even if she had taken one look at him and been overwhelmed by his face, she would be difficult to cajole anyway. He was fairly confident he was winning her over to his side with his help; she had listened to what he'd had to say earlier. She was quick and intelligent and worthy of leadership; the first time he had met someone and feel able to truly say that. It was possible that they might develop amicable terms, that she would come to trust him, and that would make it easier for him later on.

He could not fail, not if he wanted to redeem himself in the eyes of his friends—and himself. He had only ever planned to be a knight of great renown. He'd never wanted to become a great lord of some castle. The only examples he'd seen of such men were Lord Ormand, a cruel, twisted leader with a hideous temper, and his father, a man who used his face and power to seduce half of England. Tristan wanted none of that.

Only two people had ever cared for him, Leo and

Hugh, and because they had stuck by him when things had gone wrong, they'd had their own hopes for the future destroyed. He could not be the man who let them down again. No, whether she liked it or not, Lady Catrin was coming with him to Windsor so he could complete his mission as soon as this mess was over.

It should not matter that his attention kept snagging on the length of her neck and the soft skin behind her ear. He should not want to keep finding ways to accidentally touch her, but when the backs of his fingers had lightly brushed her earlier, he'd been almost powerless to stop himself from doing it again and again, if only she would let him. Of all the women to finally cause this reaction and it had to be her. The woman he had to persuade to leave her home for a King she would never meet and for reasons he could not fully justify. Not when he could see that she was no spoiled, pampered lady but an efficient, capable leader.

A movement far below finally distracted him from these endless thoughts that had no answer. One man was stepping forward, coming within firing range. Tristan reached for an arrow, stepped out from his hiding place and shot. The man was too far away to hit but the arrowhead buried in the ground not far from his feet. He scrambled backwards, tripping over himself to reach a safe distance. Tristan allowed himself a smile of satisfaction.

'Good shot,' growled a voice.

Tristan turned to see he had been joined by Wynne, the man who had hated him at first sight. Tristan moved so that he was no longer in sight of Ogmore's men; Wynne stopped a few steps away from him.

'He made it easy for me.'

Wynne nodded but did not smile. 'Lady Catrin has put me in charge of the battlements.'

Tristan already knew this. It was what he'd discussed with her. Wynne, Lady Catrin had told him, was calm under pressure, had the respect of the younger members of the castle but was probably too old to fight. He was the perfect person to oversee and to report back to Lady Catrin.

'Someone will need to be on watch all the time,' said Wynne, his gaze flicking down to the growing encampment.

Tristan nodded. 'Aye.'

'Around four men, I should think. It'll spread the load.'

It slowly dawned on Tristan that the older man was asking him for advice but phrasing it in a series of brisk, short statements.

'Aye, that sounds about right,' he agreed. Pwll Du Castle was a small stronghold on a high hill. Four men would be able to cover enough ground and that would allow others to rest. There were not enough inhabitants for it to be more. 'Arrows will need to be placed at regular intervals, so they are easy to reach.'

Wynne nodded thoughtfully. 'We will need more ore. For the arrowheads.'

'Aye, but perhaps this is not a problem for now.' Tristan was hoping this siege would end before that became an issue but, if it did, he wasn't sure Wynne was the right man for the role. They would need someone small and fast if they were to get in and out of the castle unseen.

'No,' Wynne agreed quickly and Tristan hid his smile by turning to look out at the enemy once more. He had never been asked for his advice before and there was something charming about the older man's gruff approach; it warmed him. 'Lady Catrin wishes to see you.'

Tristan nodded again, wishing his heart did not feel lighter at the thought of seeing Lady Catrin. He had barely been apart from her for any time at all and yet the prospect of returning to her side, of getting to see those blue eyes sparking at him again, made him turn hurriedly for the stairs.

'You won't be the first lad to lose his head over her,' Wynne said, before Tristan could begin the climb down.

Heat scalded his skin. 'I am not in danger of that.'

Wynne's face twisted itself into what might have been a smile. 'Only one day here and you are already running to see her.'

'You told me to.'

'And if I told you to bugger off and leave us all alone, you'd do that, would you?' The older man was definitely smiling now; Tristan could see what was left of his teeth.

Tristan blustered. 'No, I have a message to give to Lady Catrin, that's why I'm here.'

'I reckon you've had plenty of time to pass that message on, lad. You could be on your way now.'

Tristan didn't know if Lady Catrin had explained to anyone the real reason for him being in Pwll Du Castle and he wasn't about to. Wynne wouldn't be so friendly if he thought that Tristan was going to take his leader away from him when all this was done.

'I can hardly leave now. I'd run straight into them, wouldn't I?' he asked instead, gesturing to the wall to make it clear he meant Ogmore and the soldiers gathered below.

Wynne shrugged. 'I am sure you could find a way if you really needed to, but you won't because she's already got you under her spell.'

'She has not.'

Wynne turned away from him, seemingly losing interest in him. 'You tell yourself that, lad. But we both know you're lying.'

Tristan muttered to himself all the way down the steps and across the courtyard, cursing the day he had set foot in this abominable castle where even when the people were speaking English they did not make sense, and where their leader was mind-scramblingly beautiful.

Just inside the door to the Great Hall, Lloyd was half-lying on the rushes, a young woman brushing his hair from his forehead. From the young lad's wide-eyed look of adoration, Tristan assumed this must be Eluned. Tristan squatted down next to him. 'How are you faring?' he asked.

'Better. The bleeding has stopped.'

'You were brave to be among the first men leading the defence,' he said. 'I am sure that you will be up on the battlements again in next to no time.'

The men who had trained Tristan and the other knights at Ormand Castle would have expected Lloyd to get up and continue fighting with such a minor injury. A graze from an arrow would not have been deemed worthy of any sympathy and the page or squire would have been left to deal with it in his own time when he had finally completed his other tasks for the day. Tristan had seen men gravely wounded and expected to keep going. There had been no softness where he had grown up, no hint that anyone felt any compassion. Tristan and his two close friends had supported one another, another reason Robert, their fellow squire and the man who had framed them for a crime they had not committed, hated them. But watching these two young people who clearly adored each other and who would hopefully not face anything more serious than today made him want something different, if only for a short while.

'He was brave,' Eluned told Tristan earnestly.

Lloyd managed a small heroic smile. 'It was nothing,' the young man said modestly, and truthfully in Tristan's opinion. 'Anyone would have done the same.' Again, Tristan agreed with this but he did not say it. Not when Lloyd's love was looking at him with such adoration.

'I must attend Lady Catrin,' he told them both. 'Rest and regain your strength, Lloyd. We will need your bravery again.' His words were only slightly tongue-in-cheek. The fortress was not so full of men that they could take losing any of them in their stride. Every person was going to have to play a part in the defence, but if this came down to a siege only, then the most determined side would win and there need be no more bloodshed. Tristan just hoped that this would be over quickly.

The Great Hall was not big. On his left was a large fireplace with ornate carvings. Lady Catrin was at the far end, watching his approach. He ignored the way his heart kicked when he caught sight of her. If he kept pretending his body was having no reaction to her, perhaps it would stop.

'That was sweet of you,' she said as he drew closer.

'What do you mean?' He had never been called such a thing before.

'The way you inflated Lloyd's contribution to this

morning's defence. It might finally settle things between him and Eluned.' She was smiling softly towards the young couple.

'I hoped it would make him less likely to build that rack for me after all.'

'Ah, yes, of course. Well, I think you are all right on that score now. If you had heard him during our latest gathering, you would realise that, to him, you are second only to God in your greatness.'

'From possible torture victim to potential deity in less than a day, that is a heady rise indeed.'

Her smile grew and Tristan had to resist the outlandish urge to fall to his knees and offer her everything. He had nothing he could give her, so the instinct was utter folly in every regard. 'You wanted to see me,' he said instead.

'I did. What is Ogmore doing?'

'He is having tents set up.'

She grunted, any trace of amusement leaving her face. 'That does not bode well.'

'It doesn't,' he agreed. 'It means he is preparing to be here for a long time. Do you have any spies amongst his people?' They needed to know what Ogmore was planning, how many supplies he had and how determined he was to see this through to the bitter end.

His heart dropped as she shook her head. 'Since my father died, there has been nothing but bad blood between my people and his.'

'How did you hear the rumours of a siege?'

'There is a fishing village nearby. Ogmore lays claim to it but the people there dislike him as much as I do and he provides them with no defence or any other support. He turns up to take some of their fishing haul and that is it. It is from them that we hear news but they did not warn us of the extent of the attack. It is likely they did not know. Why do you ask?'

He was almost reluctant to say because he knew what her response would be. 'We need to know their plans.'

'I agree. How do you propose that we do that?'

He bit back a groan. He really did not want to tell her the next part of his plan. It was a good plan, as well as it being the only logical step forward, but as leader she would want to be involved and it would be dangerous. 'We need to listen to what they have to say for themselves.'

She frowned, the small crease between her brows adorable, and...he was a fool for thinking so. 'By taking a hostage, you mean?'

'We could.' Tristan had considered that tactic but he'd dismissed it. 'I do not think that is the best strategy, however. We would need someone fairly high up in Ogmore's chain of command and once the Lord realised what we had done, he'd be likely to change his plan, so any information we garnered would become redundant.'

'I would not count on that,' she muttered. 'He is not in possession of the smartest mind.'

'We cannot be sure that he does not have someone new advising him.'

'Hmm.' She narrowed her eyes at him, the same way she had done every time she'd thought he might be a spy.

'It is not me.'

She sighed. 'I know, but it would be easier if it was. I could torture you and find out the answers I want to know.'

'A hostage would also mean another mouth to feed,

unless you are happy to kill him once we have the information.' She grimaced. 'I thought not.'

Servants bustled into the room and began pulling tables from the edges of the room, getting ready for the people to come and eat.

'Would you be able torture someone?' he asked. He couldn't decide. She was fierce and protective of her people and he had truly believed that she would run him through with her sword when they had met. But he also saw how compassionate she was to her people. Being a leader meant difficult choices, but somehow, he did not think that she would torture anyone.

'I hope never to be put in a situation where I need to find out. But don't try to change the subject. How do you intend to find out Ogmore's plans?'

He bit back another sigh. 'The best way would be to listen to him.'

'We will not be able to hear from the ramparts. They are too far away.'

'This is true,' he agreed.

'You intend to leave the castle and find out.'

'It is the only way.'

'I will come with you.'

There it was, the reaction he had been dreading and expecting.

'It is far too dangerous and before you get that murderous glint in your eyes, it is not because you are a woman.' Although that was part of it, but not in the way she imagined. He might not have lost his mind over her as Wynne had suggested, but he did not want anything bad to happen to her. He already knew he could not bear it if she got hurt. He would never tell her that, never let her know that she already had a hold over him so that the idea of her with even the slightest cut on her skin made his stomach squirm. She could use that against him and he never gave all of himself away; not even Leo and Hugh knew everything about him. 'It is, once again, because you are their leader. If you get caught then this is all over.'

She shook her head. 'No. I need to be the one who goes. There is no one else suitable.'

'Almost anyone else would be better,' he countered.

'You are not going to be able to walk across the drawbridge,' she said. 'Without me, you will not be able to find your way out because no one else will tell you.'

'Lloyd will.' He turned back to look at the young lad but he had left, obviously recovered enough from his injury to wander off with his ladylove.

'Lloyd may think that you are the greatest thing to ever arrive at Pwll Du Castle, but he will still obey me if I tell him not to help you. Besides, the way is hidden to anyone other than the castle leaders and only they have ever walked it. Lloyd would likely not be able to help you even if he did want to. Listen,' she said, stepping closer, so close that he could smell her, a mixture of woodsmoke and flowers. 'You will be accompanying me and so nothing will go wrong.'

'I do not follow your logic.'

'You need me to stay alive so that you can complete your mission. You will protect me at all costs.'

He didn't point out that if he got the two of them out of the castle then he could just steal away with her and his mission would be completed. He was not so hellbent on his mission that he would forgo the knight's code of chivalry and leave the people of this castle under siege with no protection. Besides, she was right. He would fight to the death for her, only he was afraid that had nothing to do with his mission and everything to do with her.

Chapter Seven

Dusk was falling. The day had been hot and stifling, with no means of escape from the relentless heat. Even now, with the sun finally dipping below the parapets, warmth was radiating off the stone walls, slowly roasting the inhabitants. The children were already fractious about not being able to swim in the stream that ran so close to the castle. With no arrows flying overhead, it was hard to explain the danger to them. A group of mothers had taken to pouring buckets of well-water over the heads of the children, their squeals of laughter incongruous amongst the grim-faced adults.

Catrin waited for Tristan to meet her at the entrance to the Great Hall. He had not been pleased with her insistence that she come with him but it was important to her that she do this, and not just because she did not fully trust him yet. She understood the dangers, but this was the only sort of risk she was willing to take, one which protected her people. She knew that if Ogmore got hold of her, her people would surrender for her safe return and that the siege would be over when it had barely begun. But she had seen Tristan fight; she was sure that he would protect her if something went wrong. Not that he would need to because she had proven herself equal to Ogmore's men on more than one occasion. She could do so again. She hadn't fought Tristan when they'd met, she rather thought he might be stronger than her, but she had held him at knifepoint and had won that bout without having to engage in a fight. This was a risk worth taking.

She had not spoken to Tristan since the morning, when they had agreed to spy on Ogmore together. Or rather, he had reluctantly accepted that he had no option other than to bring her along with him. She had seen him though. He had spoken to almost everyone in the castle, not to give them instructions but to listen to their fears or to praise them for whatever they might be doing, no matter how small.

He'd strode along the battlements, conferred with Wynne and checked over Dafydd's armour. He'd carried buckets of water and armloads of firewood. He'd encouraged Lloyd, who now followed him like a shadow, trying to imitate the larger man's stride and swagger. And all the while, he'd sent her people to her with reports and updates.

He had been a godsend and she knew she would have to tell him that, that she would have to find a way to repay him that didn't involve her giving away something she wasn't prepared to lose, like her freedom. She hadn't seized control after her father and brother's deaths from the ague only for it to be taken away from her so easily. To bow to someone else's leadership was to invite chaos into her life and she would never be under someone's erratic control again.

From across the courtyard she caught his gaze, holding it as he walked towards her, his movements powerful and concise. Her mouth went dry, her whole body stilling as he neared, waiting, although she had no idea why. She cleared her throat. 'Are you ready?'

'Is there still no chance you will change your mind?' he asked.

'None. But I shall return these to you.' She held out his sword and dagger. She'd hidden them after he'd become her prisoner yesterday but it would not be wise to make this journey without them.

He took the sword from her without comment, buckling the scabbard around his waist. Then he reached out for the dagger, his fingertips brushing over her palm as his hand curled around the handle. Sparks raced up her arm from the contact; he seemed to have no reaction. Instead, he was fixated on the blade, his thumb brushing over the inscription she had been unable to read, before he tucked it into his belt.

'It's this way,' she said, stepping away from the Great Hall and leading him to the far corner of the courtyard. This part of the wall that surrounded the castle was on the opposite side to where Ogmore was laying siege.

'Will we emerge in the river?' he asked as she pushed open a narrow door.

'Not quite,' she said. Just inside the doorway was a lit tallow candle. She picked it up and then closed the door behind them. He made a small hiss as the darkness swallowed them, with only the small flickering flame to show them the way. 'Hold this for a moment,' she said, passing the light to him. 'Could you bring it closer to the door?' He moved slowly so as not to snuff out the candle, and eventually she was able to see what she needed to. 'That's perfect.' She turned the key and tested the handle before stowing the key on a ledge high above them. Should anyone follow them back from Ogmore's camp, hopefully this last defence would slow them down.

She had been down this tunnel many times, had made herself memorise the twists and turns from the texture of the walls, so she left him with the candle to help him on his way. He followed her in silence, the only sound their breathing and the crunch of their boots on the floor below. They came to another door. This time he held the candle to the lock before she asked. This one was harder to turn; she needed to twist the key with two hands. After a couple of tries, the door swung open.

'You'll need to crouch down,' she told him, stepping into the tunnel that ran beneath the river. 'My ancestors did not take into consideration that people might be taller than them when they had this escape passage made.'

He grunted, stepping in behind her and pulling the other door shut behind them before locking it and hiding the key in a hollow. It was even darker here, where no natural light could reach, and cold. Someone had lined the tunnel with stone but water still seeped around the edges, running down in a steady flow, disappearing into the ground below.

Catrin shivered. In her younger days, this tunnel had been an escape from life in the castle, a way to meet the man she had thought she loved with all her heart. It had represented freedom and she had loved to stand within the cool walls, knowing that she would soon be in Ioan's arms. Now she knew that had been a foolish girl's dream. The only freedom one had was from the stability of making and living by one's own choices. Putting her complete trust in one man had only brought her pain.

The tunnel continued downwards for a while before flattening out. Their boots scraped on the stone floor, echoing all around them. 'Will the darkness end soon or are we doomed to walk these tunnels for the rest of eternity?' asked Tristan.

'It is only one tunnel.'

He grunted in response.

'You do not like the dark,' she guessed. There was only the sound of his footsteps in response, which was answer enough. 'It is not far now,' she reassured him as they began to climb back upwards.

Again, he didn't answer. She quickened her pace until finally shingle crunched beneath their feet, meaning they were at the end of the tunnel. She led him through a quick series of twists and turns until they were standing in a shallow cave, light filtering from a narrow entrance.

She took the candle from him and placed it in a sheltered spot on the floor. She had no way of lighting it so she had to hope that it would stay that way while they did whatever they had to do. If it went out, she would be able to find her way back but she had the feeling Tristan would not like walking through complete darkness.

The entrance to the cave was in some woodland to the east of the castle. Ogmore's men were to the south, meaning they were unlikely to be lurking anywhere nearby. Even so, she peered out of the entrance until she was sure the only things moving outside were small animals in the undergrowth.

She slipped outside and Tristan followed her. He sank to the ground as soon as they were out in the open, his head resting in his hands. She could not see his face but sweat was beaded across his brow. She wondered what had happened to him in the past to make such a strong and competent man react like this to the darkness. She hovered by his shoulder, unsure as to whether to say anything or pretend she hadn't noticed. Then she remembered the way he had stroked her back earlier, the comforting slide of his hand tethering her to the world when everything had threatened to spiral out of control.

She reached down and rested a hand on his shoulder. He didn't comment but he didn't move away either, so she took that as encouragement. She ran her hand across his back to his other shoulder and back again, her touch soft and gentle. He let out a shuddery sigh and dropped his hands from his face. She did it again, reminding herself that this was a touch of comfort and that it wasn't an excuse to feel the curve of his muscles beneath his shirt. She could have gone on doing it all day, but after a few leisurely sweeps across the expanse of his back, she stopped. She squeezed his shoulder once and then let go.

He cleared his throat. 'Can we pretend that didn't happen?'

'Of course.' She wasn't sure if he meant the stroking or the fact that he was clearly unnerved by walking in darkness. She was not about to question him.

He wiped the sweat on his forehead away with his sleeve. 'Where are we?'

'In the woodland on the left of the castle if you're looking out at Ogmore.'

He pushed himself to standing and glanced at the canopy of leaves above them. 'There is still some evening sunlight left. I thought we were in that tunnel for days.'

'We've walked under the river and into the woodland, it's not far at all.'

'It seemed to last for all eternity,' he muttered.

As she thought they were pretending it hadn't happened, she made no further comment. Instead, she began to pick her way through the undergrowth, Tristan following her closely behind. Even though they did not have far to travel, the going was tough. There was no natural way through the tightly packed trees and they had to climb over thick fallen branches and under boughs that had fallen as if drunk. High above them, squirrels leapt back and forth, chattering excitedly as if intrigued by what the two humans were doing. They were as silent as they could manage, avoiding dry twigs that might snap and give away their presence.

After what felt like an age, Tristan tapped her on the arm and nodded through a gap in the foliage. Catrin knelt, the dried mud hard beneath her knees, and peered through the ferns that were growing up wherever they could find space. She pressed her fingers against a large green leaf, moving it so that she could get a better view. They were very close to Ogmore's encampment.

'We'll wait here until after sundown,' said Tristan softly.

She nodded, that made sense.

He crouched down next to her, his wide shoulders brushing against hers. 'We might as well make ourselves comfortable,' he said quietly.

Together they lowered themselves until they were sitting down. For a while they sat in silence, listening to the sounds of the camp. Occasionally, someone would shout something out, mostly in Welsh. Tristan would look at her and she would shake her head, the comments were generally curse words that made no sense out of context.

Tristan removed his dagger and brushed a thumb over the inscription again.

'What is it about this blade that is so important to you?' she asked.

'It was a gift.'

'From a lover?'

'Jealous?' He smirked.

She rolled her eyes, even though she was a little bit. 'Why on earth would I be jealous?'

He shrugged. 'You seem too curious.' The arrogant devil was probably used to women fawning over him; she would not be like that. When she said nothing more, he continued. 'No, it's not from a lover. It was a gift from a friend. Leo gave one to me and one to Hugh.'

A large bird of prey burst out from a dense thicket of trees, its powerful wings beating the air as it quickly rose high above them, disappearing from view as the canopy of leaves shielded them.

'Who are Hugh and Leo?' she asked.

'They are knights like me, who trained at Ormand's castle. We were seven when we met, scared and alone, far away from everything that we knew. Leo was a bullish little upstart who thought he was better than everyone else.' Tristan grinned at the memory. 'Hugh and I didn't like him to start with, but he was as clueless as the two of us and somehow we became friends. They became like brothers to me.' A fly buzzed around his ear; she leaned over and brushed it away, her fingertips lightly touching the soft skin of his neck.

She cleared her throat, dismissing the oddly intimate moment. 'Where are they now?'

'In Wales, like me.'

'And yet not with you.'

'And yet not with me,' he agreed, his concentration once again on the handle of the dagger, his head bowed.

'Do they also find you intensely irritating?'

That won her a brief smile. 'No.' A pause. 'Possibly.'

'What did you do?' she asked.

'Nothing,' he replied, but there was something about his answer that wasn't convincing.

'Hmm.'

The corner of his mouth lifted. 'Why so sceptical?'

In the time Tristan had been with them he had seemed to take the knight's code of chivalry very seriously. She could not truly believe that he had done something that had brought him dishonour, but he became still and subdued when he looked at the faded inscription and there was no denying that he'd looked like a man with the weight of the world on his back when she had seen him trudging along the path yesterday.

'Did you seduce Leo's love?' she asked, unable to think of anything else that might cause such misery.

He frowned. 'I'm not sure Leo even likes women. I have never seen him with one.'

'Hugh's woman then.'

He flinched at her words and she wished she hadn't pushed; she would prefer not to know the answer. The thought of Tristan touching someone, stroking their skin or whispering secrets into their ear made her stomach turn over.

'I would never, *never*, seduce another man's woman.' The words came from deep within, as if from his very soul. 'Hugh was in love with a woman, not that he ever told me or Leo. I don't know why because he shared everything else. Perhaps because he thought she was out of his reach, but frankly any woman would be privileged to have such a man as their husband. For whatever reason, he kept his feelings to himself, but Leo and I knew him well enough to see what was happening.'

'What was it about this woman that made her too special for a good knight's love?' Not that it should matter to her, but still...it might be a long wait until they could move unseen through Ogmore's camp and there was only so much staring into the dense trees in front of them that could keep her entertained and, if she was honest with herself, she was intrigued. She had never known life outside of Pwll Du Castle and it was fascinating to hear of a world different from her own.

'She was Ormand's daughter.'

'The lord who trained you.'

He grunted disparagingly. 'He was the man who owned the stronghold in which I was trained, which is not quite the same thing. He was only interested in creating the best, strongest knights in the land. He put all his pages and squires through rigorous training, some of it brutal, some of it unnecessary. I say *he*, but Ormand was very rarely involved in anything other than punishing us should we fail. For the most part, we didn't see him. The strange thing about him was that as Leo, Hugh and I honed our skills as knights, he disliked us all the more for it.' Tristan shook his head. 'I cannot understand the man at all, none of us could. He also liked to sow discontent amongst his men. The bond I formed with those two men was highly unusual and caused resentment. But, back to Ormand's daughter, Ann.' He stretched out his long legs in front of him, his gaze intent on his boots. 'Ann decided that she was in love with me.'

'She was able to look past the disgusting eyebrows, then?'

It was fleeting but she didn't miss the slight twitch of his lips. 'It must have been my sparkling personality.'

'Do you think so? Perhaps she has a thing for men whose eyebrows could be used to weave full tapestries.'

It was fascinating to watch him try to hide his smile. He succeeded but only just. 'Fine, have it your way, she was enamoured of my hideousness.'

'Don't be too hard on yourself, your right ear is passable.'

He turned to face the opposite direction but not before she caught his smile breaking loose. 'Do you want to hear the story or not?'

'Do go on, I shall try not to interrupt.'

'Her mother also fancied herself in love with me.'

She couldn't hide her snort of laughter. 'Oh, dear.'

'Indeed.' The tips of his ears turned pink. She did not want to find that adorable but there was something endearing about seeing such a large man undone by the simplest of statements. 'Even that might not have been too bad. I doubt Ormand saw much of his wife, it was hardly a love match. The problem was Robert.'

'Robert?'

Tristan nodded. 'Ormand's household is huge and Robert was another squire training with us. Robert was in love with Ann.'

'The daughter?'

'Yes.'

'There were two men in love with her and two women in love with you.'

'I don't think there was any love involved with Ann and her mother. They didn't know me.' Her heart squeezed. She knew what that was like; enough men in her past had tried to win her over with flowery praise, but they knew only how she looked and not how she thought. 'They only wanted...well, you can guess what they wanted from me.' He wrinkled his nose. 'The only person who probably had any true feelings was Hugh, who I believe genuinely loved Ann. He's a good, decent man, who tried to hide his feelings when it became obvious they were not reciprocated. He became more subdued when she blatantly showed her attraction to me. I avoided her as much as I could because the pain in his eyes was often too much to bear.'

Tristan's eyes narrowed as he stared ahead and something uncomfortable fluttered in Catrin's stomach. It could not be jealousy but the twisting snake in her stomach felt a lot like it. It wasn't that she envied Ann. It was clear that Tristan had no feelings for this unknown woman; she must be coveting Tristan's relationship with his friends. She had never had anything like that, had never had someone close enough to her the way Tristan had. She'd thought she'd found it once, with Ioan, but he had betrayed her and she had closed off that part of her for ever. She didn't think she missed it, she couldn't get hurt if she let no one close, but the pang she was experiencing in her heart now made her think that perhaps she did. There was nothing she could do to change that now, there was no one who could be her friend, not even Ffion. It was one of the sacrifices she had made when she had become leader. A decision that kept her world safe and free from heartache.

'Once Robert was involved, the situation deteriorated rapidly,' Tristan continued. 'He went out of his way to make my life miserable. It got to the point where I could not leave anything anywhere. My sword was hidden in the barn, buried deep within the hay. I washed only to find that my clothes had been dumped in water and left sodden. I froze that day because it was winter but I still had to train outside when the land was covered in frost.' He shuddered. 'I hid from Ann and her mother whenever I could but sometimes there was no escaping them and they would make suggestions that I...' He shuddered again. 'Even if I had been the sort of man who enjoyed attention like that, I would never have bedded another man's wife or hurt a friend in that way. It would be dishonourable.'

She reached out and lightly touched his arm; his muscles flexed under her touch. 'That sounds awful,' she said softly.

His gaze flicked to her hand and away. For a moment, his lips moved silently and then, slowly, ever so slowly, he reached up and covered her hand with his. The shock of the warmth against her skin was alarmingly pleasant. His thumb traced over her skin, sending tingles racing through her; she couldn't have moved it even if she'd wanted to.

'Even that wouldn't have been so bad. But the more obvious their twisted devotion became, the more Hugh retreated into himself and the angrier Robert grew. I hated that Hugh was in pain but I hoped he would get over it in time, especially once we were on a knight's campaign. I thought Robert would take his anger out on me, try to slit my throat in my sleep or something like that, but he went a step worse.'

'Worse than being murdered?'

Tristan smiled sadly. 'At least there may have been some honour in death. No—' he squeezed her hand '—I do not mean that, of course I want to live. I have much that I still want to do and I could not achieve that if I was dead and buried. But at the time it felt worse than death. Robert framed me for a crime I didn't commit. Again, it would not have been so bad if it had just been me, but Leo and Hugh were implicated as well.'

'What was the crime?'

'The destruction of a beautifully illustrated Bible. It was to be a gift for the King from Ormand. It had taken years to make.'

'That's awful.' Books were precious. Destroying one made her heart hurt.

'Yes,' he agreed bleakly.

'How do you know it was Robert?'

'I will never know for sure, but I could see the gleam of triumph in his eyes as the three of us were accused and the grin he wore as we were sent away from Ormand's castle. I'm sure he was hoping we would hang for such a crime but, in the end, there was not enough evidence. That, coupled with our vehement denial, got us a lesser punishment.'

'Which was?'

'To be sent to Wales to complete three tasks. If we succeed, Sir Benedictus, the leader of the King's Knights, will see us if we travel to Windsor, and if he sees us then…' Tristan shrugged. 'I know there is no guarantee that he will let us join the prestigious band of knights, but to be considered, to have that chance...it is all I have ever wanted. And also...'

'Also?' she prompted him as he stared out into the distance.

'I want to redeem myself in Hugh and Leo's eyes.'

'Do they blame you for Robert's crime?' They would hardly be the friends he thought them if they did. It was clear to her that he had done nothing wrong.

'Of course they do not. They have made it clear they hold Robert accountable for everything.'

'Then why do you need to atone for something that is not your fault?'

'They are great knights; they should not be cast aside because of me.'

'They weren't.' How could he not see this? 'It was because of this Robert and the lord who was foolish enough to believe him.'

'No, I...'

'Let's look at this from a different perspective. Will you blame them if they fail in the missions they are on?'

'Absolutely not,' he said emphatically.

'Then why are you holding yourself to such a high standard?'

His eyes blazed. 'All my life, I have been judged by my face. People presume I have it easy because others believe they have fallen in love with me. I have never been taken seriously but, if I do this, if I follow through on everything that I have said I will do, I will finally have proven to everyone, as well as myself, that I am worthy.'

It was amazing to her that a man who was strong and brave and witty could not see that he already had so much worth, but if he could not see it then it was not something she could tell him. It was something he would have to learn for himself.

She pulled her hand out from under his and he let it go without protest. She bent her knees and rested her arms on them. She was glad Tristan had told her his story, but now she knew that he would be relentless in achieving his desired goal of ensuring that she left her beloved home. If they became friends, if she started to like him more than she already did, then it would make no difference in the end. She had put aside worrying about King Edward's request that she leave her home in the face of Ogmore's siege. Now wasn't the time to let her thoughts spiral either but she would have to face up to it soon. At least Tristan was not like Ioan, the man Catrin had thought she was in love with all those years ago. Tristan had been honest about what he wanted from her from the beginning. When he followed through with that, the betrayal would not cut her to the core.

The light of the summer evening slowly faded, the branches above them rustling as birds settled down to roost. A bat flickered overhead, followed by more darting through the woodland.

The noise from the encampment grew rowdy. 'They are drinking, I think,' said Tristan after a while.

'Shall we make our move now?'

'Let's wait a short while longer. The more they drink, the less likely they are to notice two people moving through their camp.'

'The less likely they are to discuss plans too, I should think.'

'It is improbable that we will stumble across a council

of war with every detail of their campaign discussed,' he said dryly. 'We can only hope for snippets at best.'

'We've risked all this for fragments of conversation?'

'Anything is better than nothing. We can check their stores of food, spoil them if possible, the same with their weapons supply.'

'How do you intend to do that?'

'I do not know until I see what I am working with.'

Catrin pressed her lips together. Not preparing for something down to the last detail could lead to disaster. With Tristan on their side, the stock of weapons had not dwindled to dire proportions yet, but they would have done if not for him and that was because she had not planned properly. Not knowing what they would need was no excuse. She had to do better.

'It could be something as simple as slitting a bag of wheat and allowing the mice to get to it. We know next to nothing and until we do, we cannot make a plan.'

Catrin's breath shuddered; she'd thought she'd known what she was letting herself in for when they'd left the castle. But as the time drew nearer for them to walk amongst the tents of her enemy her heart slammed against her ribs.

She turned away from Tristan, but he seemed to sense her unease. 'You can still wait here for me,' he said.

She shook her head. She would not be a coward, even if words had deserted her. She was sure that Tristan was not working with Ogmore but she still needed to put herself first for her people. It was what she had promised herself when she'd become leader and that did not change, not even when the action terrified her. She had no sense of evening passing. The only thing she was aware of was the heavy beat of her heart and the sweat gathering at the nape of her neck.

'It is time,' he said after what could have been hours or the mere flicker of a moth's wing.

She stood, brushing her skirts even though she could not see if leaves were scattered on them or not, needing to do something with her hands to stop them from shaking.

'Stay close behind me,' Tristan told her.

He waited until she nodded before turning and moving, not out of the woodland but just inside the edge. For a large man, he moved almost silently and she stayed close to his back, stepping where he stepped. He paused when he was past the camp, turning to look back at it.

Fires burned between tents, throwing pools of light and pockets of dark. Beyond that, the dark walls of Pwll Du Castle towered above them. There was no sign of life within her home and fear stole her breath. She knew everyone was in there, knew they were safe for now, but she was so used to the castle being full of vibrant laughter. Seeing it so still was a punch to the gut.

Tristan pointed to a large, low tent without a fire in front of it. It was set slightly away from the other tents and further back from the ramparts. 'The stores, perhaps,' he whispered.

She nodded. It would make sense to place vital supplies away from where they could be hit by projectiles from her people or, more realistically, Tristan. Her people did train but, without a knight, none of them had the skill Tristan had already displayed.

He motioned for her to stay where she was before he stepped out of the tree line. He paused out in the open for a moment, his head cocked to one side. When no alarm was sounded, he gestured for her to follow. The two of them slowly made their way across the short expanse. Catrin's breath was choppy, her heart racing, but they reached the larger tent with no one shouting out.

No guard was posted outside. The two of them stood towards the back of it, listening for the sounds of anyone moving inside, but all was still. Ogmore obviously believed himself safe from an attack during the night. If it wasn't for Tristan, he would be right. Neither she nor anyone inside the castle would have thought of walking amongst the enemy. Together they slipped towards the front of the tent. Tristan whispered, 'Stand guard.' He gave her time to respond before he slipped inside.

Her palms began to sweat as she stared towards the rest of the camp. She could make out the dark shadows of men sitting around fires; no one was moving about but she had no idea what she would do or say if someone started heading towards her. Would she call out to Tristan or slip inside to join him? It seemed foolish that they had not discussed a plan of action in all the time they had spent in the woods.

The men of the camp were laughing and singing and her fists curled. Inside the castle her people were frightened and tired, the children bewildered and probably scared, but for these men this was an adventure, something not to be taken too seriously.

Fingers brushed her hand and she jumped. 'It is only me,' said Tristan, close to her ear. 'I have the beginnings of a plan, but let us move around a little more first.'

Before she could ask him to explain, he set off, keeping to the shadows.

'Can you translate?' he asked when they stopped behind the tent of a particularly rowdy group.

'I can,' she said, 'but it will not help.'

'Oh?'

'Hmm. These men are taken with a lady named Aliana and...well...it is not courtly love poetry they are spouting.'

'Oh, I see.'

Catrin listened to more of their vulgar talk and experienced a pang of sympathy for this woman she would never meet. The men thought they were being very amusing if their shouts of laughter were to be believed, but she doubted the lady would find the constant reference to her magnificent breasts as entertaining as they did.

'Let us move on,' she said after more of the same.

At the next few campfires they heard depressingly similar talk, although the names of the women were different. Before her father had died, Catrin had heard enough of this type of ribaldry directed at herself. Her father had only laughed when she had mentioned it, said that it was the way of the world for men to talk like that about women. That might be so, but it did not stop the degrading words from cutting her deep inside, for making her feel somehow lesser. She wanted respect for her actions to wipe out the sense that being a woman only made her good for bedding.

By the time they reached the fourth fire, Catrin's heartrate had returned to normal. These people were not monsters, they were just like all other men everywhere. Then she heard her name.

'Lady Catrin does not think so.' For some reason that comment raised a few laughs.

'She will find out the hard way that a bitch does not make the rules.' Catrin flinched as that statement was followed by a rumble of agreement. These men did not sound drunk like the others.

'What is it?' whispered Tristan.

She shook her head. She would wait until the end before translating; she did not want to miss anything.

'You think Ogmore will see it through to the end this time or will he be sent running by the bitch and her band of women?' continued one of the men.

'It will be humiliating if not.'

She bit her lip. She could well imagine that Ogmore had not taken the last two defeats lightly and would therefore be more determined for this latest conflict to go in his favour.

'Think it will take long?'

'Already missing the wife?'

There was some bawdy teasing after that but still she did not translate. Tristan did not need to know that the man had only recently married and that he was missing his wife in ways which were also not romantic but were a darn sight more pleasant than what was potentially awaiting the lovely Aliana.

'She's a woman, it won't be long before she cracks.' Catrin leaned forward; this might be about her.

'She's stubborn though and that giant of hers might be a problem.'

Yes, this was definitely about her. It was good that no one outside of Pwll Du Castle knew that Dafydd was a very gentle soul despite his size. They were frightened of the man they perceived him to be and not the person he truly was, a man who would not hurt a mouse. There was some general muttering, which revealed nothing interesting. Next to her, Tristan's body was a rigid wall of muscle but still she waited.

'It's a point of principle now; we're here until the end. He's not letting her get away with it.'

Frustratingly, the conversation moved away from the siege and onto people she'd never heard of.

'We can move on,' she told Tristan after a few long moments of listening to nothing much.

'What's being said?' he asked quietly.

She stood on tiptoes so she was speaking directly into his ear. 'They are mostly discussing women and drink, and how soon they can get their hands on one or the other.' He grunted softly. 'But at the last fire they were saying they think Ogmore will not give up until he has Pwll Du Castle in his hands. He was too humiliated by being beaten by me and my people twice.'

Tristan grunted again, the noise reverberating through her body.

There were only a handful of fires left and she did not stay long at them, as none of the men were saying anything new. But she finally recognised a voice. 'We've found Ogmore,' she whispered in Tristan's ear.

Tristan nodded. 'Let's see if we can get closer.'

They crouched low and moved through the shadows.

'They're discussing the arrows you shot earlier,' she said when they were near. 'They do not understand how someone with your skill can be living at the castle.' She listened some more. 'Oh, no,' she said after a while.

'What is it?'

'They are going to capture the cattle. Those that graze on the other side of the river. They are talking about killing them all.' Her chest was tight; her eyes stung. She would rather Ogmore took the gentle animals rather than senselessly killing them. She wanted to storm into the camp and rail at Ogmore but she knew that she couldn't. One wrong move and this was all over.

'I want you to stay here and listen. Count to twenty,' said Tristan. 'Once you've reached that number, walk slowly but steadily to the point where we left the woods. Don't look back. Wait there for me until you have reached the count of one hundred. If I don't return, run.'

He stood but she grasped his arm. 'Wait. What are you going to do?'

'Something to slow them down.' He didn't explain any further. He pulled himself from her hold and very quickly the darkness enveloped him.

Left alone, her breath seemed exceptionally loud. It seemed impossible to her that no one in the vicinity could fail to hear the rasp of it entering and leaving her lungs. She could barely hear Ogmore's words over it.

'What will you do to the girl once this is all over?' somebody asked him.

'I had thought to marry her to one of my sons, out of respect for my relationship with her late father.' Catrin's stomach revolted as Ogmore's words hit home. The Lord's oldest son was ten, the idea of being married to someone of that age was disgusting. 'But she has shown herself to be utterly unwilling to show good sense. Once the castle is mine, I shall display her head on a spike by the gateway to show people that I am not to be disobeyed.'

Catrin was glad she was crouching because she did not have far to go when her legs gave way. She was going to win this siege, she was sure of it, but for a moment she could feel a cool blade at her neck and picture her face rotting on a pike in the summer's heat. Who would Ogmore put next to her? Dafydd for sure and probably Ffion. He would not have liked being bested by the two women in the past and Dafydd was a symbol of the castle's freedom for no other reason than his sheer size. She could not, would not, let that happen. She was going to need Tristan's help because this was bigger than anything she had done before. She would have to put her trust in him.

She staggered to her feet. She'd forgotten to count but she was sure enough time must have passed. Even if it hadn't, she could no longer stay here and listen. She moved quickly back the way she had come, trying to stay silent, but the ringing in her ears made it difficult to pick her way over the uneven ground.

'Did anyone hear that?' said a voice as she passed.

She froze, fear turning her bones to ice.

'Probably a fox,' said another voice.

She scrubbed a hand over her face, having no idea whether she should run or stay exactly where she was. Around the nearest campfire there was silence except for the crackle of the wood burning. She was surprised they could not hear her heart beating. It was pounding so fast it was almost painful.

'I'm sure there's something...' said the original voice.

She heard someone moving, the thud of boots on the hard muddy ground. She held her breath, knowing she had no time to run.

She pulled her dagger from her belt and rocked back into a fighting stance. When the man rounded the tent she would have the element of surprise. She let out a long, steady breath. She didn't relish taking a life. Her hand tightened on the handle. If it was them or her, she would choose herself.

She waited, her arm held in position, ready to strike. Her body settled, her mind calmed. She was ready.

But no one came.

Gradually, she realised that the dull footsteps were heading away from her, the voices fading into the distance. She waited, head tilted. But she was right, the men were not coming for her. She forgot about moving quietly and slowly and ran.

She reached the relative safety of the tree line as chaos erupted.

Chapter Eight

Breathing heavily, Catrin leaned against the trunk of a tree and stared at the encampment. Men were shouting and running but in the mêlée she could not make out the cause of their distress. Tristan had told her to start counting once she reached the trees but numbers slipped through her mind like water through open fingers. She strained her eyes, searching for his figure emerging from the darkness, but she couldn't see him amongst the other dark figures that were rushing around.

The acrid smell of burning reached her before she saw the flames. Something was burning, something that wasn't only wood from a campfire. There was a whooshing, wheezing noise and then tall flames soared into the sky, big and bright, lighting the whole area. Someone screamed, the sound full of rage rather than fear, and a shot of triumph raced through her.

One of Ogmore's tents was aflame.

She half laughed, Tristan's audacity astounding her.

But still he did not come.

She waited. She wasn't going to count, the numbers still would not come, but it did not matter. He would appear; she was sure of it.

Confusion reigned as the flames continued to grow. The shouts of the panicking soldiers reached her but she was too far away to make out what was being said. She knew she should retreat. She had been waiting for far longer than Tristan had told her to but she did not want to leave without him. The danger of staying was outweighed by the thought of losing him. He wouldn't know the way through the woods back to the secret entrance and even if, by some miracle, he did find it, he would have to walk through the tunnel by himself, not knowing whether he would be able to get through the locked doors at the other end. She remembered his white face after he'd come through with her earlier and her heart clenched at the thought of him going through that ordeal alone. She had no doubt he had faced worse, the way he had calmly shot those arrows earlier suggested it was not the first time he'd had to fight to the death, but still she could not leave him to negotiate the darkness alone.

And yes, rationally, she knew she shouldn't care. She barely knew him and some of what she did know wasn't good for her. If Tristan didn't return to the castle with her and was unable to enter, it would mean that she didn't have to deal with the problem of King Edward any time soon. She could think about it after the ordeal with Ogmore was over, without the constant reminder that her life at Pwll Du Castle was under threat in more ways than one.

But Tristan wasn't just an unwanted messenger, not any more. It didn't matter that he had only just entered her life. Not after he had risked his life for her and her people, not when he had made her laugh and had shown more compassion than any member of her family ever had, not when he had told her his story and shown her his fear. He was more than an undesirable visitor now. And so, she stayed.

'You waited too long,' said a voice behind her.

'Tristan.' She didn't hesitate, she turned and flung her arms around his neck. 'You made it.'

He held still for a moment but then, slowly, his arms slid around her waist, his palms resting lightly against the base of her spine. Slowly, tentatively, one hand travelled up her back, pulling her closer until the full length of their bodies pressed together. He smelled of woodsmoke and leather.

'We need to go,' he said into her hair, but he did not release her.

For a long, tremulous moment, they held each other tightly. She couldn't have explained her behaviour, why it was important for her to cling to him, to make sure he was real and that he was safe. His strong arms were a safe haven.

'There!' someone shouted, making her jump. 'I think there are people there.'

Tristan swore, dropping his hands and threading his fingers through hers. 'Come on, we must run.'

He set off, dragging her behind him. The floor of the forest was uneven and it was hard to see further ahead than the next tree, but that didn't slow Tristan's footsteps as he darted away from Ogmore's men.

'You are going the wrong way,' she gasped out as branches whipped against their faces, leaves entangling in their hair.

'I know,' he called back to her. 'We do not want to

lead them straight into the castle's secret tunnel. We must lose them in the trees.'

Behind them came the sound of men crashing through the undergrowth, following them at speed.

'Split up!' she heard someone shout. 'We can surround them.'

Catrin began a fervent prayer under her breath. Tristan had been running in a straight line but he suddenly veered to the left and then after several long strides he careened to the right. She had no time to question his strategy. She needed all her breath for running and praying. Tristan showed no sign of tiring but she knew that she could not go on for much longer, not at this pace.

Men were still smashing through the undergrowth after them but Catrin thought there were maybe fewer of them. The men around the campfires had been drinking heavily. Running in the dark might have been beyond them after the initial spurt of fury. But there were still enough following them to mean she and Tristan were not safe. They were heading far away from the castle now and she did not know how they would get back in the darkness, even if they were to get away from their followers.

'They're falling back.' She was panting as they ran forward.

'True, but they will not stop. Not after what I have done.' Tristan did not sound out of breath whereas her lungs were burning violently after running for so long.

She wanted to ask him exactly what he'd done and how he had managed to rattle the enemy, but there was no breath left to speak. All she could do now was survive.

Still they ploughed forward, the forest becoming

denser. She stumbled over roots, only the grip of his hand keeping her upright.

Abruptly they stopped.

He pressed her into the hollow of a tree, his back to her as he faced outwards. She pushed her face against his tunic, trying to smother her gasps as her lungs desperately tried to get air into them.

The heavy thud of many boots neared.

Her knees turned to liquid, her body vibrating as terror surged through her.

This mission had seemed simple in the castle when the morning sunshine had been warming her face and everything had been still and quiet. Nothing had prepared her for this. If they were caught... She clutched the edges of Tristan's tunic, the material thick and hard in her fists. Beneath the leather she could feel the softness of his shirt. He stayed completely still. If she hadn't been able to feel the warmth of his skin beneath the cloth, she would have thought him turned to stone.

The running feet crashed past them and carried on.

Tristan pressed back into her as if he were trying to make them one with each other and the large tree behind. The noise of their pursuers came back to them through the forest. The men were slowing, perhaps coming to the realisation that they were chasing ghosts.

Something soft brushed against her leg, a fox maybe. She squeezed her eyes closed. If it wasn't deadly, it didn't signify if it touched her. What mattered was staying quiet. The moment she thought it, everything that she did rang loud in her ears. Her breathing, the way her cheek scraped against Tristan's shirt, even her shaking knees appeared to be making a sound. She gritted her teeth. She had survived worse; she would survive this.

'Where did they go?' called a voice, ahead of them but not far enough.

'To the east,' said another voice.

'That was a deer.'

'No, it was people.'

'How can you tell?'

Catrin counted four voices, all ahead of them, scattered at different points. Not near, there would still be time to get away if they came for them, but fear was still running through her, more potent than several glasses of the finest wine.

Footsteps crunched, coming dangerously close. She could feel Tristan's sword arm tense but the sounds moved away.

'We cannot return without them.'

'If they are hiding, they cannot be far. Let's wait until daybreak. It will not be long before dawn.'

The men moved together, their voices becoming a low rumble, making it hard to pick up individual words. Tristan turned slowly until he was facing her, their bodies still tight together. He leaned down, brushing her ear with his lips. 'What are they saying?' he whispered, his breath hot against her skin.

She'd forgotten he wouldn't be able to understand.

It was hard to unclench her jaw, her teeth were so tightly pressed together. 'They were debating whether we had headed east or whether we are hiding,' she said softly. 'Before they huddled together, they settled on staying where they are until dawn.'

He swore softly and fell silent. He didn't move away

and she was grateful for his solid presence. She wasn't sure she could stand without his body pinning her to the solid trunk of the tree.

'Do you think you can move?' he asked eventually.

Movement seemed like the greatest folly in the world. Surely they would be seen or heard. But they could not stay where they were. Come sunrise, their hiding place would be easy to see.

'Yes,' she told him, unsure if that was true. She had run further and faster than she had in a long time. Even if her legs were not weak from terror they were aching from the strain. It could not matter. She had no choice. Stay here and she would surely die or worse. Men were not kind to women whom they caught in war—she might not have seen it for herself but she had heard enough tales to have a horror of it. She'd heard enough leering remarks made about her to know how men thought.

His fingers found hers in the dark. Slowly they entwined, the warmth of his skin giving her comfort. 'If I tell you that I am impressed with your bravery will you punch me in the stomach?' he asked, a hint of teasing laughter in his voice. 'I do not wish to get into trouble for being patronising.'

She pressed her lips together to stop a surprised laugh escaping. She had not thought to find humour in these moments. 'How about being punched for getting me killed?'

'You're not going to die.' His amusement was replaced with cold, hard certainty.

'If I do, it will not be your fault.' She had been joking. He might be here to take her away from her home but he had proved himself to be on the side of the people of

Pwll Du Castle. Whatever happened in their future, she would always remember that.

'You will not die,' he repeated firmly.

The rumble of the voices of their followers continued and deeper into the forest an owl hooted loudly. Closer, she could hear Tristan's slow inhale and exhale as he breathed steadily. She had trusted him thus far and he had not let her down.

'Let's see if we can make it to the next tree,' he said. He moved away from her, dropping her hands, and a chill swept across her front. 'I will go first.'

Slowly and softly, they crept around the wide trunk of their hiding place. The floor was covered in dried leaves and twigs that crackled as they stepped, and she thought that surely the men must hear them, but it seemed they were too caught up in their argument to listen for any movement from their prey.

Despite the chill of the night air, sweat pooled at the base of her spine. The next tree was a towering dark mass, visible only because it was darker than the surrounding forest. The distance towards it seemed to stretch and distort, as if the next safe hiding place was moving.

They made it, her fingers brushed against the bark and she clung to it for a moment as if the tree itself could protect her.

'To the next one,' Tristan murmured.

She didn't want to keep going but he was already moving, so she followed. As soon as they reached safety, he moved on again and again.

'What did you do?' she asked when she could no longer hear the sound of men from any direction.

'I was right—that tent was full of food and weapons. Weapons made mostly from wood.' He huffed a short laugh.

'You set it on fire.'

'Aye.' That one syllable held a wealth of pride.

'How?'

'Ah, that was easy. I found a fire with only two men. One went to take a piss and so I knocked the other one out. Took some burning logs from their fire, placed them at various points around the tent and fanned them until they were burning well and then left.' He spoke lightly but it was evident he was very pleased with himself.

'Is that all?' she said faintly.

He laughed boyishly. 'Aye. That is all.'

She couldn't imagine the courage it must have taken to stand in the store tent and cover it in flames. He could have been caught or he could have gone down with the flames, but either it hadn't occurred to him or he hadn't cared. Or perhaps he had and he had deemed it worth the risk. Either way, there was nothing she could do to ever repay him.

'Do you have any idea where the entrance to the cave is from where we are?' he asked her.

She paused, not wanting to tell him the truth because she did not want to disappoint him but lying would serve no purpose. 'No. One tree looks much the same as the next in this level of light.'

'Do you think you could find it from Ogmore's camp?'

'Yes.' That would be easy, she had travelled that way in darkness many times. 'But do we really want to go back there?'

'I do not think we have an option. We must be within the castle walls before the sun comes up and that will not be long now, not at this point in the summer. If we are careful, I hope that we will not attract unwanted attention. It is unlikely Ogmore's men will be looking for us close by. They think that we fled further away from the castle walls. They saw us, and they are unlikely to believe we have backtracked, not when they think we are ahead of them. They will no doubt have guards stationed at the camp itself in case we come back, but I hope that we can move unseen if we stay within the woods.' He paused. 'We cannot stay out here regardless and we cannot ask for the gate to be lowered for us to be let in either.'

'I know *that*. I am not a complete fool.' Panic at their situation made her speak more harshly than she intended.

'You are not a fool at all,' he said softly.

'I think perhaps I am.'

'Are you going to argue with everything that I say?'

She rubbed her eyes, she ached everywhere. She wasn't even sure why she was disagreeing with him. 'It's possible. That's why I am a fool.'

He laughed softly. 'Come on, we must keep going. We cannot sleep here.'

'Are you tired?' she asked as they made their way slowly through the trees, no longer trying to hide but hoping not to draw any attention to their progress either.

'Everything aches,' he told her. 'I could sleep standing here.'

'Oh.' She had been expecting him to deny feeling anything other than fine. 'You don't sound it.'

'Where I grew up, tiredness was considered a weakness. I have grown adept at hiding it.'

She reached out a hand to touch him but dropped it before she could make contact. She wasn't sure he wanted sympathy, there had been no sad reflection in his voice, but that sounded harsh. Her father had shown her no love but she had seen enough compassion from others to know that he was unusual.

They only had to travel a short distance before they could see smoke billowing and smell the acrid stench of burning. Neither of them spoke as they made their way past the camp, not stopping to see the level of damage.

Catrin led the way, she could do this bit blindfolded, the darkness of the night almost similar to that state.

Stepping into the cave was a welcome relief and she managed to stop herself from sinking to the ground to rest on the cool stone floor.

'It is not far now,' Tristan told her and for the first time she could hear weariness in his tone. 'Where is the candle?'

She picked her way to the back of the cave, but it was as she had feared, the candle had long since flickered out.

They would have to make their way back to the castle in complete darkness.

Chapter Nine

Tristan said nothing when she told him about the candle. If she hadn't known to listen for a reaction, she would not have heard his sharp inhale.

'You will have to lead the way then,' he said after a moment's pause.

Once again, there was nothing in his voice to suggest that he was not completely in control of himself. The training at Ormand's castle must have been very vigorous indeed if he was able to hide his fears so well. Her heart hurt at the thought of a young Tristan being forced to act as if he was unafraid of everything. If she ever met this Ormand she would burn his castle to the ground.

There was no light at all in the cave but she knew from Tristan's voice that he was standing close to her. She reached out and found his hand. His fingers were icy cold as she laced them with hers.

'It's this way,' she said, tugging him to the small gap that hid the entrance.

She had made the journey many times and did not need a light to lead the way. In the darkness, she could hear Tristan's unsteady breathing over the sound of their footsteps and the steady drip of water. His fingers gripped hers. In the forest, he had protected her, shielding her with his body. Here, it was her turn.

'When I was younger,' she said, 'I fell in love.'

'Oh.'

'Or at least I thought I did. He was a stableboy named Ioan.'

'Oh.'

She had started the story to distract him but he did not sound very interested.

'Have you ever been in love?' she asked.

'No.'

'Love is a ridiculous notion. It makes people do foolish things, things that end in pain.' She had risked everything for love and had been burned. It had changed her, for the better, she believed. She was not flighty, did not follow whims and dreams. It made her a good, dependable leader.

'Is it?' That was more like it, she had managed to get two words out of him. The fingers in her hand were both icy and slippery with sweat.

'Romantic love, I mean. Love between family is a different matter. When you are *in love* you can think of nothing else but the other person and when they smile at you everything is ecstasy.'

'Sounds...irritating.'

The tunnel continued on its downward path; they were not halfway yet.

'It is distracting, yes.' When she had fancied herself enamoured of Ioan, she had been unable to perform even the most basic of tasks without sighing over his name. She had been a wool-brained fool who'd almost deserved her heartbreak. 'He was very handsome, Ioan.'

'Sounds like a bastard.' Four words was a huge improvement, enough for her to carry on with the tale.

'So he turned out to be, but I did not know that at the beginning. I was unhappy, you see. My mother died when my brother and I were very young and my father thought he had all the time in the world to find another wife and have more children. But, for whatever reason, the proposed marriages fell through time and again. Maybe it was because their kinsmen could see no value in an alliance in this obscure part of Wales, or maybe they met my father. I have no way of knowing. It did mean, however, that I was his only daughter. He didn't care for me overly much, aside from what kinship he could gain through my marriage. He thought that my...er...face would snare him a bigger prize than he would otherwise have been able to achieve.'

'You are very beautiful,' said Tristan.

She squeezed his fingers. 'I know.'

He barked out a laugh and she grinned into the darkness. 'The men he would invite to the castle were horrible. Old or ridiculously young or free with their hands. They would make offers but each time my father held out for a bigger prize. I believe he was hoping for an earl or a prince.'

Tristan whistled. 'I did not know I was in the presence of near-royalty.'

'Would it have made you more respectful if you had known this since the beginning?'

'Very possibly. Would you like me to bow?'

He was talking in full sentences now, although his skin was still cool to the touch. 'When we are back at the castle, you may abase yourself,' she told him and was rewarded with a soft laugh.

'Your father would not have been happy about the swineherd then.' Tristan's prompt and his engagement with the story felt like a victory.

'He did not look after the pigs; he was a stableboy. A very handsome one.'

'As you keep saying.' The tunnel was flattening out. They had reached the lowest point and would soon begin the climb back up to the castle entrance.

'It is an important point to my story.' Inasmuch as it would remind Catrin not to get her head turned by a pretty face and Tristan's was more remarkable than any she had seen. She could imagine herself becoming transfixed by those dark eyes and getting so lost in them that she'd agree to anything. Falling for a handsome face hadn't done her any good the first time and certainly would not help matters now. Obviously, that was why she kept repeating it and not because a part of her, a part she could barely acknowledge, even to herself, was trying to needle Tristan. It would do no good to make him jealous.

'I suspect my father would have killed Ioan had he known about my tender feelings. As it was, Ioan spun me stories of how we would run away together and start a new life somewhere else. I used these tunnels to meet with him.'

Tristan growled. 'I despise these wretched walls even more.'

They began to climb. She kept his hand in hers, ignoring the warmth spreading through her chest at his comment.

'I gave him gold coins,' she told Tristan, confessing

into the darkness something she had never told anyone else before; she wasn't sure why she was doing so now. 'I thought it was for our future but it turned out it was only for his.'

Tristan was silent.

'He left and he didn't take me with him.'

Still, he said nothing. Heat began to spread across her face and it had nothing to do with the strain or the temperature and everything to do with shame. Tristan obviously thought less of her for falling for such blatant lies. She should have told him only that Ioan had left or, better yet, never have said anything about Ioan. There were plenty of other stories she could have told him. It was these wretched tunnels, dragging up memories that should stay forgotten.

They came to the first door. She dropped his hand to work with the lock, stepping through it and closing it behind them.

They walked in silence for the rest of the way; she did not offer her hand and he did not reach for it. She wished more than anything that she could stuff the unwise words back into her mouth. She wanted him to respect her and she had undone everything by showing herself to once have been naïve and foolish. She could not fathom what had caused her to put her trust in someone she barely knew, the heightened stress of the night's events perhaps.

They came to the final door. She fished about on the ledge until her fingers curled around the cool metal of the key. She slotted it into the lock but paused before she turned it.

'I would ask that you do not tell anyone of what I told you. I only spoke those words to distract you from the darkness but it is not a tale I would like people to know.' These people had known her all her life, had probably noticed her infatuation with the handsome lad, but they would not have known about the coins or about all the times she had escaped from the castle to meet with him. They thought her virtuous; she was not.

'You need have no fear on that score.' Tristan scrubbed a hand down his face. 'I will not tell a soul. As for distracting me, you have done an excellent job. I'm utterly furious. I didn't think about the darkness at all because I spent the last of that climb plotting all the ways in which I can hunt down the latrine-scrubber and make him pay for ever causing you a moment's hurt.'

'He was a stableboy,' was the only way her addled mind could respond to Tristan's fierce defence of her.

'He was a pox-ridden mud-dweller.'

She laughed, relief weakening her bones. He didn't think less of her after all.

Chapter Ten

Dawn was turning the world grey as they stepped into the courtyard. Ffion leapt to her feet, running towards them, flinging her arms around Catrin. Tristan stood to the side and watched the two women. He wondered briefly if anyone would ever be so visibly thrilled to see him; he doubted it. Oh, he knew Leo and Hugh would be pleased to see him but they would not show it with hugs and tears of happiness over his safety. He did not have one person in this world who would do so. It had never bothered him before. For a long time, he had been striving to become one of the best knights in the land and a loving embrace was not part of that. It still wasn't and yet…

'You have caused chaos,' said Ffion, holding Catrin at arm's length. 'You must come and see.'

Tristan could see how tired Catrin was in the drag of her footsteps but she kept going, following her second-in-command across the courtyard. Catrin was a greater warrior than many of the pages and squires Tristan had trained with over the years. He knew, from the way she had trembled in the woods, that she had been frightened, but she had not once complained, not once asked to slow down or stop to rest. And when it had been his turn to feel fear she had stepped up and taken charge, while leading him into his own personal nightmare distracting him with a tale that had burned his veins with fury. One day, he would find this Ioan and make him wish he had never been born. For now, he could only marvel at Catrin's composure. She was a contradiction: a hard warrior leader and a caring, generous friend.

He dragged himself up to the ramparts, following the two women but only able to look at one of them. Perhaps his brain had been addled by the smoke coming from the large fire as the store tent burned or perhaps the darkness of the tunnel had taken away what brains he had, but it seemed as if Catrin was the light, his beacon in the dawn, and he was transfixed by her.

The castle's men were guarding the ramparts and they grinned at him as they saw him approach, several slapping him on the back. Even Wynne nodded at him, his gnarled face possibly smiling or perhaps he was grimacing, it was hard to tell, but he wasn't swearing at him; their relationship was definitely progressing in the right way. Tristan glanced down at the scene below.

'Oh, my goodness,' breathed Catrin as she took in the sight. 'I thought you only set fire to the stores.'

'It must have spread,' he murmured, looking at the charred remains of many of Ogmore's tents.

Smoke was still rising from the encampment but it looked as if the flames were out. His plan had worked better than he had hoped. If he'd had an army at his disposal, Tristan would ride out and finish the enemy off while they were already reeling. But he did not have access to men who could make that happen. Not only that, both he and Catrin had been awake for an entire day and night. They needed to rest before they did anything else.

Below them, men were carrying buckets back and forth from the river, still dousing the tents. Others were sorting through the remains of what was left and several were moving those dwellings that were still intact further away from the castle walls, creating a new camp that would not be as easy to watch from the ramparts. Ogmore's men were learning, too late perhaps, that they could not underestimate the people of Pwll Du Castle.

'We must sleep,' Catrin told Ffion. 'Is everyone settled? How is Lloyd's arm?'

'Everyone is either sleeping or on watch. Lloyd is comfortable.' Ffion's lips twitched. 'It was only a graze after all. Eluned is impressed with his fortitude, however, and the matter of whether or not they will wed has finally been settled. They are to do so this evening, all being well.'

'Lovely,' said Catrin, swaying slightly. 'That will give everyone a boost.'

Tristan's heart swelled and he pressed a hand to his chest, with no idea why he should care whether this couple marry or not. He barely knew them, would never see them again once this was all over. It must be exhaustion that was making him feel uncharacteristically emotional about two people coming together in matrimony.

'You two look like you will sleep where you stand,' Ffion commented, looking between them.

Catrin nodded. 'I have never experienced exhaustion like this. I think I could rest for a week.'

Tristan couldn't open his mouth to agree. Now that they were back in the relative safety of the castle walls, his body was shutting down. If he did not get to a resting place soon, he would lie where he stood. 'Wake me at midday,' he managed to say.

'Me too,' said Catrin quickly.

'There is no need for us both to get up,' he said. She had tried to hide it but he was aware of how hard the night had been for Catrin. She had not trained like he had and their flight through the trees would have been physically punishing.

'Then you should rest for longer.'

Tristan met Ffion's gaze. The other woman shook her head, gazing fondly at her leader. 'I will wake you both later.' Catrin seemed satisfied but Tristan noticed that Ffion had not specified a time. 'I have prepared the red chamber for Sir Tristan,' Ffion added.

Catrin nodded and Tristan guessed this was a better chamber than the one he had been locked in. In truth, it did not matter so long as he was not standing. Even the cold stone of the ramparts looked inviting.

They left Ffion on the ramparts and somehow, they made it inside, up a spiral staircase and into a narrow passageway lit by candles placed high on the walls.

'Here.' She pointed to a wooden door. 'This is the red chamber. There are windows.'

He was too tired to be embarrassed that this woman knew how little he liked the darkness. They hadn't known each other long, but not even those who had known him most of his life knew about his secret fear. They had been through a lot in a short amount of time but that wasn't all. He didn't know how to frame the way he felt about her, didn't know how to explain the way he was drawn to her.

His body was heavy, sluggish. Sleep tugged at his

mind and yet he still did not open the door. It did not seem right to leave Catrin, to step away from her into an empty chamber. There might be light inside but he still wanted to hold her hand. There might not be enemies within but he still wanted to protect her with his body.

Dark shadows rimmed Catrin's steady blue eyes as she gazed at him and he had the sense that she did not want to leave him either.

'I should...' he said.

She nodded.

Neither of them moved.

Her braid was a mess. Strands were coming loose, bits of green foliage were entangled with it and a rogue curl was pressing against her neck. He wanted to brush it off, to feel the smooth skin beneath it with the tips of his fingers, to run his thumb from beneath her ear to the base of her throat, but still he did not move.

'I am down here.' She gestured to the end of the corridor where a more ornate door was slightly ajar. 'If you need anything...'

He had half a mind to say that he did need her, not in the way a man wanted a woman, although, if he was honest, he did, but it was not just in that way. He wanted to curl around her, to hold her and to talk to her when they both woke from a deep sleep. He frowned; he should not be thinking this way. When this was over, he was going to have to hand her over to someone in Windsor, someone who would decide her fate. He would spend his life never knowing what had happened to her. The thought made his chest ache and he shut his eyes tightly. He was too tired to be thinking; once he was rested his normal, imperturbable emotions would rule and he would not feel much at all.

He opened the door. 'Sleep well,' he murmured, stepping over the chamber's threshold.

'You too,' she replied.

He slowly closed the door. He did not move away from it, staring at it as if it held the answer, although he was not entirely sure of the question. He lifted his hand as if to open the door again. He had not heard Catrin's footsteps move away; she must still be there. If he pulled it open, what then? If he held out his hand, would she take it?

Tiredness dragged at him but that did not stop his body from responding to the thought of her with him in here, the thought of pressing his lips to hers. His hand reached for the door handle, his fingers closing over the cool metal. Before he could pull it open, he heard the soft click of a door closing further down the corridor. He was too late; she had retired to her own chamber.

He let go of the handle and dragged himself across to the bed in the centre of the room. He did not have the energy to undress himself as he crawled onto the straw mattress. Lying face down, he allowed his burning eyes to close, his regret at not opening the door quickly enough following him into sleep.

Chapter Eleven

The clink of the blacksmith's hammer stole into Catrin's dreams, gradually waking her with its repetitive rhythm. She stretched, her muscles sore and tender. Sun was streaming through the window but the glass was not clear enough to see through, so she had no idea whether it was midday or later. Later, she would guess. Ffion did follow Catrin's orders for the most part, but she might not if she thought Catrin was being a danger to herself.

Catrin's insides clenched as she remembered the last few moments before she had tumbled into bed. She had stood outside Tristan's chamber, debating with herself whether she should follow him. What would she have done if she had? What had she been hoping for? An end to the lonely ache that resided in her? A brief, satisfying roll on the mattress? Neither of those would solve any of her problems, would probably have only added to them. Extreme tiredness was the only explanation for that fleeting lack of judgement. Thank goodness he did not know, no one knew. She never had to tell anyone or think on it again.

She sighed and pushed back the blankets. She had barely been able to pull her outer layer of clothing off before falling into bed and her clothes from yesterday were bundled on the floor.

She picked them up, nearly gagging at the stench of sweat and acrid smoke coming from them. She threw them into the corner of the room, as far away from her as possible, and began pulling clean ones from her chest. Someone must have come into her chamber while she'd slept; the jug on her table had been refreshed, the water warm as the air around it and scented with lavender. She filled a bowl and washed the grime from her skin before pulling clean clothes on.

She picked up her mirror and flinched. She tried not to be a vain woman. She knew that a beautiful face did not necessarily mean a beautiful soul beneath but she was horrified by the state of her hair. No wonder Tristan hadn't... No, she was not going to think about it, but even as she tried to push the thoughts to one side they still came.

She hadn't wanted to be parted from him. She could admit that much to herself. She could put it down to the strange bond that had formed as they had fled through the woodland, or even the way they had clung to one another as they had made their way through the dark tunnels, but she knew it was more than that. She'd wanted the comfort of a warm body next to her, perhaps a way to release tension, to end the exhilaration of the night with soft satisfaction. Although she also knew that she would not have wanted *any* warm body, that there was only one person she had wanted next to her.

She untied the bindings of her hair. It was irrelevant what she had wanted in that moment. He had closed the door in her face and he had not opened it. Likely, it had not even crossed his mind to do so; he doubtless would have been shocked to find her there. He had been as exhausted as her and had probably staggered to the bed and slept the sleep of the dead, not thinking of her from the moment she had disappeared from his sight.

Her hair was such a tangled mess it was difficult to separate the different strands of her braid. A twig fell from it and landed on her lap and then a leaf. Or maybe Tristan had seen the invitation in her eyes and had been repelled by the amount of woodland she was carrying around on her head. She began to pull a comb through her hair but it got stuck in a giant knot.

A gentle knock on her door interrupted her curse words. If it was Ffion she could get her to help with the hideous tangle that had previously been the hair on her head.

'It's open, Ffion. Come in and help me with this, would you?'

It was not Ffion who entered but Tristan, bearing a tray. Catrin's heart flipped at the sight of him. He looked fresh and rested and for some reason his forearms were showing, which did not help with her resolution not to think about him any more. Her stomach growled as the waft of meat and freshly cooked bread reached her.

'I am here to report that nothing has changed since last night,' Tristan told her, completely unaware of everything going on inside her body. 'Ogmore and his men are still trying to regroup and the damage is extensive. Your men have made a very obvious display of their defensive prowess all morning by marching around the battlements with their weapons on show.' He smiled briefly. 'Our enemy have kept out of harm's way, skulking and licking their wounds. Although they have not gone away, I feel optimistic enough to say that we have made some positive progress.'

'This is good news,' she replied.

'I also brought you something to eat,' he said, bringing the tray over to her and placing it on the edge of her table.

His dark hair was damp, curling as it hit his neck.

'You have washed,' she said.

'I took one step outside and was told that I stink.'

She laughed, tearing off a hunk of bread and biting into it. She couldn't stop the low moan of bliss as she chewed.

Tristan glanced away, clearing his throat. 'I was almost forcibly removed from my shirt by two older women I have not met before. It was a lowering moment. I always thought that I could withstand any sort of attack, but they got me in a pincer movement and...' He shrugged.

Catrin wished she hadn't taken such a large bite as she nearly choked on her giggles. 'What are you wearing?' she asked after she had swallowed her mouthful.

Now that he was nearer, she could see that he was wearing a shirt. It was loose about his torso and he'd rolled the sleeves back to his elbows, revealing what seemed like acres of skin.

'This is one of Dafydd's shirts.' He tugged at the material. 'I was given one of Lloyd's to start with but the way it stretched over my arms was a cause of great hilarity for everyone who saw it. Dafydd's clothes were the only ones that didn't look as if I was about to rip out of them. But of course, he is more mountain than man, so they do not quite fit either.'

She took another bite of bread to stop herself from

blurting out how glad she was that he had cause to show off his arms and the muscles they revealed. They should never be covered up, in her humble opinion.

'Did you not bring your own clothes?' she asked.

'I did, but the lady of the castle has hidden all my belongings and no one else appears to know where.' He winked at her to show that he was not angry.

'Ah.' Her gaze slid to the chest at the foot of her bed and he raised an eyebrow. 'Go ahead.' She gestured for him to open it.

He did as she instructed, pulling out the bag that contained the belongings he had seen fit to bring with him on his travels. She had not looked in it, had managed to restrain her curiosity, but from the soft feel of it, it only contained replacement clothes.

He placed the pack by her door and then turned back to her. 'When I knocked, you asked for help. Was it with that?'

He gestured to her hair and her hand flew to her comb, which was still entangled in the knots. Heat scalded her skin. She had been sitting here, stuffing her mouth with food while wearing a comb. No wonder he had not wanted her to follow him into his chamber; she was a mess in more ways than one and there she was thinking about it again. What on earth was wrong with her?

He chuckled softly. 'There is no need to be embarrassed. It has happened to the best of us.'

'I very much doubt it,' she said with as much dignity as she could muster. She tugged on the comb, trying to release it from her hair but it was stuck firmly.

He laughed more loudly, coming closer. As he reached

for the brush, his fingers skimmed hers and the shock of his touch ricocheted through her. 'Let me,' he said.

'Fine.' Her humiliation could not get worse anyway.

'Such gracious capitulation. I am honoured.'

She snorted and picked up the chicken thigh. He had already seen her at her worst, there was no point trying to be dainty around him. She tore into it as his long fingers began to tug at the tangled strands. 'Ow,' she muttered as he pulled at her scalp.

'I would be less likely to hurt you if you were still and not acting like a pig at a trough,' he said.

'I am starving.'

He sighed, although she could hear laughter in the sound rather than exasperation. 'No one who could see you now would doubt it.'

She refused to apologise or slow down; she was too hungry. Besides, if he saw her as a pig then at least she would know not to act like a foolish calf-sick girl around him.

One last tug and the comb was free. 'There,' he said, holding it aloft triumphantly.

'Well done,' she said as dryly as she could manage. She bit the inside of her cheek to hide her smile, he looked so pleased with himself.

'Possibly my greatest conquest.' His eyes sparked with amusement and her stomach flipped.

'I can believe that.'

They grinned at each other, her heart feeling lighter.

'Would you like help with...?' He gestured to her head. 'You must have half the forest in there.' He peered closer. 'I think I just saw a shrew peeking out from the strands.'

She laughed. 'That would be kind of you, if you do not mind the potential bites from the woodland creatures stowed within.'

He began to pull bits from the back of her head and set them on the table in front of her. 'It would be my pleasure,' he murmured and butterflies took flight in her stomach. There was no mistaking the low rumble in his voice; she had heard men sound like that before but it had never made her toes curl or her skin tingle deliciously.

Her appetite fled as his long fingers worked over her scalp, to be replaced by a different kind of ache, one that started low in her belly but spread slowly through her body, making her limbs heavy and her skin tingle.

By the time he picked up the comb, she was biting her lip to stop herself from moaning from the decadent pleasure of his touch. He lifted a section of her hair and a shiver ran down her spine as he pulled gently on the strands, the bristles tugging on the knots. He worked his way around her head, lifting and brushing. She pressed her fingers together so that she didn't reach for him but she knew he would be able to hear the way her breathing was not quite steady and perhaps he could see the way her pulse jumped in her throat.

A soft whimper broke through her lips and his breath hitched in response.

His long fingers swept along the back of her neck and along the length of her jaw, his thumb grazing her chin.

She tilted her head to gaze up at him. His lips were lightly parted, his eyes dark.

'Catrin...' he whispered.

She stood slowly, his fingers sliding back into her hair, his other hand rising to brush strands off her forehead, moving down her cheek, tracing the length of her arm, finding the curve of her hip. His gaze flicked over her face, lingering on her lips, and his breathing stumbled, a light puff of air grazed her skin. She touched her tongue to her top lip and his fingers twitched against her.

She swayed closer.

His lips brushed her brow, her cheek.

Her hands skimmed the length of his arms, over his wide shoulders to the slope of his neck. His soft grunt whispered across her skin. She turned her head and brushed her lips over his, once, twice. His grip tightened, pulling her closer. Her fingers stole into his hair and she felt his smile against her skin.

His mouth became urgent, seeking more, a press to her cheek, her jaw, finally her lips. She responded, a breathy whimper escaping her as his tongue brushed her bottom lip. She opened to him and the sweet, gentle kisses became something deeper, something ravenous and desperate.

He growled her name against the skin of her neck and her hands went to the ties of his shirt. They were knotted tight and she pulled on them, desperate to feel more of his skin against her.

His hands skimmed over her back, down to her thigh, he lifted her leg, pushing her into the table. She moved against him and he gritted out her name, a command and a plea.

Footsteps sounded on the stones outside the chamber and they leapt apart. His eyes were wide, his hair tousled. She glanced down, there was no hiding his physical reaction to their activity. She'd have smirked if she wasn't so shocked by herself. She had all but climbed him like a cat up a tree.

They were both breathing heavily and all the while the footsteps came closer. She sat down abruptly and picked up her comb, pulling it through the strands of her well-combed hair. She heard Tristan move away from her, towards the long window that stood at the far end of her chamber.

Ffion appeared at the doorway. 'You're awake,' she said.

'I am.' Catrin's voice came out as a croak. She cleared her throat. 'I am,' she said again, clearer this time.

Ffion frowned, glancing at Tristan, who Catrin now saw was staring at the window as if he had never seen glass before and wanted to learn the secrets of it.

'I have news,' Ffion said.

Catrin placed her comb on the table before her. 'Is it bad?'

'It is.'

Tristan whirled round. His hair was still standing on end but all desire had gone from his face. 'What is it?'

'Ogmore has slaughtered the cattle.'

'Oh, no.' Catrin pressed a hand to her heart; cracks were opening up in it, small fissures that hurt.

'He has left them out in the open to rot, all aside from one that he has dumped half in the water, presumably to poison our water supply.'

Tristan swore viciously under his breath and Catrin had never liked him more.

She closed her eyes. She didn't want to think of those gentle, trusting beasts lying dead on the wide open plains. This was a battle and she knew that bad things happened, but it was the senselessness of the act that seemed so cruel. If he had used those animals to feed his own people, she could have accepted it easier.

She took a steadying breath, focusing on the impact of the destruction. 'The cow in the water will be more of a hindrance to him than to us. Our water supply from the well does not come from the river; that act of vandalism will not impact us.' Her fingers curled around the edge of her table. She wanted nothing more than to storm from the castle walls and fight with Ogmore herself, but that would not bring back the cattle and would likely see her dead. She would not allow her grief to make her foolish.

'Lloyd and Eluned thought they might postpone their wedding,' Ffion told them.

'No, that would be a shame. There should be laughter and joy while we still can.' She straightened. 'I want Ogmore to hear us celebrate. I want him to know that we are not afraid of him, that we can find happiness, and I want that while he is sitting amongst the charred remains of his encampment surrounded by dead animals that will surely rot and make his life miserable.'

'I agree with Lady Catrin,' said Tristan, his voice hard and firm, as if his lips hadn't softly touched hers only moments ago. 'Let the young couple enjoy themselves.'

Ffion snorted. 'Young. They are only a year or two less than the two of you.'

'Innocent then,' said Catrin. 'Let them be innocent for a little while longer.'

Ffion's amusement faded. She looked between them both and then nodded slightly. 'I shall tell them what you think and ask the kitchens to prepare something fitting with the rations that they have.'

Catrin nodded. 'That would be excellent, Ffion. I shall join you in a moment. There is something I need to discuss with Sir Tristan first.'

Ffion's lips twitched. 'I am sure that there is.' With one last glance at Tristan's rumpled hair, she left them alone.

The silence in her wake seemed deafening. It was hard to believe that they had been grasping at each other before Ffion's arrival, that if Ffion hadn't come Catrin would have dragged him to her bed and lay with him and damn the consequences. It was as if she had forgotten everything once he had laid his hands upon her. Forgotten that her people were depending on them to end this siege, forgotten that he was in her castle to remove her from it, forgotten that she had sworn to herself that she would never take another lover. Forgotten everything.

He walked slowly towards her, the floor creaking under his weight. He stopped at the foot of her bed. She stood slowly but made no move towards him.

'That was a mistake,' she said, her fingers pointing between herself and him to clarify her meaning.

He nodded.

'Obviously, it cannot happen again.'

'Obviously,' he said in agreement.

'Good.'

'Good.'

Neither of them moved.

'I am not in the habit of kissing men,' she told him.

'I am not in the habit of kissing women.'

'Well, then.'

'Quite.'

He was ramrod-straight, his hands clasped behind

his back. His rigid position contrasted with the wildness of his hair.

'We should join the others,' she said.

He nodded.

'You should...' She gestured to his head. He frowned and she held out her comb. 'Unless you would like me to...'

'I think that would be a very bad idea.' But he stepped towards her, ducking his head so that she could reach up and run the comb through his hair. His eyes fluttered closed as she worked her way across his scalp, her actions the exact opposite of what she had just said to him and he to her.

'What are we doing?' she murmured.

'Something we shouldn't.'

She dropped her hand and he straightened. 'You look more presentable now.'

He nodded slowly. He was so close it would be the work of a moment to close the short gap between them and carry on where they had left off.

He sighed. 'I suppose we should be sensible.'

'I suppose so.' She had followed her desires once before and all it had got her was a broken heart, the absolute terror that she might have fallen pregnant and an abhorrence of taking risks. Repeating the same mistake twice would be folly that she could not put down to naivety.

She stepped away from him, ignoring the way his shoulders dropped. There was no future for them as a couple and wanting to kiss him did not change that.

She strode briskly towards her chamber door and heard the heavy thud of his boots as he followed her. 'We need to take advantage of the chaos you caused last night,' she told him as they made their way along the narrow corridor that connected her living quarters with the rest of the castle.

There was a brief pause and then, 'There should be another raid tonight.'

'I agree. Although it will be harder, they will be expecting us to do something.'

'I still think there is merit in going. I will take a group and show them the ropes. Then we can make nightly forays. Some won't be a success but any time we are able to get past their defences we will weaken and unnerve them. It will be worth the effort.'

'When you say I, you mean we.'

'Lady Catrin,' he said formally, as if his fingers had not run through the strands of her hair, 'you are too important. If they are on guard against us coming then the chances of them capturing you are far higher. We came very close to that last night and I do not think we should tempt fate again.'

She might not like what he said but it made sense. She was not a leader who stubbornly clung to the notion that she needed to be involved in everything, but it did sting that he did not want her there. A foolish notion but the truth nonetheless.

'I see,' she said.

'You are not going to argue.'

'I would like to, but your comment is logical. We must choose those who accompany you well.'

'Huh,' was only his response.

Outside her personal quarters, the courtyard was bustling with activity. From the height of the sun in the sky, she must have slept past midday but, as she was feeling rested, she could not complain about that either. She had watched the way her father had blustered and bullied those around him, seen how that had made their lives miserable and how the efficiency of the castle had been slowed by his random decision-making. She was tolerant but not foolish.

'Would you like to receive information from those who report to you?' asked Tristan as they strode out into the sun.

'I would.'

'I shall arrange it,' he told her.

'Very well. I shall wait in the Great Hall.'

He nodded and walked away. As he moved, she noticed how her people stopped to talk to him, how they smiled at his approach and looked pleased as he engaged with them. They would be hurt too when they realised the truth behind his reason for being here. She pushed it aside as a problem to deal with on another day, just like everything else she was sweeping to one side. She was becoming adept at the skill.

Chapter Twelve

The wedding of Lloyd and Eluned took place in the doorway of the castle chapel, as was becoming the tradition. The late afternoon sunshine bathed the couple in golden light. Something made Tristan's heart ache as he watched the beaming lovers exchange their vows. Ffion had said that the two of them were not that much younger than him, but looking at them it was as if they were decades apart in age. They looked hopeful and sweet and he felt heavy and tied down with guilt and anger.

He would never experience anything gentle like this, never bind his life to another person. His path was a warrior's one with battles and constant war; he'd never wanted anything different.

Catrin was standing at the front of the crowd, smiling widely, her love for the two inhabitants of her castle shining from her face. This was her home and he was a bastard because he still needed her to leave, was still going ahead, even after everything. He'd known that even when he'd stood in her bedchamber and run a comb through the long strands of her hair; it hadn't changed even though he'd touched the soft skin of her neck and held her in his arms and breathed in the scent of flowers from her freshly washed skin. His mission still stood between them as their kiss had turned from soft and gentle to something fierce and possessive. He'd known he was a miserable cur and yet he had not stopped, would have carried on for ever if they had not been interrupted by Ffion. He'd wanted to both slam the door in her face and invite her in with relief.

Tristan had never lain with a woman. He knew that would shock anyone if they discovered that about him—it was generally assumed that he'd had lovers, although he had no idea where those rumours had come from. Perhaps the women he had gently turned down had started them so as not to lose face. He had never told anyone, not even his closest friends, that it was not true, that it would *never* be true. He had watched his father destroy lives by casually moving from one lover to another, or having several at the same time. The pain that had caused had lasted far longer than any pleasure.

When Tristan finally took someone to bed, he wanted it to mean something. He did not want a quick roll in the hay to satisfy an urge. When he touched a woman, he wanted it to be because he cared for her above all others, he wanted there to be trust and true emotion between them. It was why he had never taken up any of the many offers he had received over the years. Not one of them had tempted him to break the rules he had made for himself. Until now.

Even though he had never done it, he still knew what kissing sometimes led to, had understood the path they were on when her fingers had tugged on the knots of his shirt. It wasn't that he expected to lie with Catrin, although she was the first woman he had truly wanted, the only one he could imagine breaking his self-imposed rules for. He was not good enough for her in every way. He was a lowly knight, only just starting out, and she was the lady of a castle. One day, many years from now, he might be worthy of her, but by then it would be too late. It did not stop him from imagining though, did not stop the intense craving just to touch her or even stand next to her. He was a half-wit.

He had always thought those who became consumed by the idea of making love to a woman somewhat ridiculous. There were other, more important things to obsess about, such as becoming the greatest knight in all the land. But now he understood. While she had listened to her people report to her, he had watched her and ached, ached to be the one receiving her attention, ached to be alone with her, just ached.

Kissing her was a mistake, she had said so and she was right. That did not mean that it was not the greatest thing that had ever happened to him. He would remember it for the rest of his life, would feel her lips on his deathbed. He shook his head; this was not like him. He did not get distracted by a woman; it was always the other way around. He had never understood why women sometimes lost their heads around him, still didn't really. But he now understood the sentiment, now he knew what could happen to him if he let his longing for her get the better of him. He couldn't though. This mission was his redemption and that was more important than lying with a woman. She was a temptation he would have to resist because he could not afford to become beguiled by her—do that and he could lose sight of everything else.

A feast had been put on to celebrate the nuptials. It

was not the grandest he had ever been to, the castle was rationing its food and was nowhere near as wealthy as anywhere he'd lived before, but it was the best celebration he had attended. Despite the very real threat that existed outside the castle walls, the inhabitants were happy for Lloyd and Eluned. Laughter filled the Great Hall and Tristan found himself wedged on a table with some of the families. He should have felt awkward. He didn't know these people, not really, but they seemed to have accepted him as one of their own. They told him stories and made him laugh harder than he had in years. Guilt crept over him now and then, reminding him that he was on a serious mission, that he still had to ensure he did not let his friends down, but for the most part, he enjoyed the food placed before him and the conversations that surrounded him.

But too often for his own liking he was distracted by something else altogether. He'd focus on something, putting food in his mouth or trying to talk to the people around him, and he'd find his food halfway to his mouth, watching Catrin talk quietly to Ffion, her head bowed, the flickering candle casting shadows over her face. Wynne's wife, who sat opposite him during the meal, was openly laughing at him towards the end. Even Wynne might have been smirking, although Tristan still wasn't able to read the man's expressions easily.

Tristan wasn't sure what to make of their response. He couldn't understand why Wynne wasn't leaning over the table, grabbing his shirt and growling a warning to stay away from their leader. Perhaps they thought Catrin was able to take care of herself, that he would receive a blistering put-down if he tried anything with her.

Or maybe Catrin's people trusted him now that he was helping them. Everyone had been very pleased with the raid last night and there had been no shortage of volunteers for tonight. Even Lloyd had put his name forward, but had been easy to dissuade. No man should spend his wedding night away from his bride.

By the time the evening repast was over, people were spilling into the courtyard, pockets of laughter erupting here and there. The sun was still in the sky and it would be hours before they could leave the castle tonight. The evening air hummed with insects still going about their business; the sweet smell of hay from the stables filled the air. A short stake was hammered into the ground and, with lots of good-natured slaps on the back and a few jeers, Lloyd stepped forward and began to throw horseshoes at the target. When one landed around the stake, the crowd erupted in cheers; the young man grinned as his last one fell short. It didn't seem to matter, the crowd was on his side anyway, happy for the young man on the most important day of his life.

Ffion stepped up next and showed no skill, missing every single throw, but the stern woman laughed along with those observing, more relaxed than he had ever seen her. Tristan was grinning too, his body warm in a way that had nothing to do with the evening sun.

Dafydd, his size giving him an advantage, managed a convincing two out of five attempts and Tristan cheered along with everyone else. The big man collected the horseshoes from where they had landed and held the metal towards Tristan. 'Come on, Englishman, show us what you are made of.' The giant's eyes were laughing and the crowd started up a chant. Tristan wondered what

Ogmore and his men would make of the jubilant noises; he hoped the man could hear them clearly and would know that he had not cowed these people.

Tristan took the horseshoes, the metal warm in his palm. 'I don't want to show you up.'

The crowd laughed. Catrin's gaze met his, her eyes filled with something that looked suspiciously like affection. Tristan's heart expanded behind his ribcage. A smile spread wide across his face. He hadn't been part of a group like this since…ever really. He, Leo and Hugh had formed a tightknit threesome and the other inhabitants of Ormand's castle had steered clear of them. Tristan had always thought that avoidance had been down to jealousy on the part of the others. Ormand did not train his squires with patience and thrived on an openly hostile atmosphere. Tristan, Leo and Hugh had blamed everyone else because that was easiest. Met with the open friendliness of Catrin's people, perhaps the three of them had played their own part in pushing the other men away. Not that he had time to think deeply about this now; he had a point to prove.

'That's too close, Sir Dyn Golygus,' Ffion called out.

Catrin nudged her friend in the ribs but kept her gaze on him.

'What does that mean?' he asked Dafydd.

'It means you need to move back a couple of paces.' The tall man's Welsh accent was thick. 'As for the name she's given you—' his grin spread '—it's a term of great honour.'

The crowd laughed and Tristan guessed it wasn't. He met Catrin's gaze and she nodded at him, her lips quirked in an amused smile.

He stepped back a bit and threw his first shoe. It landed to the left of the target, much to the delight of the crowd. 'That was just a practice,' he said, eliciting more good-natured teasing.

He threw again.

And missed.

He held up the three remaining horseshoes. 'These are faulty.'

Dafydd's laugh was loud and unrestrained but it was Catrin's quiet laughter that held his attention. He couldn't hear her over the others talking but he would have gone on losing all evening to keep the smile of pure delight on her face. He had his pride, however.

The next one landed on target with a resounding thwack. Everyone cheered and he knew he was grinning like a delighted fool.

The next one went over with ease.

The cheer was even louder. He cut a quick glance towards Catrin. Her gaze flicked away from him and he bit the inside of his cheek to stop his grin from spreading further. There was no reason for her not to be looking at him, everyone else was, but her thinking it was something she needed to hide was enough to make him happy, even though that was clearly another mistake.

He flung his final shoe, the crowd yelling as it landed on target.

He lifted his arms triumphantly as the crowd cheered. It didn't seem to matter to them that he was an outsider, that he had come from England into their Welsh home. He'd hit the target more than anyone else and they were pleased for him. He wasn't sure that he had ever experienced such a simple pleasure. His whole body was light, as if he was filled with air. He couldn't have stopped his smile if he'd tried, but he had no reason to want to.

Dafydd slapped him across the back, jolting his ribs.

'Does Lady Catrin take part in this?' he asked.

'Lady Catrin,' Dafydd's voice boomed out, 'Sir Dyn Golygus is challenging you to beat him.'

Whatever that name meant, it seemed to be sticking.

'I would not say that, my good man.' Tristan slapped Dafydd on the back. The man mountain did not move, even as the sensation reverberated through Tristan's arm. 'I do not think anyone will be able to top my triumph.'

The crowd oohed, the noise increasing as Catrin took the bait. She moved towards him, lithe and graceful as a cat. He collected the horseshoes and held them out to her. Her fingers brushed over his as she took them from him. His breath hitched and her gaze shot to his, the smile fading, becoming something heated, a living thing that seemed to whip between them.

She turned from him quickly, moving to the starting point and throwing the first shoe before he'd had time to catch his breath.

The horseshoe spun as it flew around the target, hitting the ground, sending up a puff of dust.

'Impressive,' he murmured.

Somehow, she heard him over the general roar of approval. She raised an eyebrow, sending the second direct to the target, having barely spared it a glance, her movements powerful and concise.

'You are showing far more grace here than you did when you tried to comb your hair earlier.' His comment was meant to goad her and it did. Her eyes narrowed, her shoulders tightened.

Her third attempt went wide. She turned to glare at him as the crowd gasped. He raised an eyebrow, somehow able to stop his smirk from being too obvious. He must have failed because her fourth attempt was too short; he was getting to her just as he had meant to. She shot him another exasperated look and this time he allowed his grin to grow wide.

'I do not know why you keep glaring at me, it is not my fault you are no good at this contest.'

'I suppose you think you are better.'

'The results speak for themselves.'

'You need to be careful that I don't throw this at your forehead.' She waved the remaining horseshoe around.

He raised a shoulder nonchalantly. 'You would only miss.'

Next to him, Dafydd guffawed and even Ffion smiled.

With a quick flick of her wrist, Catrin sent the final horseshoe over the target. Her people went wild, congratulating her as if she had won a battle against their greatest enemy.

Dafydd gripped his shoulder. 'Do not worry, boy. You played well.'

Catrin all but hopped up to him, smiling delightedly. The urge to reach out, to pull her to him and claim that smile with his mouth was so strong he could almost feel it as if it had happened.

'I hate to destroy this great celebration,' he told her, forcing himself to remember where they were and what they were doing, 'but you did not win. It was a draw.'

'Would you like to go again, Sir Great Knight? Or are you afraid that your three shots on target were down to luck?'

He should step back, allow her victory, let her feel good about it, but he found that he could not. He wanted to engage with her, to tease her and to have her attention fixed solely on him.

'I do not want to hurt your delicate feelings when you lose.'

The crowd laughed, siding immediately with their lady with shouts of, 'You will destroy him, Lady Catrin.' And, 'Show the Englishman what Welsh people are made of, my lady.'

At Ormand's castle, jeers were personal. Tristan was an excellent knight. With the exception of, perhaps, Leo, he was the best fighter Ormand had produced in years. That made him a target, the man the others wanted to beat. At the start of any practice bout, the comments aimed at him were meant to throw him off, to try to find his weakness and to deflect him from his purpose. It hadn't worked. Anything they'd said that had hit home he'd ignored, burying comments deep within him where everything that had ever hurt him lived.

Right now, surrounded by these people who were yelling encouragement at Lady Catrin and not him, the comments didn't feel like anything he had experienced before. Even though the insults were aimed at him, there was laughter in their voices, a response more to the way he'd teased their lady than a personal attack on him.

But even if the comments had been cruelly meant, he wasn't sure he would notice. Catrin's face was tilted towards him in challenge, her body poised to give flight to the horseshoes, but her eyes were shining with laughter. They were so bewitching he could not tear his gaze away. He'd play and lose a thousand times if only she would keep looking at him like this. He was doomed to a lifetime of pain when this all ended, but he would take this moment and enjoy it for all it was worth. He raised a challenging eyebrow, knowing he goaded her whenever he appeared smug, wanting more than anything to continue this game in the fading sunlight.

She smirked up at him, full of confidence. 'Will it not hurt *your* masculine pride when I win?'

He shrugged, affecting nonchalance when all he wanted to do was to slide his hands into her elaborate braid and drag his lips along the sensitive skin of her neck. 'That will not happen, so there is nothing for me to worry about,' he said instead.

Those around him who could hear their exchange laughed along with them but he was only vaguely aware of their presence. Catrin was the only person he could see, her voice the only thing he could hear.

The stake was moved further away as sunlight skimmed the edges of the battlements, turning the air softly golden. Small birds pecked at the ground nearby, searching for dropped crumbs, not worrying about how close they were to people who could crush them underfoot.

Catrin's shoulder brushed against his arm as she turned to take her first shot. She made the task look easy as her horseshoe landed perfectly. The crowd roared on her side. Tristan wanted to shout along with them, but that was not the game he was playing.

'You can go next.'

'You want to alternate?'

'Yes. It will make your downfall all the sweeter.'

Someone handed him another set of horseshoes as he

snorted with amusement. 'I fear it will highlight your tragic inability, but who am I to argue?'

Tristan's next shot hit the target; he was surprised to hear a roar of celebration. Something warm was unfolding inside him, reaching corners of him he'd kept closed off for years, his whole life really, when he'd realised no one really thought him special. He tried to clamp down on it; no good could come of developing soft feelings for these people. He was not here to make friends. Developing unwanted feelings for Catrin was bad enough, but to care about a whole community was a disaster. But even as he told himself to shut it down, the feeling spread and intensified as they both succeeded in their second attempt and the cheers of support for both of them became deafening.

Catrin threw her third and…missed. She grinned as the horseshoe clipped the target and spun away from it, her people laughing with her.

'Your chance to get ahead, Sir Dyn Golygus.' She winked at him and he took a half-step towards her. Her eyes widened and he stopped in his tracks. He had no idea what he had been going to do when he reached her, only knowing that he had been intent on touching her. Not only was that unwise, it was not what she wanted from him, not the game they had played in any of their encounters.

He got his horseshoe around the stake but somehow it didn't feel like the victory it should. He wanted to share the triumph with her, not take anything away. But if he threw the competition she would know and she would not thank him for it.

The fourth round saw her hit the target and him miss.

He was finding it harder to concentrate on the competition. All he wanted to do was to throw the horseshoe to the ground, sweep Catrin off her feet and carry her to her chamber. He was almost trembling with the effort of not doing such a thing.

Catrin waved the last horseshoe at him. 'It is time for us to find out which of us is the greater warrior.'

'We already know the answer to that.' He winked again to hide the feelings coursing through him. *It's you*, he added silently. Physically, he could match or beat her in anything but standing here, surrounded by people who were happy and healthy because of her, he knew she was the better person in every other respect.

She threw first, her horseshoe landing precisely where she was aiming, as if she had neatly placed it there rather than hurled it from afar.

He got ready to throw. She moved nearer; she was standing so close that her dress brushed against his legs. He tilted his head towards her, his gaze still fixed on the target. 'You are not playing fairly, Lady Catrin.'

'Since when were there rules to this game?' Her voice took him back to her chamber, her arms around his neck, his fingers in her hair.

'Since we are competing to become the ultimate champion, Lady Catrin.' His teasing comment, his narrowed eyes, were all for show. His body was tightening, responding in the unique way it did for her.

'Ah, I see. Well, do go ahead and try your best.'

Knowing she had succeeded in distracting him, she took a step away from him, a small smile playing around her lips. She had disturbed his concentration but he would not be a knight if he could not take a little distraction. With as much nonchalance as he could summon, he threw his final projectile. It sailed through the air and landed neatly on her last horseshoe.

'As you can see, my lady,' he said, turning to her with as much swagger as he could manage, 'my best is always better than good enough.'

She rolled her eyes at his words but she was smiling at him. 'I know,' she said quietly. For a moment, the noise of the crowd faded away. It was as if it was just the two of them standing in the courtyard, the sun turning her hair golden. Her smile slowly faded, her gaze softening.

'It is nearly time for the raid to begin,' he said, reminding them both of what was to come.

She nodded. 'Are you prepared?'

'I need to fetch my weapons and then the four of us can leave.' They were talking of practical matters but somehow it seemed as if a second conversation was going on between them, something that had nothing to do with words and all to do with the way their bodies were tilted towards each other.

'Be careful with my people,' she told him.

A fleeting pang, a quiet yearning, crossed his heart. In that brief moment, he desperately wanted not to be the greatest knight Britain had ever seen, but someone who belonged to Lady Catrin, someone whom she wanted to keep safe.

'I am always careful.' She raised an eyebrow and he conceded, 'Most of the time.'

Behind them the crowd was breaking up, the inhabitants retreating to the areas in which they slept. Lloyd and Eluned disappeared to bawdy comments from those left in the courtyard. Even with their backs turned, it was easy to spot the bright red tips of Lloyd's ears. Next to him, Catrin's eyes twinkled warmly as she watched her people teasing one another as they slowly wended their way in the long, summer evening. The scene was different from anything Tristan had ever experienced at his parents' stronghold or Ormand's training grounds. That people could be loving and kind to one another was fascinating to him. If Tristan had more time, he would stay at this castle for longer, to discover whether they were always like this. Was it truly possible that Catrin had created something different with her leadership? Or was this a bond formed under the pressure of being under siege? He could understand the latter easier than the former.

When he'd been a page, he could remember some of the little boys crying during the night, never during the day for fear of mockery. They'd wept for those they had left behind, their brothers, their friends, their parents. Tristan had stared up at the ceiling listening to their sobs, the idea of missing the place he'd been born foreign to him. He hadn't been able to understand why they weren't rejoicing their good fortune in escaping to somewhere new, somewhere they could reform themselves without the pressure of everyone knowing who was your sire while waiting for you to be his very image in looks and deed. Ormand's training had been hard, brutal even, but Tristan had never once regretted ending up there. For him, it had been an escape from a far worse fate.

Looking at Catrin's people, he finally understood those boys' tears. These people would cry if they were made to leave this place—hell, he'd be upset himself and this was not his home. It might break something in Catrin when she left this haven she'd made.

His chest tightened because, despite everything, he knew he couldn't abandon his mission. He could not face Leo and Hugh, after everything they had been through, and tell them he had failed to complete his mission because Pwll Du Castle was a *nice* place to live. That was not what he owed them. He owed them a resolution. They might have told him that they did not blame him for Lady Ann's actions, but that did not mean that he didn't. If he had somehow been firmer, outwardly rejected her, then maybe she would have hated him and Robert would not have targeted the three of them. Even if no harsh words had turned Lady Ann away from him, it was still his fault. His mother might have been harsh when she had raised him but she was right—his face caused problems.

He turned, realising that Catrin was watching him, a slight crease between her eyebrows. Perhaps he had stared too intensely at her people or she was still worried, despite his protestations, that all would be well on the raid.

'I should get my weapons together,' he said, gesturing behind him to show that he intended to walk back to the red chamber where he was now stowing his belongings.

Without discussion, she fell into step beside him. She kept up a litany of questions about what he intended to do, what his plans were if he and the men he was taking with him were followed by any of Ogmore's troops. The raid would not be difficult, it was what he was trained for, it was more to get the younger men of the castle skilled in the art.

They had been through this earlier, had gone through the plan with the men he was taking with him, and Tristan was able to answer the questions without much thought, his mind taken up instead with the way Catrin's hair seemed to shimmer in the setting sun. His fingers twitched with the urge to touch it, to run his fingers through the long strands.

They slipped into the part of the castle meant for the lord and lady of the stronghold. It was smaller than any he'd seen before but it was somehow welcoming. Only Catrin used any of the rooms within it. Her antechamber with the weird tapestry was on the ground floor, her private chapel was above that and the chambers for her personal use on the top floor. They fell silent as their footsteps echoed in the empty building. Fresh rushes were on the floor and candles lit their way.

'You should probably ration these,' he said, pointing to the flickering flames.

'I know.'

'You are not keeping them lit for me, are you? I am not so incapable that I cannot climb stairs in the dark.' Humiliation made his tone harsher than he intended.

'You are the most capable man I have ever met.'

Her bold statement deflated his indignation as they began to climb the spiral staircase that led to the top floor.

'Oh.' He had nothing else to say. Instead, he watched, transfixed by her lithe body as she moved ahead of him, her hips swaying with every step.

They came to a stop outside his chamber door. The climb had made her slightly breathless and her chest rose and fell quickly.

She tapped her fingers lightly on his door before turning and looking away. He thought she would go without another word but instead she said, 'I know why you are really here. You are here to complete your mission, which is to remove me from my home.'

His heart twisted at her blunt words. 'If there was any other way...'

She shook her head. 'We are past that. It is not your fault that you are the messenger any more than it is my fault that I am a woman in a man's world. I know it's important to you that you complete this endeavour, that you somehow believe it will redeem you or prove to the world, and yourself, that you are not a failure. Despite all this, despite the pressure you have put on yourself, you are delaying your own mission in order to help the likes of Lloyd and Eluned, a couple you don't know.'

He scrubbed a hand over his face. Put like that, he wasn't sure if he sounded noble or foolish. His liege would undoubtedly argue that he was wasting his time, but Leo and Hugh would expect him to do the right thing by the people of this castle. Besides, the siege was keeping him inside the castle walls as much as it was the people who lived here.

'Ogmore is in my way. I cannot walk out of the castle with you if he is barring the path.' It was important that she knew he wasn't entirely virtuous.

'You could always force me to surrender to Ogmore,' she said. 'It would be a quicker solution for you, wouldn't it? We could be on our way to Windsor tomorrow if you did so. You could leave my replacement to deal with the problem of Ogmore.'

It was something he had considered—very briefly indeed. It was not an option, no matter how much easier it would make his life. Ogmore, with his heavyset thugs, would take what was special about this place and crush it within an afternoon. He would probably kill Dafydd on principle, not taking time to realise that the man was a gentle soul. He would not notice the longing looks the big man gave to Catrin's brittle second-in-command, Ffion. He would not laugh at Wynne's jokes—he probably wouldn't realise that the grizzled man was making any. There would be no mercy for Catrin's people from someone who was foolish enough to try to seize a small castle when he had a large one of his own.

Tristan didn't say all this. He did not want Catrin to know how much he was coming to care for her people; she might use it against him at a later date. 'A man who senselessly kills cattle does not deserve leadership of any castle, let alone this one,' he said instead.

'You have honour.' Catrin's gaze seemed to look through him as if she could see his soul.

He shifted on his feet. He did not deserve the way she was looking at him; his actions were nothing special for a knight. 'When I became a knight, I swore to follow the code of chivalry. Handing Pwll Du Castle over to Lord Ogmore goes against everything I believe in.'

Her blue eyes were clear, even in the dimly lit corridor. 'That is why I have had the candles lit, because you are an honourable man who is helping us at a time of need and by this—' she gestured to the light '—I can make you a little more comfortable.'

He stared at her, something settling around his heart—something not altogether easy. *This* was what it felt like to be cared for by her, *this* was what had been missing from his whole life.

'I am not completely honourable,' he whispered, slowly stepping towards her.

The air around them seemed to still. Her gaze flickered to his lips and his body tightened.

'How so?' she whispered.

'If I was, I would not constantly think of the thing we promised ourselves was a mistake.'

Her lips parted as he drew her to him and her arms immediately wound around his neck, pulling his mouth down to hers. He wasn't sure who moved, only vaguely aware that he was pressing her into his door, their bodies flush as their mouths devoured one another. The delicious friction of her moving against him sent him out of his mind. He could not touch her enough, not feel enough of her tongue against his. One of them groaned, possibly him.

Her leg came around his waist, his fingers found the end of her skirts and his hand circled her ankle, her knee. Her hands moved up the loose material of his borrowed shirt, over the top of his arms to his shoulders. His movements turned wild at her touch on his skin, her fingernails dug into him and his hand travelled up her thigh to where she was warm and wet.

Somewhere in the distant recesses of his mind, words like *honour* and *duty* were trying to make themselves known but he was able to ignore them easily in favour of consuming what he wanted more than anything. His fingers pressed against the soft flesh of her thigh, she whimpered into his mouth and flames flickered through his veins. He brushed the soft curls between her legs and her head fell back against the wooden door. He placed open-mouthed kisses down her neck as his fingers found her opening. He pushed one inside her warmth and she moaned, writhing against him as she begged for more.

He returned his mouth to hers as another finger joined the first, swallowing her moans as he stroked and pushed and sent them both out of their minds.

The door to his chamber gave way and, with no arms to protect themselves, they fell backwards to the ground, landing with a thud on the hard floor. He heard her 'Oof' as his weight landed on her.

He immediately rolled sideways. 'Are you hurt?' he asked, running his hands over her arms, her stomach, her head. 'Tell me, did I crush you?' Her skirts were rucked, showing her calves, but his desire had died as she'd crashed to the ground. 'Talk to me, Catrin.'

'Winded,' she gasped out. 'Heavy.' She poked a finger in his ribs.

'I am.' He skimmed his hands over her ribs. She didn't wince, so he thought they were unlikely to be broken. That didn't stop him continuing to run his hands over her body, searching for hidden damage. If he'd hurt her... 'Are you hurt?'

She shook her head. 'No, I am fine.' She still sounded breathless but no pain laced her voice.

He looked at her face. Her lips were plump and the skin around her mouth was red. He'd done that, the bristles from where he'd not shaved marking her.

'I should not have touched you like that.' Shame was creeping down his spine, spreading to all corners of his body, settling in his stomach and making him sick. All that talk of honour and he had savaged her like a wild beast, rutting against her, intent only on his own pleasure. And hers. The noises she'd made as she'd rocked against him had been heady and powerful. He wanted to do it all over again but this time without the untimely end. But he knew that he couldn't, that his integrity, such as it was, would not allow him to take advantage of a woman whose life he was going to change, not now that he had a clear head.

She lightly rested her fingers against his temple. 'What is going on in there?'

'You said kissing was a mistake earlier.'

'I did,' she said softly.

'That was a lot more than kissing.'

'It was.' She brushed a strand of his hair away from his forehead. He wanted to lean into her touch but he held himself still.

'And it was a mistake again.' He forced himself to say the words, even though he couldn't fully mean them. Getting too attached was a bad idea for both of them, would only cause them pain in the long run. It muddied his primary mission but it didn't stop it from being the one thing he wanted more than anything else.

'I know.' A light in her eyes slowly died and his stomach twisted itself into a tight knot. Then she grinned quickly. 'I am too beautiful for you to resist.'

His laugh surprised him. 'That you are.'

'And those forearms.' She lightly tapped the skin of his arm. 'They appear to be my undoing.'

He laughed again, even as he flexed his arm, knowing he was a vain fool but doing it anyway. She caught the action and grinned again.

She stared up at the ceiling. 'We are agreed then,' she said. 'Kissing and anything else that it leads to is a lapse in judgement.'

'We are.' He nodded, even though it hadn't felt wrong in the moment.

'We should also agree not to do it again. It would be a disaster to love you.'

His tongue appeared to be stuck to the roof of his mouth. He couldn't force the words out to agree with her on this point. She was right. It shouldn't happen again.

It hurt far more than it should to hear her say that she couldn't fall for him, even though he knew that falling for her would be catastrophic. There were only two people he had ever cared for in his life, Leo and Hugh. Letting them down had twisted his insides. If he fell for her and then had to take her to Windsor, it had the potential to destroy him. But to say out loud that he would never kiss her again…no, he couldn't do it and, as the silence stretched between them, it seemed neither could she.

She sighed and pushed herself up onto her feet, rearranging her skirts so they covered her legs. 'Did you get hurt when we fell?' she asked him and Tristan realised he couldn't remember the last time someone had shown concern for him like this.

'I had a soft landing,' he said, grinning up at her.

She rolled her eyes and, muttering something about softness, she left the chamber without a backward glance. He stayed lying on the floor, smiling in the direction she had left for far longer than a man with any sense should.

Chapter Thirteen

Life settled into a monotonous pattern. Ogmore refused to end the siege. Catrin's men spent their days stalking the ramparts, weapons on display. The blacksmith churned out arrowheads, the iron taken from Ogmore's own stores. Tristan continued on his nightly raids, taking a rotation of men with him each time, using the exercise to develop different skills that would help them should this siege end in a battle. Sometimes the raids were successful in procuring goods or destroying equipment, sometimes they were not. As they went on, Ogmore's encampment became smaller, the tents tightly packed together, the store tent in the middle becoming heavily guarded.

After the first interminable week, Catrin asked Tristan to train her in sword fighting. If the attack came, she wanted to be able to defend herself properly. He was a kind and patient teacher but one who expected her to reach for perfection; her muscles protested after every session, aching in ways she had never thought possible. Others in the castle began to join their sessions and, before long, Tristan was training everyone, splitting them into groups according to ability. Even the young children practised with wooden swords, laughing uproariously at Tristan whenever he pretended to be foiled by one of their attacks.

The training lifted everyone, giving her people the sense that they were doing something, not just waiting for Ogmore to invade. Within the walls, training for battle, she believed her people were safe. Only the potential risk of their nightly raids threw a shadow over her, but with each success she began to believe in the necessity of the danger, to understand that some chances were worth taking.

When it wasn't her turn to train, Catrin would watch her people or, rather, she would watch Tristan's strong arms as he moved around the courtyard, while pretending to watch everyone else.

'Is there not something else you should be doing?' asked Ffion one afternoon.

'I want to see if Lloyd is getting any better at his blocking technique.'

Ffion flung back her head and laughed. Tristan turned his head, raising a questioning eyebrow. Catrin shook her head, her skin burning. 'Oh, come on,' said her friend. 'Even I can see that your knight is pleasing on the eye and I'm fairly sure Lowri and Gwen don't need to be washing those sheets for quite as long as they have been.' Ffion nodded to two of the older inhabitants, who did seem to be looking at Tristan more than the task they were taking so long over. 'When he does that twirl with his sword…' Ffion fanned herself and Catrin wanted to fling herself in front of the woman's eyes so that she could not look at him.

'Any fool can see he is handsome,' said Catrin. 'But he is not *my* knight any more than he is yours.'

Ffion grinned wickedly. 'Don't be ridiculous. Everyone can see that you are enamoured of each other, gazing at one another dreamily, blushing when you speak together, and do not get me started on all the touching that goes on during your training sessions.'

Catrin's heart flipped and raced like a foolish girl's at the thought that Tristan might be infatuated with her. She'd been down this road before. She was older and wiser now and she was not going to admit to any misguided idea, no matter how many times Tristan flourished his sword or smiled lopsidedly at her. Even if it were true, there was no possibility for a relationship between them to flourish. His true mission would crush it.

'He only touches me to move me into the correct position,' she said in protest. She'd never admit it but the fleeting grazes of his hands on her arms and her wrists were the highlight of her day. If she occasionally asked him to show her more than she needed, well, she was only a woman and there was a limit to her self-restraint. That he sometimes lingered more than he needed to was also something she was not going to complain about. They'd agreed to go no further—no more touching, no more kissing. It might not be fun but it was right. She might enjoy looking at his arms and the way he moved but she was *not* in love with him.

'Right, I see,' said Ffion, seemingly not done with this topic of conversation. 'Well, you must be a lot worse than the rest of us at sword fighting because none of us get the level of dedicated attention you receive.'

'He's a good instructor.'

'Aye, he is. He's even patient with the babes.' Ffion scuffed her boot on the floor. 'You could do a lot worse for a husband.'

Catrin recoiled as if slapped. 'He is not going to be my husband, not now, not ever.' He would never offer because it would interfere with his plan for her future. To entertain the idea that he might, even for a second consider it, would cause her far more heartbreak than Ioan ever had. 'I beg that you do not say such things to me or talk about it with anyone else.'

Ffion held up her hand. 'I did not mean to upset you.'

'You haven't.' She had. Catrin could no more marry Tristan than she could spin gold from wool. 'And you are right, I have other things to do rather than stand here watching the sword fighting. I will speak with you later.'

Catrin walked away from the training ground, not looking back.

More weeks passed. Ogmore and his men made no further attempt to attack the castle walls, but that was not as reassuring as it could have been. Ogmore did not need to waste his energy or his men's lives by mounting an impossible attack on their barricades. He'd removed the cow's carcass from the stream and now he had a continual supply of fresh water and would be able to hunt for food whenever he needed to. He only had to wait until the food ran out at Pwll Du Castle. Catrin and her people would be forced to leave, surrender or starve.

Her people were already becoming thinner, their cheeks hollowing out and dark shadows appearing beneath their eyes. The children were increasingly fractious as they were contained within the castle walls, the only respite their sessions with Tristan. The summer showed no sign of relenting its heat and it was hard to find a spot to cool down as the stones gave off a searing warmth even after the sun went down. Even Lloyd's smile was dimmed, a sight that made Catrin's heart ache. Lloyd was a man of exuberant emotion but he was quieting, especially when he caught his young wife pretending not to be hungry so that he had more to eat. *That* was painful to watch, so upsetting that Catrin found eating meals with her people a struggle. She continued to do so because she knew it was her role to keep up their morale, but the smile she plastered to her face was becoming tighter with every day that passed.

Every day she met privately with Tristan. They discussed Ogmore, the raids, the food, sword fighting, in exhausting detail. They did not kiss. No matter how many times she caught him gazing at her mouth or how often her eyes drifted to his capable hands. Only once did they come close to breaking their own rule. They'd been talking, standing in the Great Hall alone, and she had swayed closer, or he had, his lips had brushed her forehead, her fingers had grazed over the back of his hand. The air had stilled, the only sound their breathing. For a little while she'd forgotten everything, aware only of the heat of him.

Nothing had come of it. They had pulled apart and gone on their separate ways, but for the rest of that day the skin of her forehead had tingled with the memory of his lips.

It got harder to remember why they were holding back. On long, lonely nights, the thought of some future heartache seemed insignificant compared with the longing in her soul.

One evening she and Tristan sat with their backs against the rampart walls, waiting for the sun to go down. Her legs were stretched out in front of her, crossed at the ankle. He rested one arm on his bent knee, his dagger in his long fingers. At nightfall he would leave the castle with his band of men. They spoke, as usual, of everything. Tristan told her how proud he was of her people, how the men would have made good knights should they have been of noble birth.

Slowly, they exhausted the topic of Ogmore and warfare and fell into silence. She watched him as the sun slowly began its descent. He'd lost weight around his face and his cheekbones were now sharp. To stop herself from reaching out and tracing them with her fingers, she asked him about his fear of the dark. 'You do not seem to mind if we are outside,' she said to finish.

He pushed his hair back from his forehead; it was getting long and he had started to tie it back when training. 'It is not the dark which bothers me. I could walk around outside all night if I needed to. It's being confined and it being dark that I do not enjoy.'

'Did something happen to you?' she asked.

His lips tilted down on one side. 'A long time ago.' His gaze flicked to her and then to his dagger, which he flipped over before catching again. 'My father, Lord Peter, was, and probably still is, a man who seemed to think it his duty to repopulate England. It did not matter to him who the mother of his next child would be. It could be my mother, who is his wife, or one of his many mistresses, or the wife of a friend.'

'I see.' She wiggled her toes. 'Actually, I don't.'

'I haven't finished the story yet,' he said, his lips twitching.

'Ah.'

He flipped the blade again, the metal glinting in the sun. 'He did not care who his actions hurt. He is a charming, handsome man and everyone adores him. I thought he was wonderful but I did not spend much time with him. Whenever I did it was like standing directly in front of the sun. He was dazzling in his attentions and his smile made me feel special. But I was never enough to hold his attention for long; he flitted away like a butterfly.' Tristan smiled grimly. 'Although I am sure he would prefer to be thought of as a wolf stalking after prey or some other nonsense. It was only later, once I had left for my training, that I realised how immoral his actions were, how much he hurt the people he should have cared about. Women adored him, including my mother, who should have learned to hate him.'

The description of Tristan's father explained a lot. It was clear now why Tristan, one of the most selfless people she had ever met, believed himself unworthy. Catrin knew what it was like when someone made you feel as if you were the very centre of their world and then took that away. It left you adrift, unable to find anything likeable about yourself.

'I still don't see why this made you f...dislike the dark so much.'

He smiled at her clumsy deflection. 'My masculinity will not be dented if you describe it as a fear and, as I said, it is not the darkness so much as it is being confined in a dark place.' He shuddered as if plunged into darkness in that moment. 'My mother could not punish my father for his indiscretions. Even if she had been able to physically restrain him, she adored him too much to hurt him deliberately.'

'Am I allowed to criticise her?'

'You do not normally hold back.' He was twirling the handle of the blade, the movements quick and assured. He grinned and her stomach flipped.

It was annoying it still did that, even after all these weeks of getting to know him. Knowing him made the kick of attraction stronger, if anything.

'Yes, but saying something bad about someone is different when it is their mother.'

His smile dipped; he flicked his blade once more before resting the tip against the sole of his boot. 'There is no love lost between us.'

'Then I would say that she sounds weak. If my husband took a lover I would cut off his...' She waved in the direction of Tristan's trousers and he winced. 'If I loved him, I suppose. If it was a relief that he took his attentions elsewhere, I guess I would not bother. I could learn to live with the dishonour if I did not love him. I certainly would not continue to adore him.'

Tristan's expression darkened but whether that was because of her mention of having a husband or cutting off a man's member, Catrin could not be sure.

'My mother is a weak woman,' he said. 'I am her only son, although she had many daughters, and I looked very much like my sire. She could not hurt him, but she could hurt me.'

Catrin straightened; she hadn't expected this turn to the tale. Rage raced through her blood, burning her from the inside. 'What did she do?'

Tristan studied the handle of his blade, running his thumb over the faded inscription. 'Nothing too dramatic. I am not covered in wounds from a beating or anything too awful.' He shrugged his shoulders, trying, she supposed, to appear nonchalant. 'I am my father's image. It was obvious, even as a boy, that I was going to grow to look just like him. Even as young as six, I was aware that if I smiled in a certain way the cook would let me off taking a loaf from the kitchens. I am sure, with a face like yours, that you know what I mean.'

'Despite the uneven ears?' She referred back to their first conversation, ignoring the squirming in her stomach at his compliment. It was not as if he had paid a flowery tribute to her looks after all. There was no reason for warmth to flood through her veins at his reference to her appearance.

He grinned and that traitorous warmth spread, spilling into every part of her body. 'Despite your uneven ears.'

'I do know what you mean,' she told him. 'In the beginning I did enjoy that, but it became a burden.' He nodded and she realised that he did understand. It was hard to know if people liked you for yourself or for your face. 'I interrupted your story, however, do go on.'

'If my mother became aware of an affair she would lock me away in a dark chamber, claiming that I needed to learn that my face caused people hurt.'

Catrin gasped. 'You would only have been a little boy. What would be the point?'

'The reason for the lesson, I believe, was to remind me that although I might have been a handsome lad, that did not mean I could use my looks to manipulate women into bed. However, that was not clear to a young boy under the age of seven who did not even know what having a woman in a bed meant.' His forehead creased into deep furrows. 'It also does not make logical sense. Now I believe that his affairs made her lose control of her mind and that the only way to lash out at him was to hurt someone who looked like him.' He shrugged again but Catrin was sure he was not as relaxed as he was trying to appear. Fury was burning through her, she wanted to tear this woman's hair out.

'I was not in any pain,' Tristan continued, 'but I was young and hungry and I did not know if I would be forgotten in the darkness of a small chamber. I probably was not even left for that long, only it seemed like that because of my age. It is for the same reason that I do not care for rats either. There is something particularly disgusting about them crawling over your feet in the dark.'

Forget rage, Catrin was incandescent, her blood boiled and burned. She was a burning stake that she would drive through the heart of this woman. Since her father's death, Catrin had not wanted to leave Pwll Du Castle, she had only wanted to create a perfect home for her people, but now... Now she had another purpose. She would find this woman and she would destroy her and then she would destroy Tristan's father and once she had done that she would...

His fingers lightly touched her arm. 'Are you all right, Catrin?'

She shook her head; she would never be all right again. She was murderous. The anger and hurt she had experienced after Ioan's betrayal was nothing on this. This was all-consuming rage.

'I will destroy her.'

'Catrin…' His voice was threaded with laughter and something else, an emotion she could not name but one that she knew. The air crackled and sparked between them. His fingers flexed on his blade and she thought he might drop it and pull her towards him. She pressed her fingers to her thighs, reminding herself that they were outside, anyone could see them and she would not be able to explain herself if she were caught in Tristan's arms.

'You know that what she did was not right? That you are worthy of being seen.' He made a noise that did not convince her that he agreed with her. 'You are…' How could she explain everything that he was to her without revealing more of herself than she was willing to give? 'When we first met and you tried to use your charm on me, it didn't work because I knew what you were doing. I'd done the same thing.'

He huffed a laugh, his dark gaze fixing on her. 'Are you trying to make me feel better or pointing out that I have fewer wits than a sheep?'

'You were putting on a front, pretending to be someone you're not. Since you dropped that pretence you have been by turns infuriating, smug, helpful, generous, kind and the greatest warrior I have ever seen.'

His eyes crinkled in the corners, his smile soft and warm. He turned his head away and gazed out over the courtyard below them.

'Tell me something about you,' he said.

She could only blink at the side of his head at his unexpected request.

'Tell me something about you,' Tristan said again. 'I have told you something I have never told another living soul. It is your turn.'

Rage was still flowing through her veins, turning her vision red. She took a few steadying breaths. He was smiling faintly at her, his dark eyes full of warmth.

'I am afraid,' she said.

'You?' He raised an eyebrow. 'I have never seen you frightened of anything.'

'That is not true. I was truly terrified that night in the forest, the first time we were running from Ogmore all those weeks ago.'

He nodded slowly. 'I remember the way you were shaking but you kept on going. That is not fear, that is bravery.'

'I am afraid that I will fail.' She had never told anyone this, had never truly admitted it to herself. 'I worry that I am not enough, that despite how hard I have tried, I somehow have made this place more dangerous. Since Ioan, I have lived an ordered life. I never take risks and yet now I have to take them daily. It terrifies me. Decisions I make might send my people to an early death. If I were a man, this siege would not be happening, but I cannot change my sex. I cannot sleep at night because these thoughts swirl around and when I see how hungry everyone is, it is like a knife wound to my chest. I…'

'Hey.' His fingers lightly touched her wrist. 'This is normal, everything that you are feeling is to be expected.'

'How do you know that?' Nothing about this worry felt natural. Her father had never experienced anything like this. He probably would have sent guards out to attack Ogmore on the first day. It wouldn't have mattered to him that some of them might die. He would consider it done for the greater good. And perhaps he would have been right. Now her people were slowly dying from lack of food and she was powerless to stop it happening.

'It wasn't all about fighting technique at Ormand's castle,' said Tristan, angling his body so he was facing her. 'Some of the better instructors told us what it was like to be a leader. They explained that on campaign it is usual to doubt yourself, especially when other people's lives depend on you.'

'It is not just now; it is all the time. It is crushing, soul-destroying. I try to shut out what my father used to say about me but it is no use. I...'

'What did he say?' Tristan's voice was ice, his spine rigid.

'Oh, you know, it was probably much like your mother was to you. He thought my *pretty face* was all I was good for. If I tried to express an opinion he would laugh and then repeat it to other people as if it was all a great joke.' She picked up the end of her braid and threaded it through her fingers. 'Ioan was the first person to listen to my ideas and tell me they were worth something.' She huffed out a laugh, although she was not amused. 'Of course, he only wanted one thing from me, two things, I suppose, if you include the gold coins.'

Tristan leaned his head back against the wall, flipping the dagger over and over. 'I will not be like Ioan then and offer you false compliments. I will say, however, that since we met you have been by turns infuriating...' she laughed and he grinned wickedly '...thoughtful, tenacious, selfless to a fault and the greatest leader I have ever seen.'

The sounds of the bustling courtyard below them faded away as she allowed his compliment to settle within her. She had not lied when she'd listed his qualities and his words held the ring of truth about them; he truly did think her a leader of worth.

'I will also ask you this,' he continued. 'Has anyone within the castle walls suggested to you that we surrender to Ogmore?'

'They have not.'

'Then you have your answer.'

Did she? She wasn't even sure that she had asked a question. But she was glad he had not tried to soothe her with platitudes. She supposed that what he meant was that her people still believed in her, that they could take a little longer of this siege, that she was doing the right thing, even on the days when it felt as if she was not. That the risks they took *were* worth it.

'Are you ready, Sir Dyn Golygus?' someone shouted up to Tristan from beneath the ramparts.

'What does that name mean?' he asked.

'It's a term of great respect,' she said, giving him the same answer everyone did when he asked, all of them enjoying the crease on his forehead as he tried to translate the phrase. 'You should have paid attention when you were taught the language.'

He muttered something that sounded uncomplimentary, but when he stood he held out a hand to help her to her feet. She hesitated. Since they had landed in a tangled heap on his chamber floor, they had kept touching to a minimum. It had seemed wise but perhaps it was an unnecessary precaution.

She slipped her hand into his and everything she had tried to deny herself came rushing back. The warmth of his skin seemed to heat her body, racing through her and awakening everything that had slept since he had last held her in his arms. She met his gaze and saw the reflection of all that she was feeling in his eyes.

He pulled her to her feet and she stumbled into him, her lips brushing against his jaw. She heard his soft exhalation, felt the whisper of air against her cheek. His mouth was a hair's breadth from hers; lightly, he brushed it against hers.

She was trembling, her whole body yearning to get closer, to press against him, but she held still. It would not be fair to either of them to go further. They could not let themselves get swept up in the moment, no matter how good it might feel, no matter how much they might want it.

'You had better go, Sir Dyn Golygus. Your troops are waiting for you.'

Slowly, he released her hand, his fingers trailing over her skin. They stood close to one another for another heartbeat and then he was gone, running down the steps of the battlement to meet with the men who awaited him, and she was left alone.

Chapter Fourteen

Lloyd's shoulders were sagging, his body drooping with the tiredness he kept denying he was feeling. Tristan walked behind him, their footsteps echoing on the tunnel's stone floor. Ahead of Lloyd, Wynne led the way, the older man the most sprightly of the three of them. A week ago, Tristan had sat on the ramparts with Catrin, sharing more of his life and hearing details about hers. He had suggested to her that none of her people wanted to surrender to Ogmore because of their loyalty to her and he had believed that, still believed it. But he did not know how much more they could all take before their bodies were spent.

Tonight's raid had been semi-successful. The three of them had managed to take weapons from several of Ogmore's men. The iron in the blades would come in handy but they had not been able to take any food and it was that which the castle inhabitants desperately needed. If they were unable to replenish the stocks soon, the people would become too weak to carry on the raids. After that they would become sick and Tristan could not bear to think about what would happen after that. He did not think he would be able to witness the life draining out of these people, people who should never had become part of his life but who he cared about so deeply the thought of them suffering was more than he could handle. Worse was the thought of Catrin sickening. Already the purple skin under her eyes and the worry that tightened her shoulders pained him. He had to do more, had to win this before Catrin and her people hurt any more.

The three of them began to climb, the tunnel was coming to an end. In all these weeks, he had not come to enjoy the darkness of this journey any more than he had on the first night, but he was more used to it. It helped that he never made the walk alone and that they always carried at least two torch-lamps to see them through. He knew Catrin always made sure of that for him and it was yet another thing in the incredibly long list of things, that he liked about her. Nobody had ever given his comfort as much thought as she did.

By the time they made it through the final door, Wynne was also dragging his feet. Tristan told them both to go and lie down; he would report to Catrin. Neither of them protested. They were reaching the end of their ability to give to this cause, not because they no longer cared but because they needed more food to fuel them.

Catrin was in her antechamber. She stood when he walked through the door, coming to meet him before he was fully inside. She stood so close to him—she always did now. He didn't know which one of them made sure the gap between them was so small but he knew that he was always the last to move away, that he was no longer strong enough to keep his distance from her. She was near now, so near he wouldn't even need to take a step to touch her. Her blue eyes were full of worry and relief and happiness to see him and his heart ached.

'Is everyone well?' she asked. It was the first thing she said every time they returned from a raid.

'We are all fine, tired but no injuries.'

Her shoulders loosened. 'That is good.'

'I do not think we can go on like this for much longer.'

Her whole body tightened again. 'I agree.' She bit her lip. 'What do you suggest?'

He admired this about her. The practical way she accepted bad news. From the start he had thought her a calm woman, a warrior in mind and body, and he still did. There was no bluster, no trying to prove she was better than him by contradicting what he said. He hoped she believed what he had said to her a week ago on the ramparts, hoped that she did not think he was spouting platitudes.

'We are going to have to attack.' He'd been thinking it for nearly a week now, had dreaded telling her, but there was no longer a choice. They had to make this perilous move or risk a slow, painful death.

She closed her eyes, her long lashes casting shadows on her pale skin. 'I know.'

'It will have to be soon.'

She nodded, her eyes scrunched tight.

'While there is enough food to give everyone the strength they need to fight.'

She licked her top lip. 'When?'

'The day after tomorrow.'

She let out a long steady breath. He could see that her fingers were trembling but her voice was calm. 'Very well. You should get some rest and then this afternoon we will meet with the people to discuss our plans.'

He was struck once again by how calm she was in a crisis. If she had been born a man, she would have commanded armies, but as a woman she was being moved on by a King who would never bother to get to know her.

'I will see you at midday,' he said.

She nodded again, her eyes still closed.

He swallowed. This part of his life was coming to an end. However the attack concluded, he would either be dead or free to ride away on Darrow. Weeks ago, he would have rejoiced at the idea. Now, the thought of walking away almost brought him to his knees. Perhaps because of that, he closed the short distance between them and pressed a gentle kiss against her mouth.

He left before she could tell him once again that it was a mistake.

Chapter Fifteen

The plans were in place. The decision made. Her army was prepared, her women and children ready to flee if necessary. First thing in the morning, they were going to end this siege one way or another. She had no idea if she had made the right decision. She had put her trust in Tristan, had done so without conscious thought, the first time she had done that since Ioan had betrayed her all those years ago. Tristan had proven himself to be a different man from her former lover and her father. Now she had to hope her faith was not misguided.

Catrin wound her way up the spiral staircase towards her chamber. Her knees were shaking but it had nothing to do with the impending battle and everything to do with the other decision she had made earlier.

Tomorrow she would either lead her people to victory or she would be captured and killed. Those were the only two options. She believed in her people, believed in Tristan and the men he had trained over the long weeks of being barricaded within the castle walls, believed in herself and their ability to win. Despite that, the attack tomorrow was still a huge risk. She could die or Tristan could die and all this denying themselves pleasure would have been pointless.

With Ioan, she had thought she was following her heart when she had given her body to him and she had been betrayed. With Tristan, she was going into this with her eyes open. She knew he needed her to complete his mission. He would leave her once all this was over, leave her in Windsor if he had his way. She could prevent herself from loving him but that did not mean she had to forgo knowing what it would be like to be held in his arms. What was the point when her life might end tomorrow?

She reached his chamber and rapped her knuckles on the door.

Silence greeted her.

She held her hand ready to knock again, wondering where he might be if not here. Perhaps he had gone on the evening raid after all. Earlier, they had decided to act as normal, to raid as they had every night so as not to raise Ogmore's suspicions, only Tristan was to stay behind for the first time. He was their most experienced warrior and needed to rest, but perhaps he had been unable to help himself. Or perhaps he had heard her first knock and decided not to answer.

She was about to walk away when the door swung open.

She'd prepared a speech but at the sight of him her mouth dried and her mind went blank.

He stepped backwards, gesturing for her to step inside.

She walked in, hoping her knees would not betray her. She stopped in the centre of the chamber, her back to him. She heard the soft click of the door closing. She walked to the window. It was still light outside, although dusk would not be long in coming. She touched the cool glass lightly. Behind her, Tristan's footsteps grew closer until she could feel the warmth of his body from where he was standing behind her.

His scent washed over her and she wondered if it would be too odd to ask him to give her one of his shirts when they parted. No odder, she supposed, than what she was doing right now.

His fingers lightly moved her braid, brushing against her shoulder as he draped it to one side. He pressed his lips to the base of her neck and a delicious shiver ran through her. His lips curved on her skin in an unseen smile, his hands settling on the curve of her hips. He moved slowly, as if savouring every inch of her. She tilted her head, allowing more access, the gorgeous scrape of his stubble against her soft skin the most decadent of pleasures.

He reached her jaw and she turned her head. He captured her mouth with his lips and she slowly turned in his arms, winding her hands into his hair. For a long while they stayed like this, the whisper of lips, the slide of tongues, soft breathy moans filling the air, those wonderfully strong hands of his roaming her back.

When they had kissed before it had been all heat and fire but this was a slow burn, there was no race to the end, only the joy of exploration.

Slowly, unhurriedly, they made their way to the bed. She had no idea how long it took, but clothes disappeared on the way, his tunic, his shirt, her dress, until they were standing skin to skin. The rough calluses of his palm tracing her back, her hip, her sensitive breasts, touching her everywhere until she was a whimpering mess against him.

The mattress dipped underneath them, his heavy weight over her. He lifted his head, his eyes were glazed, his words slurred. 'Are you sure?'

She arched her back and his eyes rolled back in his head. 'I am.'

Slowly, achingly slowly, he moved into her. Her fingernails dug into his spine and he grunted. His head dropped to her shoulder, making a noise almost as if he were in pain.

'Tristan.' She breathed his name into his neck.

He grunted. 'A moment. I need a moment.'

He lifted his head, his eyes full of wonder as he gazed down at her. He smiled slowly. 'Beautiful,' he said and then pressed his mouth to hers once more. He began to move then, setting a rhythm that had her clinging to him, gasping and crying out his name. Her back arched off the bed as her world splintered, pleasure unfurling inside her, racing to every point in her body. He was calling her name, his lips against her neck, and then he was collapsing on top of her, his body deliciously heavy.

Neither of them spoke. She ran her fingers through the damp strands of his hair but he didn't move, his arms wrapped tightly around her. After a while, she dozed, his body the perfect covering.

She woke when cool air brushed over her skin, followed by the soft slide of a blanket. A heavy arm pulled her against a warm body, a press of a kiss against her forehead.

She slipped an arm around his waist and kissed his chest.

'Are you awake?' he murmured.

'I am.' She snuggled deeper.

'You came to talk to me and I ambushed you. What did you want to discuss?'

She chuckled softly. He was very sweet, her warrior knight. 'I didn't come to talk.'

'Oh.'

'I came to tell you that we might die tomorrow.'

His arm tightened. 'You won't. I will not allow it.'

'Well, if Sir Great Knight does not allow it then it definitely will not happen,' she said teasingly, becoming more awake as they talked. 'But that was not the point. The point was that either of us could die during the battle and that makes abstaining from what we have just done completely unnecessary.'

'I see.' A large hand swept over the curve of her hip. 'So you came here with the express intention of seducing me then.'

She cracked open one eye. 'I did.'

'That's good. I was lying here worrying that I had taken advantage of you when you wanted to talk about something serious.' He actually did sound concerned.

Both her eyes were open now and she leaned back slightly so she could look at his face. 'At what stage in that encounter did you think I was being coerced into it?'

He paused. 'You did seem to be enjoying yourself, but then I...'

If she had not been close to him, she would not have seen the blush seeping across his skin in the dim light of the candles.

'You...'

He groaned, dropping his head to her shoulder. 'Do I have to go on?'

'You most certainly do.'

He muttered curse words into her hair that made her laugh softly, but she was not going to let him off. They had only ever been honest with each other; there was no reason to stop now.

'Fine,' he said eventually. 'I wasn't sure because...' He groaned again. 'Because you are the first woman I have lain with and at the end you seemed to hold on to me very tightly, but by then I was so far gone, Ogmore and his entire army could have stormed into the chamber and I would not have noticed.'

Catrin stared up at the ceiling, words deserting her.

'Say something, I beg of you.' His fingers pressed into her waist.

She laughed, she couldn't help it, joy bubbled through her veins. 'You are very warm,' she said, pressing her fingers to his forehead. 'I could light a fire with the heat coming from your skin.'

'You do know it is unkind to tease a man when he is down?'

She laughed again. 'I know that I am being a bit cruel, but it is because your statement has completely shocked me. I do not understand how it is that I am your first woman but I am...' Her heart was swelling, she wondered if it would crack. 'I am honoured and that is not a joke, and I am not teasing you about that, it is true. And at the end I was holding on tightly to you because... how to explain?' She'd never imagined she'd be in the position of describing what happened to a woman while making love, especially not to this man. 'When things go well between a man and a woman, a woman will experience similar pleasure to the man, but without the… um…sticky stuff.'

'Sticky stuff,' he said faintly and then they both laughed, huge belly laughs from their stomachs that had them curling their knees and the mattress shaking.

'What you are saying,' he said when they had calmed down, 'is that it was a pleasant experience for you?'

Another giggle rippled through her. 'It was *very* pleasant.'

'Would you…er…care to do it again?' he asked, not hiding the hope in his voice.

'I would like to do it again every moment from now until the end of time.'

'Thank goodness for that,' he said, and those were the last words spoken for a very long time indeed.

Chapter Sixteen

High on the ramparts, four of her men stalked through the dawn mist. It was like any other morning of this long siege. At least it was from the outside looking in. Behind the castle gate was a different matter.

At the front of her ragtag army, Catrin and Tristan sat astride their mounts. Tristan had tried to persuade her that it would be better if she coordinated the attack from within the castle walls but she saw this for the ploy it was. He wanted to keep her safe. She understood that need. If there was a way of keeping him from the fight then she would make it happen, the idea that he might get hurt more terrifying than anything else. Neither of them would ask her people to ride without them, so they were both at the front of the attacking army. Tristan had visibly swallowed when he had seen her in her armour, his gaze taking in the altered breastplate, her sword strapped to her side. She'd thought he'd argue then, or maybe even lift her bodily and carry her into the Great Hall to await his return, but he hadn't and she had fallen a little more for him.

Behind them ranged her men, some on horseback but most on foot, their armour polished, their blades shining. Her heart slammed behind her ribs as if trying to escape. She tightened her grip on the reins, her fingers slick on the leather.

Tristan glanced across at her, one eyebrow raised.

She nodded. This was it; she was ready.

Tristan raised his left hand, a signal to the gatekeepers.

The silence of the morning was broken as the gate began to lift. Through the heavy wood, Catrin could hear the shouts of Ogmore's men as they heard the noise and realised what it meant. She glanced at Tristan. His jaw was clenched, his eyes narrowed. Without turning his face, he reached across and encircled her hand with one of his own.

'All will be well,' he said. 'I will not allow it to be otherwise.'

She squeezed his fingers. 'I trust you.'

Tristan was not to know the import of those words, how rare it was for her to put her faith completely in another person. He had shown her in word and deed that he was honourable. This was a man who would stand by his word until the very end. Last night she had gone to him willingly, not because of any pretty lies he had told her but because of his honesty.

They poured from the gates, shouting and hollering, their swords raised. Ogmore's men were not ready. Used to guarding against Tristan's nightly raids, many of them had been settling down to sleep. Scrambling to their feet, they searched for weapons amongst discarded clothes.

She and Tristan paid them no heed. In a plan devised in the Great Hall, her people rode towards them, scattering Ogmore's army as quickly as they could, spreading panic throughout. Alongside Tristan, Catrin rode towards the tent where they believed, from their many raids, they would find Ogmore and his more senior men. Ogmore was the one who had to surrender. Otherwise, this siege would go on and on until her people could take no more. Together, she and Tristan would make Ogmore submit, no matter what it took.

Darrow was quicker than her mare, Mai, and pulled ahead. A soldier ran towards Tristan, his sword raised. Catrin's breath caught in her throat, but Tristan knocked the man aside before his blade could connect with Darrow. Darrow thundered forward, the knight's horse built for speed and agility on the battlefield. Mai skittered sideways; Catrin tugged on the reins, bringing her back under control.

All around them, chaos reigned. Men shouted and yelled, metal clanged against metal and the portcullis crashed back into place as the last of her fighting men entered the fray. It would only be raised when the battle was over. If they won, they would enter victorious. If they lost, the women and children would escape through the secret tunnel and the survivors would join them later.

At the central tent, Ogmore appeared in the flap, caught sight of them bearing down on him and promptly stepped back inside.

'Coward!' roared Tristan.

At least they knew where Ogmore was. He was hiding, not joining his men in fighting hers. Or else it was a trap to lure them both in before springing a counterattack on them. But it was likely to be a combination of the two.

Continuing on horseback became impossible. Tent ropes lined the way and tumbling from their mounts was a real possibility. Tristan jumped down from his saddle and held his arm up towards Catrin. She clasped it and he swung her down, his muscled arm coming around her as she landed on the ground. He grinned at her, his smile anchoring her in the swirling storm around them.

'Ready?' he asked.

'Ready,' she confirmed.

'I will go first. He is likely to have men in there with him. Make sure you take in every corner of the tent before stepping inside. We do not want to be surprised by someone hiding from us.'

She pressed her lips to his; his response was swift as he pressed back. For a moment the world stilled and all that mattered was him. It was over as quickly as it had begun.

'What was that for?' he asked, his eyes smiling.

'Just because...' she said, not wanting to voice her fear that it might be the last time she was able to do that. She knew what Tristan was capable of, but that did not account for bad luck.

Tristan dropped his arm. She wanted to take it back, to lift it around her shoulders and to curl into him but it was too late. He was already turning away from her, striding towards the tent. She followed him.

Tristan lifted the flap of the tent with the edge of his dagger. She could not see over his wide shoulders but whatever he saw had him stepping forward. She followed closely behind, making sure she did as Tristan had told her to and checking for places where men could potentially hide. There were lots. In the far corner she could make out a tuft of hair where a man crouched behind some barrels, but there could be others. It was not possible to see behind various mounds of detritus. She sniffed, the smell inside was stale, lived-in. The remains of a meal were scattered on the floor.

Ogmore stood in the centre of the tent, his sword raised. His right-hand man stood next to him, also in a fighting stance. Tristan faced them, his sword still in its scabbard but his dagger clutched tightly in his hand.

'Surrender, Ogmore,' Tristan told him, 'and all of this will be over. You can go home, spend some time with your wife, wash and have a decent meal.'

Catrin tried not to roll her eyes. Tristan was trying his charm on this man. It might have worked if Ogmore had more wits than a chicken.

Ogmore blustered, 'I'm not going anywhere. That castle is mine.'

'It belongs to whoever King Edward wants to rule it. I *know* that is not you.'

Ogmore's pallid flesh reddened. 'Well, it sure as hell cannot be her.' He gestured at Catrin with his sword.

'That is Lady Catrin and you will address her properly,' Tristan told him, his eyes narrow.

Outside, someone howled. It sounded like Lloyd. A shiver ran through her. She could not tell if that was a cry of victory or agony. With every moment that passed in this godforsaken tent, her people battled.

'Lady Catrin—' Ogmore spat her name out '—has no place leading a castle. She should be bearing children like other women her age, not giving orders.'

Catrin had had enough. If life had taken a different turn, that would have been her role. She would not have minded, would not have known any different. But now she did know and she would bow to no man unless they had earned her respect first.

'Do not be so ridiculous, Ogmore. Whether or not I have children is none of your concern. What takes place inside my castle walls is as irrelevant to you as the goings-on in France. Return home and we shall pretend none of this has happened. If you do not leave willingly, Sir Tristan here will battle you, and I can assure you that will not end well for you.'

A rustle near their feet was all the warning they had of a young knight. The lad emerged from a pile of discarded stained clothing, striking wildly at Tristan. It was over before it truly began, the knight lying unconscious at Tristan's feet within a few moves.

Catrin's knees shook but she managed to control her voice. 'As you can see, this proves my point.' She gestured to the man on the floor, pleased to see that her fingers were still, even as her insides trembled.

'I will not surrender to a woman,' said Ogmore with a snarl.

'Very well,' said Tristan, the metallic scrape of his sword being drawn from its scabbard filling the tent.

Ogmore turned white but he held his sword aloft, standing his ground.

Catrin peered around the enclosed space. There must be more men hiding in here because Ogmore and his right-hand man were not equal to Tristan, and Ogmore must know that. She pulled out her own sword. She had practised sword fighting with Tristan daily for nearly a month, had even battled when she had fought Ogmore in the past, but she had never killed a man. She swallowed and slowly stepped to Tristan's left.

Tristan took a careful step towards Ogmore, who brandished his sword awkwardly in front of him.

Catrin prodded a bundle of clothes with the point of her sword. She tried again, harder this time when she met no resistance. It was as it seemed; there was no one hiding here.

Tristan moved against Ogmore. Ogmore stumbled backwards, his right-hand man moving in front of him, blocking Tristan's sallies. Catrin moved around the edge of the tent, using her sword to check potential hiding places.

The man who had been hiding behind the barrels came out and joined the fray. Tristan was now three against one but Catrin knew they were not a match for him. It was only the unknown that was causing her disquiet. She wanted to watch but she knew the best help she could be to Tristan was to root out anyone who might attack him from behind.

A loud crash and a grunt and the right-hand man joined the other man on the floor. It was back down to two against one.

She continued forward.

Another crash and Ogmore was frantically blocking Tristan alone.

'Now!' Ogmore screamed. 'Now!'

Catrin whirled around, searching for whoever Ogmore was yelling commands at.

Four men burst from hiding places and she screamed. They were bearing down on Tristan, who whirled and parried, his body flowing so quickly his movements were a blur.

'Not him!' Ogmore screamed at his men.

Before she had time to register what Ogmore meant, two of the attacking men came towards her.

'No!' Tristan shouted as he knocked the blade out of the hand of one of his remaining attackers. 'Move, Catrin, move!'

She managed to get her sword up in front of her body, moving into a fighting stance. Her two attackers were more skilled than Ogmore. They came at her with their blades raised, moving quickly.

She wasn't going to call Tristan for help, he was working against three men, had already dispatched at least four. She would not be a distraction for him.

Her body shifted into position, remembering stances and moves she had practised a thousand times, maybe more. She was no helpless damsel in need of rescue. She was Lady Catrin and she was going to fight for her freedom.

Sweat coated her forehead, her arms ached as she clung to her sword. Another of Ogmore's men appeared in the tent and another. Tristan was fighting four men again. It was six against two.

She stumbled over a discarded helmet, falling to her knee. She pivoted and a blade whispered past her ear.

'Catrin,' called Tristan, his eyes wide, 'get out of here!'

She didn't want to leave him, but she knew that she was a distraction. Ogmore wanted her—captured or dead. If she left the tent, Ogmore's men would follow and Tristan would be able to incapacitate Ogmore easily. Then it would be over.

The exit was barred by men twice her size. She tried to roll sideways and then stopped. She was a fool. The tent was fabric, the walls easily torn. Pulling her dagger from her boot, she stuck it into the tent's side and pulled. The material ripped easily, the tearing sound grating against her nerves.

She swiped away an incoming sword.

'Hurry!' Tristan yelled to her. The floor around him was littered with fallen men, but others kept appearing from outside.

The hole she'd made for herself was big enough. She started to push her way through, she would have made it too had Dafydd not barrelled past the outside of the tent, accidentally knocking her back inside with his bulk.

A hand grabbed her ankle with a vicelike grip, yanking her all the way back in. Tristan roared with rage as she was roughly forced to her feet, large hands grabbing and pulling her arms behind her back, heedless of her pained gasp.

'Stop!' a voice growled near her ear, foetid breath brushing over her face.

The command was not for her, it was for Tristan, who had pushed his latest attacker aside, his body coiled to spring towards her.

Tristan straightened, breathing heavily. Sweat was running down his face, strands of hair clinging to his cheeks. 'If you hurt her, I will kill you.'

'You are not in a position to make demands,' said Ogmore, straightening his clothes and standing tall, as if he had not just been cowering behind one of his men. 'We have Lady Catrin. We have won.'

Tristan made a move towards her. The thug holding her pulled on her arms and pain rippled through her. She bit her lip to stop herself from crying out, but he did it again and she whimpered. Tristan froze, his jaw so tight it looked painful.

'Step away from her,' said Tristan, 'and I will not kill you.'

'Step away from her and I *will*,' replied Ogmore, snarling.

The grip tightened on her arms, yanking them back and up until she was hunched over at an awkward angle, staring at the floor of the tent. 'We have starved here, plagued every night by your people,' her captor muttered near her ear. 'It will be a pleasure to bring you to your knees. Begging will be entertaining for me, but it will not get you any relief.'

Ants scurried across the ground, hurrying towards the discarded food. Her stomach roiled at the stench of the man holding her. She shut out the sights and sounds around her, concentrating only on the hands that gripped her.

Tristan moved, his blade swirling in the periphery of her vision.

The man holding her roared, 'Stop! Put your blade down or I will put mine through her throat!'

Ogmore frowned. 'I don't think that…'

'No,' said the man. 'You paid me and my men to win this wretched castle for you and this damned woman has kept us in this stinking hellhole for over a month. This ends now, today, and if you are too lily-livered to do the job, Ogmore, I will get it done and *I* will reap the rewards.'

'Now look here,' said Ogmore. 'I have been more than generous with my payment and I…'

'Your money means nothing. We have been here for weeks with nothing to show for it.'

Catrin's gaze flickered upright. Tristan was staring intently at her face. When he caught her gaze, his eyes darted to the right and then back to her, instructing her silently on something else they had practised many times. She edged her foot forward, balancing her body in the way that Tristan had taught her. She had only one opportunity to get this right.

'I never promised you a quick resolution.'

'You said the castle would be easy to take, you said there was only an untrained woman in charge, you said…'

Catrin threw all her weight to one side, pivoting and twisting as she went. Instead of falling to the ground, her arm came under her assailant's leg and, using the element of surprise, she tugged, sending the man crashing to the floor.

She leapt up, the unmistakable sound of bone snapping filling the tent. She raced towards Tristan to find Ogmore kneeling in front of him, blood pouring from a broken nose.

The mercenary was staggering to his feet. She had not hurt him in her attack, only taken him by surprise. But Tristan was already on him, his sword meeting the man's dagger once, twice, and then it was over. The only sound in the tent was Ogmore's moan as he clutched at his face.

Tristan strode over to her, running his strong hand along her arm. 'Did he hurt you?'

'Not really.'

'Your skin is red.'

'Only where he was touching me. It's nothing, really.'

Rage lurked in Tristan's eyes, but the mercenary was out cold, so, short of killing him where he lay, there was little left to do.

'Shall we tie them up?' she asked as Tristan ran his hands over her, checking she wasn't hurt.

'Mmm.' He ran fingers along her brow, his gaze searching her face.

She caught his hand in hers. 'I am fine.'

He smiled faintly. 'I know. I can see that. The way you moved, we'll make a knight of you yet. But I do not think I will forget the noise you made when that…' He glared at the prostrate mercenary. 'When he grabbed you. I should kill him for that.'

'The fewer people who die the better, but I would like to get these men away from my castle.'

Together they trussed up Ogmore and the men who had fought with him and lost. Dragging Ogmore outside, his people surrendered quickly when they saw that their leader was restrained by Tristan. From the way their bodies sagged, she guessed they were exhausted and keen to return to the luxury of castle living once more.

'Can you spare me and a few others?' Tristan asked as Ogmore's army slowly trudged into the woodland, not bothering to collect their belongings from the tents that were now tattered and broken. 'I should like to see Ogmore and some of his more unsavoury companions home.'

Catrin nodded, forcing a smile. 'Will you return?'

He paused. 'Of course I will. There's…' He trailed off, his face settling into a smooth mask. She was afraid to ask him what else he had been about to say, although she could guess.

She knew this victory meant there was no reason for him not to complete his mission. She knew they would have to talk about it. She needed to know what would happen to him if she refused to leave Pwll Du Castle, or what would happen to her people. She supposed she ought to know what her future held too, but a weariness dragged her down and she found that she did not much care. That would come, she knew that, but, after weeks of the siege and a battle, she couldn't find the energy.

Tristan allowed Ogmore to ride on his own horse out of the encampment, although he had the mercenary who'd held her slung across Darrow. From the murderous glances Tristan kept throwing at the man, he was lucky he was not being dragged along behind the stallion.

'I suggest we keep this one hostage for a while,' he said, pushing Ogmore's right-hand man forward.

Catrin nodded. 'I'll have him locked up.'

The man protested until she handed him to Dafydd, his skin paling when he caught sight of the giant man.

The sun was high in the sky as Catrin's people sorted through the mess of Ogmore's encampment. The castle rang with laughter for the first time in weeks, children ran outside and threw themselves in the stream, squealing with delight as the cool water rushed over their bodies. There was not much of value in the abandoned tents; Ogmore's men were coming to their end as much as Catrin's had been. Whenever food was found, a cheer went up amongst her people and Catrin knew that, for the first time in weeks, they would dine well tonight.

'It's not enough food,' said Ffion when no one else was around to hear her. 'We are on our knees.'

'I know.' Catrin had made her way around the whole

of the camp and although there was food to eat, it was not enough to see them through the weeks ahead.

'We will need to send out a hunt.'

Catrin agreed but her bones ached. 'Not today, the people are tired and need a moment to celebrate their release.'

'Tomorrow then.'

Catrin nodded. Everything was being pushed back until tomorrow but right now she was too weary to deal with anything other than getting everyone back into the castle, happy and sated on food and some of the wine she had found.

Later, when the feast was over and her people were sleepy from the spoils of war or singing on the ramparts, there was no in between, she curled her arms around Tristan's neck and the two of them celebrated the win in their own way.

Chapter Seventeen

Tristan leaned his back against the bedpost at the end of the mattress, staring down at Catrin. The morning light was pouring through the long window. They'd not thought to pull the curtains around the bed last night and he was able to watch as her chest rose and fell peacefully. Her cheeks were hollow, throwing the delicate bones of her face into stark relief. She looked soft and vulnerable, as breakable as an autumnal leaf, but he'd seen her fight yesterday and knew there was a core of steel beneath the surface. He wished, almost to the point of desperation, that they had met years from now. If he had proved himself as a successful knight he would have something to offer her, maybe a refuge for her to stay that meant she did not have to face whatever fate King Edward had in store for her. But he hadn't and the future had never looked more uncertain.

He'd complicated this mission.

He should have resisted her. God knew, he'd tried, but in the end it had been futile. Maybe if he had thought to protect his heart he would have been saved the pain of what was to happen next. But he hadn't and he cared about Catrin more than he had ever cared for anyone. He wanted her safe, he wanted her happy.

Seeing a knife at her throat yesterday had almost brought him to his knees. Only his years of training had made it possible for him to keep calm, to do what had needed to be done. He knew that horrific memory would be added to the nightmares that plagued him.

He was quite sure Lord Ormand had sent him here to charm Catrin into following the King's orders because his liege believed Tristan's face would persuade women to bend to his will. This scene would not have surprised him. His liege had probably expected Tristan to romance Catrin into giving up her home, perhaps to whisper sweet nothings into her ear or to take her to bed. He wouldn't have cared what that might do to Tristan or the woman he manipulated, only that it got the desired result.

But Tristan wasn't the man everyone thought, he didn't jump into bed with a different woman each time. He'd seen the devastation his father's antics had wrought on those around him and he did not want to be the same man. He'd held off giving himself to a woman for that very reason. He'd wanted his first time to mean something, not for it to be a quick roll to satisfy some primal instinct.

With Catrin, he'd achieved exactly what he wanted. He wasn't sure if the two nights they'd had together had meant as much to her, but to him it had been everything. Being with her, lying with her, having her curl up by his side while she slept had been the pinnacle of his life. He feared it would be his brightest memory too. That only made everything he had to do much worse.

Catrin shifted in her sleep, her long fingers curling

on the bed next to her. She had not eaten much as the siege had progressed, preferring to give her portion to other people. Even at the feast last night she had held back, a small wistful smile playing on her lips as she had watched her people celebrate. She was selfless to a fault. She would not see that, though, would not see that by always putting other people first she was denying herself. That she did not need to doubt that she was liked and respected. She had already earned that by her thoughts and deeds. She could afford to take something for herself and yet he would use that selflessness to his own ends to make his own mission a success.

He and Catrin had been through all this together and now he must ask her to leave her castle and come with him to Windsor, where he would have to leave her to whatever fate King Edward chose. The meagre amount of food he'd managed to eat last night turned over in his stomach. He was not sure he could do it, even knowing that Leo and Hugh's futures depended on him. To rip this woman from her home would be the very height of cruelty.

'I know what you are thinking,' she said.

He started, so lost in his thoughts he hadn't even realised she had woken. 'You do?'

'You are wondering when it will be suitable to broach the topic of your mission with me.'

How well she knew him.

'Close enough.'

She pushed herself into sitting, pulling the sheet to her chin. 'I have decided to go with you without complaint.'

His fingers twitched in his lap. 'You have?'

'You said there would be an exchange of coins.'

He pushed himself off the mattress and paced to the foot of the bed, his bare feet scraping against the rushes on the floor. 'That is what King Edward promised. He is an honourable man and I am sure he will keep his word.'

She nodded slowly, her hair tumbling over her shoulders. 'And if I refuse to leave his castle, I assume he would take it by force.'

Tristan glanced down at his boots; he'd abandoned them last night, could not even remember pulling them off. In the desperation to have Catrin under him or over him, he hadn't been fussy, only frantic. The boots were worn now, scuffed on the edges. The days of travelling through the country had been hard on them.

'I can only guess at what King Edward's actions might be should you refuse, but I suspect that you are right. He cannot be seen to be disobeyed while he is preparing for war. Any suspicion of weakness would need to be squashed in the first instance. I know that he is ruthless in controlling his castles. He wants to unite Britain under one rule, but I also know that he is a man of his word. He will not go back on his offer of money or keeping you safe.'

Her fingers flexed on the sheet. 'Do you think he plans to marry me to some lord?'

The edges of Tristan's vision turned red. He was glad of the mattress for somewhere to lean as his legs turned to liquid. The King would not care what happened to her—a nunnery, a marriage—what would it matter to a man of such greatness what happened to one small woman with no political power? It was unlikely the King would even see her. His courtiers would see a woman of great beauty and would no doubt marry her off to someone. She would be someone's wife—someone who wasn't Tristan.

A black pit was opening up inside him, threatening to consume his soul. He knew he'd added a complication to this mission by taking her to bed. He'd known from the moment his lips had first touched hers that he would find life without her gut-wrenching but he'd had no idea that this darkness would try to drown him.

She was still waiting for him to answer and for a fleeting breath he wanted to fall to his knees and beg her to marry him instead. But he had no right to ask her such a thing. He had no home to offer her and, even if he had, he had things he *needed* to do. He had to see this mission through to its end, he had to redeem himself because, without that, he was only half a man, not fit to be anyone's husband, let alone hers.

'I do not know,' he said softly.

Her eyes dipped, studying the blanket. 'It would be best if it were done soon. I do not think I can be here when the new lord and his family arrive.' Her voice wavered but her bright blue eyes pierced him when she turned her gaze back to his.

'Very well. Would you like me to...' His voice trailed away; he had no idea what he was going to offer. It was not as if he could make the announcement to her people for her. The only thing he could do was to take himself away from her, to give her time to come to terms with everything she was losing.

She shook her head to his vague offer anyway.

'If you need me, I will be outside.' Where else would he be? He could only wait for her to be ready. He knew she would not be long; she had made her decision and she would stick with it. That was the way she was: fire and determination.

He dragged himself to the door, each step heavier than the last. This was the right decision. Hell, it wasn't even a decision. He was following the mission he'd been sent on. Even though he knew this was the right path, it was agonising. Far worse than a blade to the stomach, worse even than the look on Leo and Hugh's faces when they'd realised they were being framed for a crime they had not committed, worse than the long weeks after it had happened when he'd known it was his fault and that there was nothing he could do to make it right. The aftermath of this was going to be an unending agony.

Catrin watched Tristan leave her chamber, head bent, shoulders slumped. She was reminded of the man she had first met, the one who had seemed weighed down by life's burdens. He'd shed that demeanour almost immediately after he'd been captured, rallying as he'd used his talents, first against her and then against their common enemy. He'd quickly become one of them as he had fought to keep Ogmore from taking the castle.

She knew that giving her the news that she had to leave her castle weighed heavy on him. If he'd forced her, argued with her, then it might make this easier. If she didn't know that making her leave her home was going to hurt him, then perhaps she could find it in herself to hate him or at least dislike him a little. If she had something to fight against, she might have been able to feel something more than this bone-deep sadness.

She was going to have to leave her home. No, that wasn't the problem. This was just a place, a place she loved but she was not tied to it. As a child she had thought she would leave when she married and had not worried too much about it. It was the people. She would have to walk away from Ffion, would never know if her dear friend would realise giant Dafydd was in love with her; she'd never meet Lloyd and Eluned's children, would never watch Wynne become a grandfather. All these lives would carry on without her, they would never know how much she loved them.

She scrunched her eyes tightly closed. She would not cry. Her people must never know the pain it would cause her to walk away from them; she did not want them to feel the guilt of her sacrifice. They wouldn't survive another siege, she knew that. The food stocks were so depleted that even without a siege this coming autumn would be hard, not to mention the lean winter months that would follow.

She pushed the covers back from the bed and stood. Looking down at herself, she could see a red patch on her belly where Tristan's beard had scraped the skin. She lightly brushed her fingers over it. She wished it would stay there as a reminder of him, but she knew it would be gone by the afternoon.

By leaving Pwll Du Castle without protest, she would also help Tristan. Tristan, who had put his life in danger for her people without thought for himself, who needed to complete the mission successfully so that he could redeem himself. If, by doing this, she could help him too, she would not mourn. This was the best for everyone, if not for her.

Chapter Eighteen

'You're making a terrible mistake.' Ffion followed Catrin around her bedchamber. All her personal rooms had been stripped of anything she considered hers. She'd handed most of her things to other people, keeping only the practical items such as her clothes and her sword. Nothing else had any meaning. It was the people she would miss, not the embroidered bedclothes or the ornate wooden chest that had housed her belongings. 'You should stay,' Ffion continued as if Catrin had not heard her the first time, or any of the other times over the last two days.

'I cannot and you know why. I am not going to explain myself again.'

'You don't have to be a martyr to your people.'

'I am not making a worthy sacrifice on a whim, Ffion. King Edward is not some little lord who I can ignore. He is our sovereign. If we disobey him, we could very well lose our necks.'

Ffion glared at her, arms crossed over her chest. 'We would fight for you, you should know that.'

Catrin's heart squeezed. She knew that her people did care for her. They had made it very clear, when she and Tristan had told them about his reason for being at Pwll Du Castle, that they did not want her to leave. She had worried they might turn on the knight who had brought the message, but it seemed they wanted to keep Tristan with them as well as her. Over the last month he had earned their loyalty. But this was not a fight any of them could win and she would not ask her people to put themselves in danger, not when they needed time to heal.

'King Edward has offered gold in return for me leaving peacefully. This will help replenish our food stock. Without it, it will be a very hard winter and if there is another siege, this time by the King's men...' She shook her head. 'We will be doomed, Ffion.'

'But your knight will help us.'

'I keep telling you, Ffion. He is not *my* knight.' Much as she might want him to be, he had his own mission he needed to complete and she was not going to ask him to give it up, not for her. 'He is a messenger for King Edward, that is all.'

'The man looks at you as if you hung the moon and stars. He would travel to hell and back if you asked him. You seem to think that nobody owes you anything, that putting everyone else first is somehow better, but it is not. Why won't you ask him to do this?'

'You truly want me to ask Tristan, the most noble man I know, to commit treason?'

Ffion opened her mouth to argue but closed it slowly. 'I only think...'

But Ffion was cut short by Tristan's appearance at her chamber door.

'My lady,' he said, his voice formal and strained in a way she had not heard before. 'A Lord John has arrived, sent by King Edward. He is cousin to one of the King's greatest knights, Sir Benedictus, and has been in the King's court for many years.'

Her heart thudded painfully. This was her replacement. She hadn't thought that she would have to meet him, had planned to leave before it happened. Now she would have to smile and pretend her heart was not breaking; pride demanded it.

Tristan's jaw was tightly clamped, his eyes narrowed.

'Is he awful?' she whispered.

'No.' Tristan's response was curt, there was no hint of the teasing knight she knew. 'From what I have heard, he is a fair and pleasant leader and, meeting him today, he seems perfectly amiable.'

She made her way to him, her fingers trembling. There was something that was not right about the situation, something that was eating at Tristan from the inside. 'Will he treat them badly, do you think?'

The heat in Tristan's eyes flared. 'Why don't you care for yourself for a change?'

She jolted backwards, as if slapped. 'It does not matter what he is like for my sake. I will not be here.'

Tristan looked towards the long window, his shoulders rigid. 'It seems word of your beauty has travelled, Lady Catrin.' She tensed, unsure why he spoke so formally after all they had been through together. 'Lord John is an unmarried man.' A heavy weight settled in the pit of her stomach at the implication of his words. His lips were thin, the cords of his neck tense, no hint of the man who'd curled around her in the desperate nights they'd had together. 'He has hastened here, aware of King Edward's initial demand, hoping to catch you before you leave. He is desirous of forming a marriage alliance with you and King Edward has sanctioned the match.'

The world around them stilled, everything fell silent.

She could stay. Her home could still be her home. Her life would be secure, safe.

All she had to do was marry a stranger.

Her gaze locked with Tristan's; she could read no emotion in his dark eyes. No laughter. No pain. Only an unending emptiness. If he was waiting for her to suggest an alternative solution, she could not think of one.

'I...'

'He is waiting.' Tristan cut across her. He turned on his heel and stormed away from her.

'It would seem you are right,' said Ffion into the shocked silence. 'He is not *your* knight after all.'

Chapter Nineteen

Round, Lord John was round. His head was so perfectly circular he reminded Catrin of a full moon, but his smile was wide and his eyes lit up when he caught sight of her. Next to her, Tristan might have been carved from rock.

'You are more lovely than a thousand blooming flowers,' said Lord John as she stepped towards him in the courtyard.

Tristan growled, the sound low and primal, but when she turned to him his face was a mask of calmness. This was a side to him she had never seen.

'That is a fine compliment,' she said, because she did not want to appear rude. Tristan flinched as Lord John's smile grew wider still.

Behind him, her people quietly made their way into the courtyard. No, they were not hers any more, they were Lord John's. Summer had finally relaxed its grip on the country and a cool breeze swirled about her ankles.

'King Edward has sent me and several others—' Lord John nodded to a small band of knights and what had to be clerical officials who had gathered by the gate '—to run this splendid castle and I have ridden here post-haste that I might catch you before you journey to Windsor, for I believe there is no need for you to go.'

Catrin could only nod, her throat constricting.

'It seems absurd,' continued Lord John, undeterred by her silence, 'that you should cross the country to Windsor when you might stay here as my wife.'

She heard the ripple of surprise move through her people but, for her, it was as if everything was happening from a long way off or to someone else. Inside, she was as blank as a still pond on a windless day.

Next to her, Tristan said nothing.

Neither of them moved.

This was the perfect solution for Tristan. He had completed his mission, she could ensure that Sir John wrote a letter to the King extolling his virtues during the siege, showing every way in which he had been a perfect knight. It also meant that she did not have to leave her home, her security would be assured. With such a recommendation from a man King Edward clearly valued, Tristan would no doubt become the knight of renown he wanted to be. He'd be redeemed in the eyes of his knightly comrades. It *was* the perfect solution. All she had to do was agree.

Her mouth was dry, her knees were shaking violently. How they were holding her up, she was unsure. She glanced at Tristan. He was staring straight ahead, his gaze fixed on some point behind Lord John. Accepting Lord John's suggestion was the right thing to do and yet it was as if her very soul was being ripped into pieces.

Used to making her own decisions, she wanted someone to make this one for her. The most important words she would ever have to say and she wanted to have no choice. If there was another option, then surely Tristan would voice it now.

He said nothing.

Behind Lord John, Lloyd's gaze was flicking between her and Tristan, a deep frown on his face, but that wasn't what held her attention. It was the way in which the bones of the young man's shoulders were clearly visible under his clothes. It was also in the way that those clothes, where they had once fitted him perfectly, were far too big for him now. He was not the only one of her people to be in such a state. Next to him, his new wife was pale, her hair dull. They needed food, they needed rest, they needed stability.

She licked her top lip. 'Of course. I would be delighted to marry you.'

Lord John's face split into a beatific smile as her world ended.

Tristan still said nothing.

Chapter Twenty

It was not yet dawn. The castle slept but Tristan did not want to wake anyone. He could not wish anyone farewell. He could not bear a repeat of Lloyd's wounded questions. The young man could not understand why Tristan was leaving and not marrying Catrin; to him it was the obvious solution. Lloyd claimed it was what everyone had assumed was going to happen. No one else followed him around, badgering him to explain himself, but Dafydd had been unable to form any words at all and somehow that had been worse. Wynne had barked that Tristan was a young fool who would rue this day for ever and had left it at that.

He knew the people were upset that he was leaving. They had been through much together and this parting would cause them pain. They would forget about him soon enough. But when Lloyd had questioned him over his feelings about Catrin, Tristan had walked away. He did not know how to answer what he felt for the lady of the castle. He knew only that it would be like a knife to the gut to watch her marry someone else, to know that person lay next to her. He could not put himself through it, could not pretend to be happy for her when he was dying inside.

He knew marriage to Lord John was the right choice for her, that she would be content in the world she had created for herself, but he could not witness it. If that made him selfish, then so be it. At least he would be able to ride into his future knowing he had acquitted himself well. He had saved the castle from capture, had kept Lady Catrin safe and he had not begged her not to marry a man who was perfectly suited to her. This was the perfect solution for everybody.

Lord John seemed like a decent man. He was clearly thrilled with his future bride and Tristan was fairly sure Catrin would be able to bend him to her will easily. Not that Tristan could imagine them married, not without the image of him torching the world because of it.

Darrow whinnied in annoyance and Tristan realised he had tightened a strap too much. He set to loosen it, marvelling that his hands were steady even as it seemed as if his whole body was trembling inside.

'You are leaving,' said a quiet voice from the stable door.

He almost couldn't turn his head to look at her. He did not want her to read the emotion in his face, did not want her to know that he was as close to weeping as he had ever been. It would be one of the last times he saw her so, although it would burn, he still turned.

'I am.'

'Were you going to say farewell? No, you don't need to answer that. It is clear that you were not.' Her voice was as calm as ever but her eyes were pained.

He longed to stride over to her, to cradle her face in

his palms and tell her that he wished life was different, wished he was a better man.

'I thought it easier not to.'

'For whom?'

'Both of us.' He'd thought it would be harder for him, but he did not say that. They were both getting what they wanted after all. His heart should not be splintering into a thousand pieces.

'Ioan did not say farewell,' she told him.

He closed his eyes. He did not want to be likened to that bastard. 'Then I should have woken you before I left, but perhaps appearing in your bedchamber would not go down well with your betrothed.'

She shook her head, dismissing his comment. 'It is irrelevant now. You are going and I have come to bid you farewell, whether it is something that you want or not. At least if I see you ride off, I will not look for you.' Her tone was reasonable but he knew from the fire in her eyes that she was angry with him, and that was unfair.

'This is not easy for me, Catrin. I do not *want* to leave you, knowing you are going to marry another man.'

Her arms folded across her chest. 'You have not told me that. You have told me nothing.'

'What precisely do you want me to say?' The words in his heart would only cause them both pain.

Red was rising from her neck, spilling across the skin of her cheeks. 'I do not know. Only I...' She looked away from him, her lips pressed tightly together. 'I know that you have completed your mission successfully and that you can go on and do whatever you want. I am happy for you, or at least I am trying to be. But I would like some acknowledgement from you that leaving *me* is hard, or if not hard then at least a little unpleasant.'

Tristan stalked towards her, coming to a stop when his boots touched the edge of hers. 'If you think that this is not *the* most painful thing I have had to do then you are sorely mistaken. It is taking everything that I have, absolutely *everything*, not to fall to my knees and beg you to come away with me. The thought of you married to another makes my heart feel as if it has been ripped from my chest, but I am not going to beg, Catrin. Do you know why?'

She shook her head, a solitary tear running down her cheek. He resisted the urge to wipe it away. If he touched her, he would come undone.

'Because you agreed to marry another man as I stood next to you. I do not blame you; it is the perfect solution for you. Hell, I will admit that it is the ideal resolution for me too. Here you are safe, it is what you know. I have nothing to offer you, nothing but my name. So I am going to take that name and that letter your future husband kindly wrote for me and I am going to Windsor to become the greatest knight the world has ever known.'

Another tear fell and his heart splintered.

'Then I wish you joy in it.' Once again that cool, calm voice did not match the expression on her face.

'And I wish you joy in your home.'

He would have kissed her then, would have held her face in his hands and plundered her mouth until they were both crying out for more, but their future saved itself in the arrival of Sir John, who seemed unaware of the tension rolling between his affianced and the knight who had happened to help keep her safe in her time of need. Lord John slapped him on the back, wished him a good journey and hoped that their paths would cross again in the future, for England needed men like Tristan, according to the affable lord who had probably never fought a day in his life.

All the while, Catrin stood next to her betrothed, a faded ghost of her normal self, and as Tristan rode away he knew that his beautiful lady was watching him leave, another man by her side, and it hurt as if the fires of hell were licking at his soul.

Chapter Twenty-One

In front of Catrin, a man of God spoke the words that would bind her to another person for the rest of her life. She stood stock still, her best gown causing the skin of her arms to itch.

If this was the safe thing to do, why did it feel so wretchedly awful?

In the two days since Lord John had arrived, Catrin had moved through life as if wading through a thick bog. The knowledge that she could stay in her home was like clinging to a log to stop her from drowning, but now it appeared her lifeline was sinking with her and all that made her who she was fading with it.

Tristan had gone. Had not stopped her when she had agreed to marry Lord John, had taken his letter outlining all the ways in which he had been a hero and ridden towards his golden future without a backwards glance. It was foolishness in the extreme to keep thinking about him. It was absurd to think about the words he had growled, *'I have nothing to offer you, nothing but my name,'* over and again. It was the height of folly to think that he might have been offering that, in his own way. Because if she believed that, then she was making a mistake, one that could not be undone.

'I can't,' she said. She held out a hand to Sir John. 'I can't marry you. It's not you. You seem like a decent man, I am sure you would be an amenable husband, but... I can't.'

Sir John's wide smile fell. 'I see...well, this is... If you need more time, I...'

She shook her head, her heart racing. This might be her greatest mistake or it might be the best thing she had ever done. There was no way of knowing until it was done. She did not take risks, but now, when this solution was, on the face of it, perfect, she was going to.

'It's not time, it's not you. I already said that, but I think it is worth repeating. It's just... I can't... I have to go.'

'What? Go where?' Sir John's kind face was creased with concern, no doubt worried that the woman he had been about to marry had completely lost her wits. In time, hopefully, he would see this as a lucky escape.

'I don't know yet. But...you will look after these people, won't you.'

Lord John puffed out his chest. 'It has always been my intention to make sure this area prospers under my rule, but I will swear it to you, my dear lady.' He held out a hand as if to take hers, but she stepped backwards. His pleasant face drooped. 'If marrying me is such an abomination to you, then of course I will not press it. You can still live here, this is your home. We can come to some arrangement, I am sure.'

It was a solution of sorts, but it was not enough. She

would never be happy if she did not follow her heart, she knew that now.

'You are kind. Too kind, given the circumstances, but it is not that. I have to go.' She turned to her people, tears blinding her. She blinked them back. She never cried, or at least almost never. She did not want to now, not when she was choosing to do something for herself, something wild and unpredictable, something that might end in terrible pain but might also bring her blissful happiness. She could hear them murmuring but she could not make out the individual words. It didn't matter, she knew they cared for her but they would be all right without her. 'I must leave,' she told them. 'I love you all and I will miss you more than you will ever know, but I have to go.'

Before anyone could stop her, she ran from the Great Hall, heading for her chamber. She had not unpacked much since she had planned to leave with Tristan and she had almost everything she needed, coins, clothes, something to eat. She gathered it all together quickly, finding something more suitable to wear for travel. In every moment that passed, Tristan was getting further away. She would have to follow him to Windsor, but she would prefer to catch up with him before that as she didn't know the way. She had no idea what she was going to say, no idea if he would welcome her turning up in his life, but she wanted him to know that she loved him, that although Pwll Du Castle was the place that she lived, he was now her home for he held her heart.

By the time she made it back down to the courtyard, the gateway was full of her people, some of them holding travelling packs. More belongings for her, she assumed.

'Have you come to say farewell?' she said to Ffion, who was standing closest to her.

Ffion shook her head. 'We have not.'

'Then what are you doing here?'

'You cannot go roaming around the countryside by yourself. You will get yourself killed within days or you'll run into a band of men and they will...' Ffion pulled a face. 'I do not want to even say the words. The point is, it will not happen.'

Catrin could not believe that her people would turn on her like this. She'd thought that they cared for Tristan as much as she did, that they wanted her to be with him. They had said as much to her after he had left, wondering what on earth she had been doing letting him go without a fight. And now they were forming a physical barrier to prevent her from leaving. Well, there was another way out of the castle. She would just wait until everyone was asleep and then she would leave.

'Do not even think about taking the secret tunnels out of the castle,' Ffion told her, obviously able to read her mind. 'I have taken the key and given it to Lord John.'

Catrin never cried. Never. But her eyes were burning and she had to clench her jaw tightly to stop herself from doing so now.

'I love him. I have to go to him.' She should have told him how she felt, she should not have let him go thinking that she was happy to marry another man just to stay in her precious castle. She'd chosen stability over her love for him and that had been the wrong choice. Her people would be all right without her. They were capable and strong and they had one another. But who would take care of Tristan?

Her plea of love did not seem to have appeased Ffion, who crossed her arms over her chest. 'You know the way to Windsor, then? And all the ways in which to fight off armies of men by yourself?'

'Of course not, but Tristan cannot be too far away. He only left two days ago.'

But Ffion only shook her head. 'You cannot travel the countryside alone. Not one of us will let you. On this, none of us will be moved.'

Chapter Twenty-Two

The ocean in this corner of Wales was a different blue from the one where he had grown up. It was jewel-like in its colour, almost as stunning as Catrin's eyes. Tristan stared at it from his high vantage point. He would give almost everything to swap places with one of the birds who flew high above the waves just for a moment. To soar and to swoop would give him a moment's respite from the pain in his chest.

Catrin would be married now. Lord John did not want to wait and there was no reason to do so. Catrin would stay in her home with her people and she would be content. There was no other option for her, or at least Tristan had not offered her one. She was not meant to roam the world alongside him. Leaving had been the right thing to do and, with his letter of recommendation from Lord John, Tristan would be able to travel to Windsor with his head held high. He might even be granted a meeting with King Edward himself. There was nothing to stop him from becoming the greatest knight the world had ever known, his ambition ever since he had started his page's training. He could travel to Europe, fight in the war that was certain to take place on French soil. He was about to get everything he had ever wanted and yet...

He dropped to the ground, his legs unable to support him any longer. Reminding himself of everything he had always wanted was not blotting out the image of Catrin's face, the way her blue eyes smiled at him, the way her teasing mouth laughed at him and her expression as they'd exchanged their final words in the stables.

He bent his head, resting it on his knees. He could have stayed at Pwll Du Castle. True, he would have had to watch Catrin married to someone else but at least he would have seen her, been able to talk to her daily, to hear her laugh. There were other knights there now, pages would come and he could have helped train them. Staying just so that he could catch glimpses of her might have made him pathetic but at least it would have been less agonising than knowing he would never see her again.

And it wasn't only Catrin. Lloyd was an enthusiastic puppy, he needed someone to guide him, to train him to become a man. As pleasant as he seemed, Sir John was not the person for that. And there was Dafydd, the man mountain who hated fighting, Tristan could have protected him from that, the two of them could have worked together. Wynne was getting older, he'd need... well, Tristan couldn't think of anything but he'd miss the grizzle-faced cur as much as all the others. He knew they'd miss him and he hadn't even said farewell to them.

Pride had made him leave, pride and a plan he had formed when he was a *child*. When he'd arrived at Ormand's castle he'd been a lost little boy; having something to work towards had kept him from falling apart. It had made him part of a tight-knit band of brothers and he had stuck to the idea in the face of a crisis. Now he'd seen a different way of life, knew that he didn't have to live from one battle to another, that there was happiness in the glint of someone's eyes when they laughed at him, that being held by the woman he cared for was a special kind of heaven. It had changed him but he had no idea what to do with that.

'Hmm,' said a voice nearby. 'You do not look very happy.'

His head whipped up. 'Leo!' He leapt to his feet and flung his arms around his friend, never so glad to see another human being as he was in this moment.

Leo laughed his big sunshine laugh and Tristan squeezed him tightly.

'I don't think you have ever been so pleased to see me,' said his friend.

'You are right.' He dropped his arms and turned to Leo's companion, expecting to see Hugh, the third knight in their trio, but instead he was met by the gaze of a bemused stranger. He looked from Leo to the stranger and back again as if expecting to see the answer written in the space between them. 'Where is Hugh?' he asked.

'Hugh has decided to stay at Ceinwen Castle with his wife.'

What? Leo's words were so unexpected Tristan was momentarily winded. He felt his mouth move but no words came out. Eventually he managed to say, 'His wife?'

Leo's eyes sparkled with laughter. 'Yes, Hugh has married and is very much in love with his new bride.'

'But...' No, it couldn't be. That was not part of the plan.

'I think we can safely say he has recovered from his

heartbreak over Lady Ann.' Leo slapped him on the shoulder. 'His wife adores him too, she told me so herself. We do not need to worry on that score either.'

A weight he had not realised he was still carrying lifted from Tristan. All this time the guilt of Lady Ann thinking she loved him rather than his friend had been crushing him and he hadn't realised how heavy the burden was until it was lifted. Tristan had completed his mission successfully, had wanted to redeem himself in the eyes of the man who had been like a brother to him and knew that he had achieved that goal. But this was even better.

'And this is?' Tristan gestured to the young man standing a little away from them.

'This is Sir Rhys,' said Leo proudly.

'Right.' Tristan continued to stare at the youth. His smooth skin suggested he was too young to have reached the necessary age for gaining a knighthood. Something wasn't quite right. 'Leo,' he said slowly, 'Sir Rhys is a woman.'

Leo laughed again. 'Your powers of observation are as excellent as ever, Tristan.' Sir Rhys's skin flushed pink. 'Although, I think, my love,' said Leo, addressing Sir Rhys, 'that we are going to have to work on your disguise a little more. Tristan is an excellent knight, second best in the land some might argue, but noticing things is not his strongest point.'

'Firstly,' said Tristan, holding up a finger to stop his friend from rambling on without addressing the main points of that wild statement, 'I am the best knight in the land, not second. That honour falls to you.' Sir Rhys's lips twitched and, whatever the story here, Tristan decided he liked her. Anyone who enjoyed teasing Leo was a friend of his. 'And secondly, what did you mean by "my love"?'

'Ah.' It was Leo's turn to flush red and Tristan's stomach twisted with what that might mean. He wanted his friends to be happy but the snake coiling in his stomach could only be down to jealousy. 'I have also married.' Leo's chest puffed up in pride. 'Tristan, meet my wife, Lady Arianwen. Only refer to her as Rhys, though. We are on the run from her family. It's a long story—'

'Married? You and Hugh are both married?'

'We are.'

'I thought...' Tristan shook his head. He could not believe that his two friends had married while he was still alone, having found someone and lost her all in just over a month. 'Is Hugh happy? Does he have the life he wants?'

Leo shrugged, the amusement fading from his eyes. 'Hugh would only have married if it was something he truly wanted to do. You know him as well as I do. I cannot tell you whether or not he is happy, he was in the middle of an argument with his new wife when I saw him, but I believe that he will be. Having seen him, I think this is the life he was meant to have.'

'And you?' Tristan asked. 'Your plan was for us to go to Windsor and now...' His gaze flicked to Rhys, who was gazing out at the ocean, pretending not to listen to their conversation.

'I will still travel to Windsor,' Leo told him. 'I want a life as a knight, but my wife wants that too. We will live as if we are two men until we want to stop and perhaps settle down somewhere with land of our own. We have not decided. Before you ask, I am very happy.'

Tristan nodded. He was pleased for his friends, he really was. And that they had found their own futures without relying on him was even better. He could hold his head up high, he had followed the knightly code of chivalry, he had honour and he had his pride. He had his whole future ahead of him. He could truly become the greatest knight in the land and not just joke about it with Leo. This should be the greatest moment of his life. Happiness should have been flooding through him, but it wasn't. His bones were heavy, his chest was hollow.

'I am almost surprised to find that you *aren't* married,' Leo said, laughter back in his voice.

Tristan's stomach twisted. He wasn't, but that wasn't because he hadn't met someone with whom he could imagine spending the rest of his life.

'She married someone else, or at least she will, any day now. It could be happening right at this moment, for all I know.'

Leo frowned. 'Who could?'

'Catrin.'

Leo glanced back to his wife, who lifted her shoulders slightly.

'You will have to help me out here, Tristan. Who is Catrin?'

'The woman I should have married, or at least offered to, but Lord John came along and I thought it was for the best that I leave. She loves her home, you see. Pwll Du Castle is the most special place in the world. The people living there *like* each other. Can you imagine such a thing?' He shook his head. He had lived it and he still couldn't describe what it was like to live in a place where laughter was commonplace. He had never seen it before and if Rhys was on the run from her family he could guess that she couldn't imagine a life like that either. He knew Leo had no experience of such a thing. It was rare and precious and should be preserved—that was one of the reasons he had left, so that her dream could be preserved. 'You know that I was sent to persuade Lady Catrin to leave her castle?'

Leo nodded. Turning slightly to his wife, he said, 'Tristan is not at his best at the moment. You should see him in all his glory. Women fall over themselves just to be near him, not even to talk to him.' His friend wrinkled his nose in disgust. 'It's nauseating. It was deemed he would be the best person to persuade a lady to leave her home but, as she is not with him, I am guessing that he failed.'

Tristan glared at his friend. 'I didn't fail at anything. Lady Catrin was prepared to leave, not because of my face but because I helped her with...it doesn't matter. It's a long story but I didn't fail. She said she would come with me but, before we could leave, Lord John, the man King Edward sent to lead Pwll Du Castle, arrived. He took one look at Lady Catrin and decided she would make an excellent wife. It was the perfect solution as Lady Catrin did not want to leave in the first place. She is...' He paused. There was no way in which he could accurately describe Catrin, no words that would do her justice. 'Catrin deserves her home and that's what Sir John can give her.' Tristan turned away from the sea and gazed in the direction of the path he had ridden along. 'It was the right decision.'

There was a brief pause. Tristan tried to reassure himself that his words were true, that it had been correct to leave Catrin in her castle, but with every moment that passed he thought that perhaps he was wrong.

'Right, excellent,' said Leo briskly. 'Let's get going then. If we ride quickly we can be in Windsor within a week and the rest of our life can begin.'

'Leo!' said Rhys.

'What, my love?'

'Can't you see your friend needs to go back to Pwll Du Castle and at least tell this Lady Catrin that he is in love with her?'

In love? Tristan wasn't in love. He cared about Catrin. He wanted the best for her, would forever remember the bright colour of her eyes and the way that her lips twitched when she teased him. The thought of never seeing her again made it seem as if his heart had been ripped out of his chest, but that didn't mean he was in love. Tristan's mother had loved his father and that had sent her out of her mind. Tristan wasn't like that. He wanted only the best for Catrin, even if that meant her being with another man. He could live with the pain it caused him to know that she would bind herself to another because it meant that she got to keep her dream of staying with her people. He would resist his longing to return to her, even if for a moment, even if it was only to make a fool of himself by telling her how he felt, because he knew that he would only cause her pain by doing so and that was the last thing he wanted.

As he stood there listing all the reasons why he did not love her, he realised that he really did have wool for brains. Of course he loved her, had loved her for some time now. He should have told her before he'd left, she deserved to know that at least. It would make no difference, she would still want to stay in her beloved castle, but everyone deserved to know they were loved. Hell, if she loved him, he would want to know about it.

'It doesn't matter if he loves her,' said Leo to his wife, as if Tristan could not hear him. 'She's probably married to someone else now. There's nothing he can do. He can't ride back the way he came, tell her he loves her, ask her to ride with him to Windsor or somewhere else where both of them could live. I mean, I am sure that Hugh would welcome a man of Tristan's second-best talents to his castle while he and Lady Catrin planned somewhere else to live, but of course Tristan knows that all of this is impossible.'

Tristan ignored the heavy sarcasm in Leo's voice, even as hope took flight in his chest. No, it was foolish to hope; wanting something badly always ended in pain. Life had taught him that, or at least it had until he had met Catrin. Being with her had been different. She had shown him that life could be happy if you were prepared to work for it.

'The only way forward is to ride to Windsor,' Leo continued. 'Gazing in a lovesick way in the direction of Catrin's castle is not getting us anywhere. Come along, Tristan, let's get going.'

Tristan glared at the man he'd formerly thought a friend. Behind Leo, his wife was pressing her lips together as if to stop herself from laughing at her foolish husband's words.

'If she is married—' Tristan bit out the words '—riding into the courtyard telling her that I love her will not solve anything, will it?'

'See, my love—' Leo gestured to him '—Tristan has it

all worked out. He can't love her because, if he did, he'd do something romantic and brave like climb down the side of a castle to rescue her. You know, something that shows that he cares about her even if it doesn't necessarily mean that he will spend the rest of his life with her.'

Tristan had never wanted to punch a man more, although he did have one question. 'Are you referring to something you did when you talk about scaling a castle wall? Because you don't like heights.'

Leo frowned. 'I never told you that.'

Tristan shrugged. 'I think you'll find my powers of observation are better than you believed.' He wasn't about to tell his friend that his fear of heights was as obvious as Tristan's loathing of the darkness. He'd prefer to keep some mystery about himself.

'Well, you're right, I loathe them, find them blindingly terrifying, but I love my wife and I would do anything for her.' Leo waited, as if expecting Tristan to confess the same for Catrin, but this was different. Tristan *would* walk through endless dark tunnels for her, but that was not what she wanted or needed.

'But don't you see,' he said instead, 'leaving her at Pwll Du Castle *was* the best thing I could do for her. She wanted to stay there and now she can. It might cause me pain to be separated from her but it would be worse for her if I made her come with me to stay by my side. She would be away from everything she holds dear and what can I offer her in return? Life as the wife of a travelling knight.'

'Did you give her that option?' Rhys asked.

'I…' No, he hadn't, but it had been obvious that if she'd wanted to stay with him permanently then he would welcome the idea with open arms. If she had wanted to come with him, wouldn't she have told him so? Although…he had only just realised that this overwhelming feeling in his chest was love, so perhaps…

'You were right, you cannot love this Catrin,' said Leo. 'If you did, you would be willing to risk your dignity to tell her that you do, you would be willing to risk everything for even the most slender of possibilities that she might be able to spend her life with you.'

Tristan puffed out his cheeks and then released the breath slowly. His friend was right, damn him. If he loved Catrin, truly loved her, then there was only one way forward. He whistled for Darrow. His stallion lifted his head and then trotted towards him. Tristan flung himself into the saddle.

'What's it to be then, Tristan?' Leo asked, climbing back onto his own steed. 'Windsor or Pwll Du Castle?'

Tristan glared at his friend. 'You know damned well which one.'

Chapter Twenty-Three

'There's an army ahead,' Rhys said, already pulling her sword from its scabbard.

They had been riding for a morning and Tristan already had a healthy respect for Leo's wife. She took no nonsense from his gregarious friend and the way that she was holding her sword now, she could easily pass for a fully-fledged knight. The lack of beard might cause her and Leo problems in the future, but that was not for Tristan to worry about.

'I don't think it's possible,' he said in response to her statement. 'There is not an army in these parts.' He did not think that Ogmore would be able to pull a band of men together so soon after the battle with Catrin's people and the countryside was not populated enough for an army to move about undetected. If there was one in the vicinity, he would have known about it before now.

'There is a band of people moving towards us,' said Rhys. 'What else could they be?'

Even if it was an army, Tristan was not going to stop for them. He'd ride straight through them if he had to. Now he had made up his mind, nothing was going to stop him from getting to Catrin. He had to tell her that he loved her and that even if the marriage had already taken place, if she wanted him, he would move heaven and earth to make that happen. Or he would run away with her, like Leo had his wife. He was open to any suggestion at this point, so long as he could stay in Catrin's life. An army wasn't going to stop him getting to her.

The three of them did not slow their speed, riding towards the army, or whatever it was, at a rapid pace. Tristan didn't need Leo to accompany him on his quest, but Leo seemed to be intent on enjoying the adventure, his friend far more carefree than Tristan had ever seen him.

As they rounded a bend the people riding towards them came into focus and everything inside him stilled. He brought Darrow to an abrupt stop.

'What is it?' Leo said, reining in his own horse slightly ahead of Tristan.

'It's not an army,' he said. 'It's something impossible.'

'Well, we can all see it, so it is not impossible.'

Ahead of him, the group was also slowing. Tristan kicked Darrow into a slow trot; the leader of the group in front of him did the same thing. They met in the middle.

Tristan swallowed. 'Where are you going?'

Catrin shifted in her saddle, her skin pale but her blue eyes shining. 'To look for you. Where are you going?'

'I was coming back to you.'

She smiled wildly and his heart turned over.

'Did you marry him?'

'No.'

The air whooshed out of Tristan, relief making him weak. His knee touched hers as he urged Darrow forward.

'I'm very glad about that.' It was an understatement

but it was hard to think clearly now that she was in front of him and they were touching. He opened his arms, 'May I?'

She nodded. He leaned across and pulled her from her saddle, sliding her down in front of him so that they were face to face on Darrow. He drank in the sight of her like a man denied water for days.

'I should not have left. I thought I was doing the right thing, leaving you in a place where you are happy, but I am not as noble as I thought. I want you. I want to be with you in every way that is possible.'

She laughed and his heart lit up like a thousand candles in the darkest of corridors. 'Then I will always be with you.'

He pressed his lips to hers, heedless of their audience. He pulled back slightly. 'I love you.'

'And I you, despite the hideousness of your eyebrows.'

He grinned, his heart tripling in size.

'What is with…?' He nodded to the group of people surrounding Catrin. It seemed many, not all, but many of her people were travelling with her.

'We're all coming to Windsor with you.' Lloyd was practically bouncing with excitement and Tristan's heart clenched. He'd not known it but he had been searching for a home for a long time. Now he didn't have a roof over his head, but it appeared his home was coming with him.

Catrin rolled her eyes. 'I have tried to persuade them to turn around. When I tried to leave the castle by myself, they wouldn't let me ride the countryside alone. I do not know how I am going to keep them all fed. It's an impossibility actually, but they will not listen.'

'Lord John seemed perfectly pleasant,' he said, because really the idea that a portion of the castle's population had walked away from their home for him and Catrin was overwhelming.

'He wasn't you,' said Catrin. 'And it seems they love you nearly as much as I do. I am not sure what we are going to do, but it seems I am not the only one prepared to give up everything to be with you.'

Tristan rested his head on her shoulder, the sweep of her golden hair hiding the tears he swore would not fall in front of everyone.

'Goodness,' said Sir Rhys from somewhere behind him. 'To look at them is like looking at the sun.'

Ffion grunted. 'You get used to it.'

Lloyd nodded in agreement. 'You do. He is not at all how you think he will be, he's not bad at all.'

'And Lady Catrin is lovelier than her face,' Lloyd's wife chimed in.

Beneath him, Darrow shifted restlessly, around them people continued to talk about them, but all that mattered was the woman in his arms. He lifted his head to see Catrin's eyes full of laughter.

'Will you still love me if I don't become the greatest knight in all the land?' he asked.

'You already are.'

'That's true.' He grinned, lacing his fingers with hers. 'I have been following my dream for a long time, so long I forgot to ask myself whether it was what I really wanted. I realised today that I can give it up without a thought, but you…you, I cannot. That is why I was coming back to you. I want to be where you are and it doesn't matter to me where that is.'

Her fingers tightened on his. 'We cannot go back to

Pwll Du Castle. Lord John is a good man, but I think there are limits.'

'Then I suggest we carve our own future with a dream of our own, one that we have decided on together.'

She leaned forward, brushing her lips against his. 'That sounds like a perfect plan.'

Epilogue

Wales 1347

Tristan moved around the edge of his wide training ground, yelling encouragement to the young squires who sparred with their partners under the late afternoon sun. 'You nearly had him Reuben,' he called to the youngest squire, who at only fourteen was showing considerable promise. 'Lift your arm higher next time.'

'Yes, Sir Dyn Golygus,' the squire replied, renewing his attack.

'I hear people say that to you all the time; what does it mean?' asked Leo, coming to stand next to him.

'It's a term of great respect,' Tristan replied without thinking. It wasn't. After ten years of living in Wales, Tristan understood the language but he would never admit to knowing that phrase was a comment on his being a good-looking man. Certainly not to one of his oldest friends who would tease him mercilessly about it.

Next to him, Hugh, who had also spent time living in Wales, snorted in derision. 'It means that he is handsome,' he told Leo.

Leo frowned. 'It is not as if anyone needs reminding of that, even though he has grey hair.'

Tristan ignored them both, concentrating on his trainees. He could see the moment the young men became aware of Leo's presence, chins lifted, chests puffed out. Leo's name was already legendary and the trainees clearly wanted to impress the knight who they had heard many stories about.

When the training session was over the three men turned and made their way towards Tristan and Catrin's private quarters. Building work had finished there only a few months earlier and Tristan was looking forward to showing his old friends around.

Life had not turned out the way the three men had planned when they were not much older than boys. Leo's life was the only one that nearly resembled what they had imagined, although campaigning with a wife had never entered the burly knight's head before he had met her. Tristan knew Leo would never leave her side, that his campaigning days were probably coming to an end soon as the two of them wanted to start a family. Whatever their future held for them, Tristan knew his friend was happy.

Hugh had unexpectedly inherited a large stronghold, his father and brothers dying and leaving him the sole heir. He and his wife had moved to England five years ago and seemed intent on repopulating the area with their already large family. Tristan missed them both fiercely but he knew that their life at Croxton Castle was what they both wanted.

As for him...

Twin girls, the oldest of Tristan and Catrin's growing

brood, burst out of a room in front of him, so like their mother it gave Tristan sleepless nights just imagining how many suitors he would have to fight off when they came of age. 'Papa,' they called when they saw him, each grabbing a hand and tugging him towards the door. 'Come and see Blodwen, she has taken her first steps. Mama thought you would not want to miss it.'

Tristan hurried forward, stepping into the long room that was for his family only, a privilege of being the Lord and Lady of the castle and one Tristan never took for granted. Blodwen was teetering on unsteady legs, her gummy smile wide when she caught sight of him. Catrin glanced up as he approached, her eyes creasing at the corners in a soft, silent greeting.

'Five girls,' said Hugh quietly, his voice laced with humour. 'I know you have promised your trainees to the King but are you sure you are not creating your own army to protect your daughters?'

Tristan laughed. 'It has crossed my mind.'

The King had granted Tristan and Catrin land on the coast of Wales, with the provision that Tristan created a knights training stronghold loyal to the Crown. It was yet another way Edward hoped to ensure peace in Wales. It more than suited Tristan, who found that he enjoyed encouraging men to reach the best of their ability. If called upon he would fight for his country but he knew that this was his home, the exact place he wanted to live out the rest of his days.

Tristan and Catrin, with their ragtag group of followers, had stayed with Hugh and his wife while they began building work, moving into the new castle during the twins' second summer. It had been a busy time, full of laughter and hard work and the birth of five daughters. It wasn't what Tristan had planned but it was far better than he could have imagined.

When Leo, Hugh and their wives dispersed to their visiting sleeping quarters and their daughters finally settled down to sleep, Tristan wrapped his arms around his wife and dropped a kiss on her forehead. She turned and curled deeper into his arms, already soft and sleepy.

'I think I might be expecting again,' she murmured into his chest. 'Perhaps it will be a boy this time.' She fell asleep almost as soon as she had finished speaking, nestled against him.

'I love you,' he said softly. He settled down, his arms still holding her close. He closed his eyes, already looking forward to another child joining their home.

* * * * *

*If you enjoyed this story, make sure to
check out the previous instalments in
The Knights' Missions miniseries*

The Knight's Rebellious Maiden
The Knight's Bride Prize

*And why not pick up the A Season to Wed miniseries,
featuring Ella Matthews's captivating romance*

Only an Heiress Will Do *by Virginia Heath*
The Viscount's Forbidden Flirtation *by Sarah Rodi*
Their Second Chance Season *by Ella Matthews*
The Lord's Maddening Miss *by Lucy Morris*

Get up to 4 Free Books!

We'll send you 2 free books from each series you try PLUS a free Mystery Gift.

FREE Value Over **$25**

Both the **Harlequin® Historical** and **Harlequin® Romance** series feature compelling novels filled with emotion and simmering romance.

YES! Please send me 2 FREE novels from the Harlequin Historical or Harlequin Romance series and my FREE Mystery Gift (gift is worth about $10 retail). After receiving them, if I don't wish to receive any more books, I can return the shipping statement marked "cancel." If I don't cancel, I will receive 5 brand-new Harlequin Historical books every month and be billed just $6.39 each in the U.S. or $7.19 each in Canada, or 4 brand-new Harlequin Romance Larger-Print books every month and be billed just $7.19 each in the U.S. or $7.99 each in Canada, a savings of 20% off the cover price. It's quite a bargain! Shipping and handling is just 50¢ per book in the U.S. and $1.25 per book in Canada.* I understand that accepting the 2 free books and gift places me under no obligation to buy anything. I can always return a shipment and cancel at any time by calling the number below. The free books and gift are mine to keep no matter what I decide.

Choose one:
- ☐ **Harlequin Historical** (246/349 BPA G36Y)
- ☐ **Harlequin Romance Larger-Print** (119/319 BPA G36Y)
- ☐ **Or Try Both!** (246/349 & 119/319 BPA G36Z)

Name (please print) _____

Address _____ Apt. # _____

City _____ State/Province _____ Zip/Postal Code _____

Email: Please check this box ☐ if you would like to receive newsletters and promotional emails from Harlequin Enterprises ULC and its affiliates. You can unsubscribe anytime.

Mail to the Harlequin Reader Service:
IN U.S.A.: P.O. Box 1341, Buffalo, NY 14240-8531
IN CANADA: P.O. Box 603, Fort Erie, Ontario L2A 5X3

Want to explore our other series or interested in ebooks? Visit www.ReaderService.com or call 1-800-873-8635.

---

*Terms and prices subject to change without notice. Prices do not include sales taxes, which will be charged (if applicable) based on your state or country of residence. Canadian residents will be charged applicable taxes. Offer not valid in Quebec. This offer is limited to one order per household. Books received may not be as shown. Not valid for current subscribers to the Harlequin Historical or Harlequin Romance series. All orders subject to approval. Credit or debit balances in a customer's account(s) may be offset by any other outstanding balance owed by or to the customer. Please allow 4 to 6 weeks for delivery. Offer available while quantities last.

Your Privacy—Your information is being collected by Harlequin Enterprises ULC, operating as Harlequin Reader Service. For a complete summary of the information we collect, how we use this information and to whom it is disclosed, please visit our privacy notice located at https://corporate.harlequin.com/privacy-notice. Notice to California Residents – Under California law, you have specific rights to control and access your data. For more information on these rights and how to exercise them, visit https://corporate.harlequin.com/california-privacy. For additional information for residents of other U.S. states that provide their residents with certain rights with respect to personal data, visit https://corporate.harlequin.com/other-state-residents-privacy-rights/.

HHHRLP25